WITHOUT
TRACE

Gerard Murphy lives in Carlow where he lectures
at the Institute of Technology Carlow. His first novel,
Once in a New Moon, was published
to critical acclaim in 1997.

BY THE SAME AUTHOR

Once in a New Moon

DEATH WITHOUT TRACE

GERARD MURPHY

The Collins Press

Published in 2005 by
The Collins Press,
West Link Park,
Doughcloyne,
Wilton,
Cork

© Gerard Murphy 2005

ISBN: 1-903464-83-8

A Cataloguing-In-Publication Data record for this book
is available from the British Library

Typesetting: The Collins Press

Font: A Caslon Regular, 11 point

Printed in Germany by Bercker

ONE

Amazon watching during the working day. The femme fatale. Theories
on the fragility of modern marriage. Madigan is told of an affair and
agrees to take on an investigation. The possibility of an improvement in
his financial status uplifts his spirits.

It was the last days of the millennium, already an hour into darkness. Madigan was girl-watching from the window of his office in
the brewery. The December city groaned under the weight of cars
and buses getting their occupants home at the rate of half a car per
minute.

Madigan had been inputting beer-tasting results into a computer. He needed cheering up. To pass the time before the traffic
eased up he thought about logging onto his favourite porn star's
website (Shrine of the Cyber-Geisha) but thought the better of it.
Using the brewery computers to access porn could get him into all
sorts of trouble. In any case, porn would not cure him of the particular disease he was suffering from that evening, for Madigan
reeled under that diminution of thought, the shrinkage of existence that comes after the end of marriage.

Besides, he'd had a dream the night before that his ex-wife
was coming at him with a meat cleaver. It was one of those not-
so-good recurrent dreams that he had from time to time. The fact

1

that he'd got used to such dreams made them no easier.

To make matters worse, a mash tun had been down all day. It was that kind of week: a week when everything goes wrong, when even the rain doesn't know how to fall decently but has to dump itself like a lurching drunk upon everybody. Besides, the new century would belong to the children of the well off, the girls who were waiting for the buses and their boyfriends, trying on various faces and doing their best to learn how to be people.

He had been trying to give up smoking and had taken up jogging at lunch times. This meant that life got a little screwy in the afternoons and he was always trying to catch up with himself so he could get back to his second job.

He hated his work at the brewery and hated his other job too. But a man has to live and in those so-called boom times not many can live without a second income, especially someone in his position, with an ex-wife and child to support, even if he rarely saw them anymore.

As he looked out, the rain came down and draped itself off the lamp-posts. Drivers read their evening newspapers under the swish of a thousand wipers, college girls crammed into the bus shelters while secretaries pulled on their raincoats and put up wet umbrellas. This was Dublin, well past the rare oul' times, with fat webs of smog snagged in the headlights of cars. Only a fool would give up smoking in a town like this.

He was just about to make a cup of coffee in the brewers' sample room when he noticed a black BMW convertible pull up in front of the brewery gates. It had bang up-to-date plates and was so shiny you would never see your reflection for the chrome would suck you in.

This was odd, he thought. Everyone wanted to flee like rats out of the place at this hour of the evening and here was somebody trying to go in. A young woman in a dark raincoat got out

2

of the car and vanished in a flurry of quick heels up the steps of the brewery. He didn't see her face. Madigan gathered up the sheets from the last tasting panel and went into the cubbyhole where his kettle whistled that coffee was ready for making. He would input the rest of the tasting results tomorrow and was shovelling the Nescafé when he heard the knock on the door.

'Come in. It's open,' he said, in the great tradition of private eyes everywhere. Fellows like Madigan, lonesome men down in their luck, were always open for business.

The door creaked and, silhouetted in the light of the corridor, stood a tall, dark-haired woman, the woman who'd got out of the BMW. She was no more than 31 or 32, young enough to still be a looker, though old enough to know every trick in the trade.

He switched the light back on. (He had switched off the lights in the main sample room out of habit so he could look out the window without being seen.)

She looked like she might be a young executive, with a long black trench coat, high heels and just a hint of make-up. She wore a pair of tiny blue stones as earrings. Her hair was pulled back and tied behind her head, her eyebrows were sharp and her eyes were calm pools in which you could trawl for trout, if you were small enough. She was better than beautiful, better than porn. She was every cliché in the book.

'Are you Madigan?' she asked.

'I've been called worse,' he replied, as he sat down at his desk and chased his mouse around the mat to turn the computer off.

'Take a seat.' He pointed to his assistant Ted Plunkett's chair, which had been vacant for over an hour. 'You're not going to do your varicose veins any good standing around in those heels. I hope you massage your feet at night.'

'I don't like flippant comments,' she said brusquely. 'I don't have time for them.'

'Suit yourself,' he said, expecting her to start off on some business or other concerning the brewery. 'The man who made time made heaps of it, and the man who made twine made balls ...'

'You are Madigan, aren't you, the private investigator? You don't look a bit like Richard Widmark.'

'I'm not as good looking, though you might say we're related, in a way. He played Dan, Dan Madigan from the New York branch of the family. The NYPD. I play myself.' Madigan smiled. 'He was also one of the few people to rise from the dead. Did you know that?'

'Which you don't do?'

'I don't do resurrections, no.'

'Pity.'

Madigan offered his hand. She did not take it. 'I'm Mike Madigan, missus,' he said with a sigh, 'Mike Madigan, the brewery foreman. Of course, I can be anyone you like, if the price is right.'

It had been a bad week, what with all the vats having to be filled for the pre-Christmas brewing schedules. Now, to make matters worse, she lit a cigarette and the smell of smoke wafted into his nostrils, making him sick with longing for a drag. He tried to appear calm over the effect the smoke was having on his nerves. 'And with some of the scams the boys get up to around here, you'd need to be a bit of a private eye.'

He put his feet up on the desk and began to examine her more carefully. She was a fine specimen all right, virtually six feet in her high heels and her hair made her taller still. She was the kind of woman you would die for, if you were in the mind for dying. Her face was full, sensuous and hungry. He thought that whoever was getting in there was having one hell of a good time. And to think that people believe you have to be dead to be in heaven. One slight flaw he noticed, however: her lips were as tight as clothes pegs. When she spoke she had to flatten her words like coins to get them out. She had an accent he could not quite place, it was Irish, American, mid-Atlantic, it seemed to come from everywhere at once.

'Well, it looks like I'm wasting my time here. I must have been mistaken. You don't seem to be the man I'm looking for. I hope I haven't taken up too much of your time.'

'Oh, it's all right, missus, it's a pleasure being intruded upon by someone like you.'

'Well, don't take too much pleasure in it,' she said. 'I'd hate to see you go blind on my account.'

Suddenly he wanted to hear what she had to say. Someone shooting straight like that went right to the pit of his stomach. He loved a challenge in a woman; he considered it his greatest flaw.

As she turned to go, her trench coat creased above the knee and for a whole second he could see a stretch of smooth, creamy thigh. She was wearing a very short black skirt, suitable for Leeson Street of a Saturday night, he thought, but not exactly what you would wear in a brewery at the end of a working day, unless you were planning to sleep with the boss. As for Madigan, in the state he was in, it was like throwing aircraft fuel on a burning hangar.

'Hold it, missus,' he spluttered, 'don't go yet. You may have the right man after all.'

Those were words that were to haunt him for a long time to come. For several months to be exact, several months which would see him nearly kill and nearly be killed, several months in which he would get a look at a side of society most people, including himself, would much rather avoid.

But now he just wanted to hear more of what she had to say.

'I doubt if there are two of us in this city. I have been known

5

to do a little private investigation. Very much on a part-time basis, as you can imagine, with the job I have here.' He waved his hand at the bottle-strewn room and the rows of glasses in which sat the furry dregs of old tasted beer.

What he referred to as private investigation was merely a bit of discreet snooping he did, mostly at night. He did it partly to pass the time and provide him with a little light entertainment, partly to make a few spare bob to keep his wife from coming down on him like a ten-ton truck and partly to keep his son in a decent school; for he was at that stage of life when the soul is just that bit smaller than the mortgage.

His usual snooping job was to keep an eye on errant husbands and report any evidence he found of affairs or visits to shady ladies and so on. So most of his clients were women whose husbands were unfaithful. There were a lot of them in a city where women outnumbered men by seven or eight to one.

This lady didn't look like one of his routine clients though. She showed none of the usual signs of emotional distress, no tear-stained cheeks or bags under the eyes from sleeplessness, no crazed look of vengeance, hate, despair or heartbreak. She was cool as an empty trawler slipping out of a fjord in Greenland.

'OK.' He saw the leg again as she turned around. 'I'm looking for a private investigator. Do you think you can help me?'

'Depends on what it is you want to investigate and depends on the money.'

'Money will not be a problem.'

From her jewellery, he believed her. By their precious stones thou shalt know them.

'But I want it to be private. Not a word to a soul. If I hear that this gets out, you'll not get a bean.'

'Why come to me?' he asked. 'Why not go to the police?

They're paid for this kind of thing. We do pay taxes, after all.' He looked carefully at her. 'Or most of us do.'

'If I could go to the police, do you think that I'd be here?' She waved her arm around the room as if it was as alien to her as a labour exchange on dole day. 'I don't like your type, Mr Madigan, and I can assure you that if I had any choice, I would not be here. Unfortunately, you're the only one I have heard of, who practices your particular kind of trade. So I'm here out of necessity rather than choice. I hope you catch my drift.'

'Like a kite catches string on a windy day. But I don't come cheap.' It was clearly her first time at this game, or she'd have gone to the professionals in the snooping business. So he decided to ask her for ten times his usual going rate and figured she'd have no problem in forking out.

'I'm 250 an hour, and 200 extra for every piece of solid evidence I come up with.' He based his inflated rates on what he knew everybody from plumbers to dentists were now charging since the boom took off and everybody wanted to pocket as much as they could while the going was good.

'I can afford you, Mr Madigan. You can be assured of that.' She took a long, soulful pull of her cigarette and let the smoke out her nostrils like the steam of thought.

He ached for the taste of her smoke and the feel of her legs and arms pulling him into her.

'OK, lady, what's your story? What do you want me to investigate?'

'I think my husband is having an affair.'

Here we go again, he thought. What a circus! The whole bloody city was having affairs, in offices, in cars, in closets, in warehouses, in toilets on trains and planes. He had seen it all in his line of work. The damn place was gone to the dogs. The whole city was riding like rabbits and it was not pretty. Especially not for him, because in spite of all the screwing that was going on, he was getting none of it. He felt like a beggar looking in at a bloody feast and did not relish the prospect of watching another fellow having a good time, while he spent his own life choking the chicken.

'So, you think your husband is having an affair? What's the big deal? Everybody else's husband is having an affair too. Join Joe Public's gang. Statistically, 80 per cent do at some stage. Why should yours be any different?'

'Because he's mine, you idiot.'

'Fair enough, I suppose.' She did have a point. After all, what kind of man could even contemplate being unfaithful to a woman like that? Still, he thought, if he had learned anything from his time in the business, it was that appearances are often deceptive. 'What makes you think he's having an affair?'

'Well, if I may be completely blunt with you ...' She took another deep pull of her cigarette, leaning over and blowing smoke in his face, letting him look down the long valley of her bosom.

'Please do. Please be completely blunt with me.'

'Yes, well. He doesn't want to, how shall I put it in language that you would understand? He doesn't want to ... fuck me, any more.'

'That sounds serious all right, missus. Anyone who would no longer want to ... well ... fuck you must be missing a marble, or perhaps two.'

'I don't have time for your kind of compliments, Mr Madigan. Do you think you can help me or should I go elsewhere?'

He could think of a hundred ways he could help her. He could think of a thousand ways she could help him. 'Have you considered asking him why he no longer wants to sleep with you?' he asked instead.

'I have. He says he's overworked. Too tired for sex. I don't believe him.'

Madigan would have believed him. He knew all about the effect of overwork on one's sex life and had separation papers to prove it. 'Maybe you're wrong. Maybe he is overworked. It does happen.'

'No, he couldn't be overworked. He doesn't even know the meaning of the word.'

'Why, is he a shovel leaner, a corporation worker or something?' Madigan attempted a joke. 'Or is he on the live register?' However, he knew that a woman like her would make sure she was married to a doctor or a solicitor or one of the lads who bring in fat lump-sums from floating or selling off their companies to big corporations. Now, if she was married to a doctor, her story would make a lot of sense for, in his experience as a sort of social worker around the edges of broken marriages, doctors were so overworked their wives must spend all their nights in dildo paradise. But he was wrong again, though merely on a technicality.

'He's a professor, actually.'

He knew the pitch of the sound of that 'actually' from years in the brewery. The women who used it, wives of senior executives who lived in the suburbs, would climb over a mound of corpses to get their way.

'What does he "profess"?' he asked with a smile. He was cheering up now because she had finished her cigarette and he had switched on the extractor to let the smoke join its cousins in the smog outside.

'He's Professor of Neurobiology at the university.'

That would go down well at cocktail parties.

'So, your husband, this professor, is having an affair. You think. Do you know who the lucky woman is, that is, if there is a lucky woman.'

'Yes. This is her here.' She past him a tattered photograph of a dumpy-looking woman in a party dress. The photo had obviously been taken at a Christmas or New Year's bash, for the woman was wearing a paper hat and bits of plastic streamers were draped across her shoulders.

'So, you know the lady-in-waiting. The husband no longer wants sex. You sound home and dry to me. If you are so sure of everything, what do you want me for?'

'I want concrete evidence that he's screwing her, a photograph, a video tape, something like that. You people can set up cameras, so I'm told.'

'We can. But could I first interest you in a little advice? I know about these things, I've been watching this carry-on since you were in your gymslip. Turn a blind eye. Lay off the guy. If you want to keep him, don't put pressure on him. These things always blow over. If you're right, and I'm not saying you are, he's hot in her pants right now.'

'Is this how you carry on all the time, Mr Madigan?'

'Only when I feel the need to, and I feel the need to now. OK, he's on the nest, right? He's happy. He's having a second childhood. He didn't believe such happiness possible. And he's afraid and ashamed in front of you because your very presence brings him back to earth, right? And, of course, he can't look you in the eye.'

'So you're an amateur counsellor as well?'

'I'm a man of many talents, lady, and if you ever get to know me, you'll find that saying the obvious is one of them. You lean on him now and you'll lose him. You put the squeeze on him and you'll lose the whole shebang. But in a week, in a month, in six months, she'll come to him with a petulant puss on her, demanding to know when he's going to dump you for good. He'll put off the decision, and put it off again, and again, and again. Eventually, she'll get tired of waiting and some night she'll take the face off him and tell him he's every kind of bastard under the sun. She might try cutting up his clothes or throwing acid on his car. And that night, or some night shortly afterwards, he'll crawl back into bed with you and give you the screw of your little life and all will be hunky-dory in the professorship again and all who sail in her will be happy in the generally unhappy way that is life. Do I make myself clear?'

She said nothing.

'And,' he went on, 'you'll then have the advantage of being able to make him pay for this every day for the rest of his life. Power like that doesn't come easily, and it doesn't come cheap. Besides,' Madigan eyed her carefully, 'he must be out of his neurological mind.'

As he said this, she leaned back on her chair and watched him, a calm smile came over her lips.

'What makes you so sure I want to keep him?'

'Your type always want to keep an errant husband. I've seen it a thousand times.'

'My type? What type is that?' She spoke with such a defiant smile that Madigan figured she could hear the truth again.

'Listen, lady. I've seen hundreds of women like you. The professional classes of this town are full of them. They go to college to snare a doctor, a solicitor, an accountant. They drop their smalls for a ring. Then when they're married they are landed out in suburbia with a couple of kids. The husband works all the hours that God sends, and the wife is left there with the washing machine for company. So she hits the pills or the gin ...'

'Do I look like somebody on tranquillisers, Mr Madigan?'

'I don't know what you're on, missus, but whatever juice you take that makes you so cool while you dig the dirt on your old man, I wouldn't mind having a quart of it the next time my wife calls around.'

As he said this, she stood up, towering over Madigan at his desk. His mind was clocking 90 miles per hour down fantasy road. He sat closer to the table; no point in showing her his appreciation.

'Listen, Mr Madigan.'

'Call me Mike.'

'Listen, Mr Madigan, this conversation is getting us nowhere. Will you take the job or won't you? Time is important to me. I need an answer.'

'OK, let's get this clear. What you want is for me to get a photograph of your husband and this ... this woman, in a compromising position, right? No more?'

'No more.'

'No court appearances or anything like that?'

'No court appearances, nothing else. Just some documentary evidence, that's all.'

'It might not be that easy, you know. We could be into big bucks here.'

'As I said before, Mr Madigan, money is not a problem.'

'OK, I'll do it. But first I'll need some info': names, photographs, addresses, phone numbers, hotel, motels, small romantic country B&Bs ... It might also be useful to have access to your husband's bank accounts: Visa, Access, Amex, anything like that. Knowing where people spend their money is usually half the battle.'

'I don't have that stuff here. But I can meet you, say, tomorrow night? How does Bewleys at 8.00 sound to you?'

'Make it 8.30. Thursday is a bad day on the books here. By the way, I never got your name.'

'I didn't tell you my name, Mr Madigan. My name is Pamela, Pamela O'Neill Crowley.'

The double-barrel moniker did not surprise him. It was fairly typical of the social-climbing classes. She held her hand out. It was the first gesture she made that approached normal human contact. Her handshake was firm, the fingers long and strong and slightly plump. They were fingers for rings and she was wearing a fistfull, though no wedding band. Her long nails gave him a thrill along the back of his hand.

'I hope this business transaction will be to our mutual benefit, Mr Madigan.'

'Oh, I'm sure it will, Pamela, I mean, Mrs O'Neill Crowley.'

'It's Doctor O'Neill Crowley, actually. But I'm sure we won't fall out over trifles.'

He showed her to the door.

'Until tomorrow night then, Mr Madigan.'

'8.30, Mrs ... Dr O'Neill Crowley.'

He closed the door behind her and went back to his desk to file away the sheets he had been working on before she came in. His coffee was as cold as the rain outside. He realised he had forgotten to offer her some. He still had the photograph in his hand. 'I must be losing *my* marbles,' he said to himself, when he realised he had also forgotten to ask her the name of the woman in the photo. He looked at the picture again. Some men don't appreciate their luck, he mused. The woman looked like somebody's mother or a maiden aunt or a nun in civvies or the cleaning lady that you just don't see. Then again, depending on where you're coming from, kindness can be a very attractive quality in a woman. He put the picture into his wallet.

As he shut the filing cabinet and locked up the tasting room for the night, he noticed there was a spring in his step, which had not been there since he gave up smoking. For once, he went out into the smog without loathing it.

TWO

Rosie. A man's home is his castle. Madigan explains why he gave up smoking and expounds on his dislike of all things feline. A visitor. Bills. Madigan hears from his estranged though by no means fondly remembered spouse and thinks about marriage.

When he reached home, Madigan parked Rosie, his old 1989 Peugeot, on the kerb outside his flat. Eaten with rust, low on her suspensions, Rosie's days were numbered. Madigan had decided to invest in a motorcycle as the only way he could circumvent the total gridlock that was now Dublin. Still, old Rosie had a good heart, a new enough 3L Peugeot engine under her bonnet and the latest Citroën shocks. She looked suitably tatty for a car of her age, but he kept her like that to encourage the belief in car thieves that she wasn't worth stealing.

Rosie could reach 60 in under a minute, which was useful for getting out of scrapes. He could lose the best of the Ford Mondeo cop cars, but a motorcycle would be even better.

He switched off the ignition and looked longingly at the crushed cigarette butts he had smoked in the good old days before he had decided to be healthy. He could not bring himself to throw them out. Like a lonely pervert, he fingered the ash and smelled his fingers.

Two

It would be easy to look upon Madigan as one of life's losers. After all, his wife had left him and he was stuck in a dead-end job. But he didn't see it like that. Madigan did not believe he was defeated, at least not yet. When he found himself in the losing corner like a boxer, with his coach frantically waving a towel in his face, his reaction was to think about where to land the next blow. Anything else and you might as well wash 50 Nembutal down with a bottle of vodka and log off. As he saw it, though he knew about loss and he knew about defeat, he was not beaten. Besides, he had other things to think about, his craving for cigarettes for one thing.

He remembered the fright he had got a few weeks earlier that made him decide to give up smoking. He nearly burnt his apartment block to the ground that night. After drinking a quart of whiskey on the way home from work that Friday evening, he had left a butt lighting on the table. The place was like Ground Zero the following morning; a gossamer of carbon floated over the table and chairs. What saved him from being burnt to a crisp, along with Lily Bowen who lived in the flat below, was the fact that the fire melted a hole through a plastic cold water pipe. The resulting deluge saved both the kitchen and Madigan's life, even if it did cause the most appalling havoc.

He decided there and then to quit smoking and reduce the drinking to what he could actually afford. He poured the bottle of whiskey that he had kept hidden in his otherwise unused oven down the sink. He would go in for clean living, calm Karma, embrace the boredom.

As a result, he gradually began to notice things about his flat he had not noticed before. That it was a lot filthier than he had realised, for instance. Nicotine deprivation gave him new eyes. He was like a blind man who can suddenly see. Dust might be the carpet of the happy but he decided he would have to do something about cleaning the place up.

Passing Lily's flat, he heard music coming from inside. Neapolitan opera. Lily had had a passionate affair with Caruso for as long as he had known her. The strains of '*La Donna È Mobile*' emerged scratchingly from under her door. She also had a long-term love affair with cats and housed at least ten of the creatures in the dim narrow confines of her flat.

As he past, her door opened and one of the cats, quick as a whisper, ran out under his feet and down the stairs.

'Come back Keen, *peesch weesch, peesch weesch*. Oh dear, where is that rascal gone? Come back Keen, *peesh weesch, peesh weesch*.'

The smell of cat's piss escaped from her room like a cloud released after an ammonia leakage.

'Evening, Lily.'

'Oh, it's yourself, Mike. Oh dear, Mike, my Keen has run away. The vet said I should have him neutered. They're calmer that way, you know. But I couldn't do it. Couldn't do it, couldn't cut his poor little thingies off. Not to my poor Keeny. Now he's gone. What am I going to do, at all, at all?'

'I wouldn't worry about him, Lily. I'm sure he'll be back, probably with his tail, at least, between his legs.'

'Oh, I do hope so, Mike. But the little fellow gets into the most terrible fights. He'll never be right now for the Prime Cat Show, all skinned and sore and missing pieces of his fur. Oh dear me!'

'Lily, Keen knows what side his bread is buttered on. I'd put any money he'll be back before bedtime. Calm yourself, go back inside and listen to Enrico. Keen is well able to look after himself.'

Lily, pale with fright, lack of air and sunlight, was every day of 70. She was bent double from feeding and stroking the cats and had begun to look more than a little feline herself. Her face was pointed and reminded him of an old though not quite whiskerless tabby. She was living proof of the theory that people begin to look like their pets if they have them for long enough. Madigan never cared much for pets; he often thought he wouldn't mind having a dog but was afraid he would begin to look like a cocker spaniel or a dachshund after a while. Better safe than sorry.

Lily had buried her husband about 30 years previously and thereafter never missed an opportunity to bring him into her conversations. 'John just loved Enrico, you know,' was her way of introducing him. And after a while, Madigan would get so bored, he would imagine spiders coming out of the walls and forget whether she was talking about her dead husband or some dead Italian tenor.

He was fond of Lily, though. Outside of work she was his main human contact since his wife had left him. She acted as a kind of secretary, answering callers to the door and picking up mail so it was not left lying around on the doorstep. She kept an eye on the place when Madigan was away, which was a lot, considering his two jobs. His flat had yet to be burgled and that was probably a record for this particular part of Dublin.

'Anyone looking for me, Lily?'

'Let me see, Mike. No, I don't think so ... oh yes, there was one. Oh, you'd like this one, Mike. She was a fancy lady, if ever I saw one. Oh yes, oh yes, a fancy lady for sure. She was looking for you, Mike. I said to myself, I said; that fellow Mike Madigan, the women are always chasing him. What a terror you are, Mike, what a holy terror.'

For a moment a girlish smile crossed her catty face, and he could imagine what she must have looked like when she was young: kittenish might have been the word for it.

'What did she look like?' Madigan asked and described his visitor of an hour previously.

'That's exactly her, Mike, that's exactly her. She's a fine girl, Mike. 'And,' she whispered into his ear and gave a little girly laugh, 'I noticed she wasn't wearing a wedding ring. You see how I look after you, Mike? I wouldn't hang around now, if I were you. Fine girls like that don't grow on trees, you know.'

'You're dead right there, Lily. Wherever they grow, they don't grow on trees. Did any mail arrive for me?'

'Just one or two bills; the usual.' Lily went into the interior of her flat to retrieve the mail. The smell of cats nearly overwhelmed him. He had always avoided going into her flat on that account and when for any reason he had to, he held his breath for as long as he could, till he felt he was a one-man diving bell.

'Here you are.' she said, handing him the bills. 'I'll have to go now to listen to Enrico. Don't be too bold now with those girls, do you hear me. A fine handsome man like you should be thinking of settling down again.'

And she shook her thin face like an old lost child and shut the door behind her. Madigan could hear the rattle of bolts and chains and locks as she secured herself against the world. He had put in those locks for her, after she had read some newspaper report of an elderly couple who had been beaten to death for a few hundred pounds they had stashed under the bed. He also got her to open a bank account in which to put her pension money. He would have done more for her but there was no more to be done.

His mail was the usual: three bills: the gas, the electricity and the taxman. There was also a mortgage statement for the house he no longer owned. £5,000 he had paid out for it over the previous year. Not bad for one with two jobs and half a life.

Madigan went into his flat. There was no change there; it had not been broken into or robbed. The miracle of his immunity to theft continued to amaze him. He put on the kettle to make himself a cup of tea, thankful for small mercies, and slit open the envelopes. He owed 50 for gas and 30 for electricity and the taxman had sent him a form for self-assessment. 'I'll have to be more careful in future about the way I'm paid,' he thought. 'No more cheques, no bank drafts, no postal orders, just cash up front, or cheques made out to cash.' He was always a bit lazy and overstretched and tended to forget such things. It was easy in the old days when everyone in Ireland was on the make, when the only economy that actually functioned was the black one. Endemic corruption held the fabric of society together. Now political correctness was coming down like a ton of bricks and was landing on all the scams that had once kept the country going. The State was now trying to put a veneer of cleanliness on itself. Madigan longed for the old days. Corruption was better than mind control.

He slapped two rashers and three sausages on the grill and made tea when the kettle was boiled. He liked to make cooking easy for himself by leaving everything open on the kitchen table at all times. There was not enough time for opening and closing the packaging of the world.

He switched on his voice mail to see if there were any messages.

There were. Two.

'Bleep bleep, Mike?' A female voice: Joyce Hamilton, beaten down by loneliness, a former client, she was about to cough up the readies. 'You were right about the bastard. What do I owe you? Please send the bill ... I hate these things ... Bleep bleep.'

He opened the 'rape page' of the evening paper and popped a segment of burnt sausage in his mouth. GIRL INDECENTLY

ASSAULTED AT KNIFEPOINT, the headline said, the usual run of things. The papers were full of rapes, child abuse, pederasty, bishops fathering babies, fathers screwing daughters, priests molesting youngsters, sports coaches feeling up little girls. No newspaper would sell without two pages of lurid court cases. Such things went on, of course, but not to the extent you would think from reading the papers and certainly not to the exclusion of everything else. Still, sex sells, and ever since money had replaced religion in people's minds, it was the only other thing that everybody was interested in.

'Bleep bleep. Michael. This is Sally. I need £100 for school books for Liam. I need it by the end of next week. We've been through all this before. So I expect no problems this time. I'll meet you at the usual place, a week from tomorrow.' Sally, wife of his life, former lady of the manor, was doing her weekly whine. 'Why are you never in, for God's sake? You'd think you'd be at home at least sometimes. I hate talking into these things ... It is so impersonal ... Bleep bleep.'

Madigan switched off the voice mail. Not half impersonal enough, he thought. When he was married, Madigan had come to the conclusion that he was Sally's wheelbarrow: he carried a lot of stuff and she pushed him around. She'd tried to make him middle class and when she failed, she blamed him. And she failed because he was unable to change; he was half a puppet with only one string, the one between his legs.

But now she had another string and his name was Liam, their son. He often wondered what she told Liam about his father: that I am the biggest bastard on the face of the Earth, I suppose, he thought. Ah well, some things never change.

Still, there was a time when he had had it bad for her and could not escape, even if a little voice inside his head said it would never work. There was a time he would have died for Sally. And then there was a time when he did nearly die because of her. Sally was simply too strong, too driven, too determined, a working-class girl moving up in the world, when all Madigan ever wanted was a quiet life.

Sally had big aspirations: good carpets, maple floors, velvet curtains, antique fireplaces, a nice house in the suburbs. She wanted Liam to have a nice middle-class life, just as the middle class themselves want their children to be pianists or ballet dancers or to bring down the house at Carnegie Hall. And who could blame her? Everybody wanted to get onto the rising raft. If you were not moving up in the world, you were moving down.

And that was where the problems started. He was not aspirational enough for Sally. He was content with what he was and happy to do his own thing. This made for spectacular fights, spectacular failures, spectacular truces and spectacular sex – until, with sex-weary limbs, they had run out of the energy needed for such fireworks. Of course, he loved it for a while. In the land of the blind the one-eyed man is king.

He switched the tape back on, out of curiosity, and played the rest of it. No more messages. That at least was a relief.

Trouble brewing. Madigan hides his face amid a crowd of stars. Lamb
dressed as mutton. He meets the femme fatale for the second time and
is charmed by changes in her demeanour. Gathering information.
Expensive tastes.

On the afternoon of the Thursday when Madigan was supposed
to meet Doctor Pamela O'Neill Crowley, things were crazy at the
brewery. A motor driving one of the mashers had broken down
and the mash sat and hardened into a four-foot cake of congealed
sludge. By mid-afternoon three brews were already behind schedule and two men had to be sent in with shovels to excavate the
dead stuff out of the mash vessel. It was 8.00 before the whole
shebang was up and running again. By the time he crawled
through the late evening traffic and found a parking spot for Rosie
in the Temple Bar end of town, it was already well past 8.30.

Bewleys Café served up cigarette smoke and the smell of fry-
ing rashers and sausages. Madigan had not eaten all day and his
nerves, his hunger and the craving for a cigarette were all assailed
at the same time. Girls in black frilly dresses cleaned the tables
like the semi-innocuous afterthought of a Victorian wet dream.
Around the tables lounged what past in Dublin for the chattering
classes: ageing student types, all scruffy-clothed and long-haired

and wearing scarves and second-hand leather jackets, lamb dressed up as mutton.

He had lived that easy life once himself, when talk was the only currency he had in his pocket. We all grow out of it in time, he thought, marry, settle down, and become frustrated husbands, tired wives or demanding harridans. We pretend for a while to be free and then cash in our chips for the mortgage and two cars in the drive for the distant suburbs.

He looked at the young and not so young singles and thought about what lay ahead of them. They deserved their youth and the illusion of freedom. If they shacked up for a few years with a shrill harpy, or stood over a smoking motor with half a million quid's worth of beer going down the drain and the head-brewer screaming like a stuck pig, then they would get a taste of what life is really about. Whenever they hit the cartwheel of commerce, he thought, that will be time enough for them to grow up.

He was late. He searched around for Pamela O'Neill Crowley and when he couldn't see her he queued for something to eat.

'Hi.' He was paying for a plate of chips and beans and rashers when he heard her voice behind him.

He turned around. There she was, a smile stretched between her cheeks, warm as a two-bar heater. She looked different. Even her lips seemed to him to have filled out. She seemed friendlier than the first time they met. She was wearing tight black trousers and high boots and a white cashmere sweater with a gold brooch at the neck. Bishops would have gone stark raving mad and thrown in the crozier for her. And she was wearing (Madigan tended to notice these things) a fat wedding ring.

'That's a nice get-up you have on,' he said for the want of something better to say, working on the basis that a compliment never went astray, no matter what your business.

'I'm glad you like it,' she replied and flashed the smile again. What spring had thawed the frost of our first wintry meeting? he wondered. Maybe it was that January must always give way to February or perhaps a rise in temperature had caused some sort of strange avalanche in her soul.

'My word, but you must be hungry,' she said, looking at his tray-full of food.

'Famished. I didn't get a bite all day. Major hassle at the brewery. Sorry for being late. Same reason.'

'That's all right. I've only just come in.'

Madigan waited for the catch.

'Do you want anything: tea, coffee?'

'Would that come out of your expenses?' she said with a laugh.

'Naw, it's on me. I buy goodwill at the beginning. It softens up the customer.'

'OK. I'll have a large coffee. Black.' She went to search for a free table. Madigan followed her movements. She walked with grace and gave the impression she would feel at home anywhere. And she had a big walk, like that of a model or a ballerina, a thoroughbred at a donkey derby. Her hair was swept back. The clothes she wore were tight, but not too tight. It would break his heart to nail her if he ever found she was up to something nasty.

'I think we're both a little out of place here,' he said as they sat down.

'Yes, we're both over dressed. But I refuse to dress down, even for places like this.'

'You're right.' He laughed. 'I'm overdressed, and that doesn't happen very often,' he said, looking down at his shabby work suit, stained as it was with splashes of beer and wort. As he wolfed down his dinner, she watched him with a bemused expression on her face.

'My God, you are a hungry fellow, aren't you? Are your other appetites as big as your stomach's?'

'Depends on what appetites you mean,' he said between mouthfuls of rasher.'

'Hmm, a coy one. Anyway, I suppose we'd better get down to business.'

'OK, you lead on.'

'As I was saying to you the other day, I think my husband is having an affair.'

'Because he doesn't want to fuck you, right?' He chewed on.

'More than that, he has begun to act strangely. My husband is a serious man. I suppose you could call him grumpy. I sometimes think I married him because I wanted to see him smile.'

'There are far worse reasons for wanting to get married.'

He could think of hundreds.

'Did you succeed?'

'No, I think I failed, in that regard anyway.'

'What about the lucky lady, where does she come in?'

'Oh, the photograph? That's Maude. She works for him. Typing, filing, that sort of thing.'

Madigan could see by the way she said it that she had no great love for typists. Somehow, you felt there were lots of groups of people she did not have a whole lot of time for. 'You seemed pretty sure she was seeing him on a more, how shall I put it, intimate basis, when we spoke last night.'

'There's something going on there, Mr Madigan. He talks about her a lot and he spends a lot of time with her.'

'The old urge-to-bring-the-beloved-up-in-every-conversation trick?'

'You seem to know about these things, Mr Madigan.'

'I know about a lot of things.'

'I'm sure you do.'

'Unexplained elation and this business of talking about some-body like there was nobody else in the world is a dead giveaway. Of course, he could be just very devious. Maybe this Maude is just a smokescreen.'

'I don't think so. William was never devious. Foolish, blind, trusting, passionate, but never devious. You see, that's the prob-lem. I was always sure I had him in the palm of my hand. In the early days of our marriage, William would have died for me. It was wonderful.'

'I could understand that.'

'These are the few things I brought along. Here. This is William.' She showed him a photograph of a bearded middle-aged man with, to say the least, a tendency to overweight.

'He looks a little old to be your husband.'

'He's 42. It's the beard that puts ten years on him. Here are his expense accounts, and I found his recent bank statements, as you asked.' She handed over a bunch of Visa and Amex accounts. 'This is our address and phone number, and Maude's address and phone number.'

'What exactly do you want me to do?'

'Just watch him in the evenings and at night when he says he's working late, that's all.'

'Can't you ring up yourself to see if he's there or not?'

'I do. Sometimes he answers and sometimes he doesn't. And the phones in there are only half-manned after 5.00. I need a spare pair of eyes, and that's where you come in. You seem reluctant, Mr Madigan. Are you still willing to take on the job?'

'Yes, sure. But I'd still say you'd be better to let him be.'

'You will be paid to spy and not to judge, Mr Madigan.'

'Suit yourself. You're footing the bill.'

'Just you remember that.'

'I get paid by the week.' Madigan said. 'And I don't cheat on my expenses. I'll check out all the purchases he made here, and keep an eye on the Department, as you call it, the Department of Neurobiology, Dublin City University?'

'Yes. Goodbye for now, Mr Madigan. You will be in touch?'

'Every week, on the dot.'

With that she got up and swung out of the café without saying another word. Two hundred heads turned their way: a hundred men who would lynch him on the spot if they thought they could get away with it and a hundred women who would have lynched her.

Four

Madigan in the Groves of Academe. The new poor. Spying. He describes the Professor and his secretary and discovers a large bag of sweets. Two GAS men. A calling card.

The following night Madigan decided he would earn his keep by doing a little spying on the Professor.

The university was an out-of-place development, built on an estate at the edge of the city near tower blocks where nobody had a job. It had started life as a college for the working classes, but soon became swamped by middle-class kids, who had more ambition and drive, and more shekels than the others. What began as an idea to pull the lower classes out of their lassitude became instead an opportunity for the lads a few rungs up to tighten even more their grip on the ladder. Though the world was obsessed with having, the have-nots wanting to have and the haves wanting to have more – there were still those who never even got near the foot of the staircase.

Madigan, a Marxist of the Groucho rather than the Karl variety, understood this place and was wary of the poor, who lived in tower blocks and dead-end estates, yet he could not blame them for thieving and pimping and running drugs. If he was in their shoes, he would do the same.

He soon found a sign that read 'Department of Neurobiology' and waited in his car with the lights off. It was dark on the campus. Two other cars were parked outside the building. The trees waved at the sky like skeletons at a party. High railings, erected to keep out the inhabitants of the tower blocks, sliced the lights of the passing traffic. The sky shone with an orange glow and small black clouds rode, as if plying a sea of ooze. After a while, out of sheer boredom, he began to see monsters in that sky and trolls of scummy cloud squatting over the spires of the cathedrals. He fancied the glow was the glow from the mouth of hell and that all the spitting rain from the damp western winds could not quench the misery that groaned in the purgatory that lay around the tower blocks. He wanted a cigarette so much he would have killed for one, but had to stub out his longings. It did not come easy.

A light was on in one of the ground-floor windows of the building beside him. After a while, he noticed figures moving about inside. Madigan recognised the faces from the photos: the Professor and the lucky lady, Maude. They were alone in the building.

They moved back and forth across the window carrying sheaves of files. The photocopy machine lit up every few seconds, making florescent ghosts march across the windowpanes. Whatever was going on must be important, he thought, especially since people were prepared to work late on a Friday evening to get it done.

There was no sign of an affair, though. Maude was middle aged, heavy, with tweeds. The Professor was a weird-looking character, much bigger than Madigan had expected, with a long grey beard and a ponytail. He wore something that looked like a monk's outfit made out of denim and moved like a big tent around the room, a blue haystack on castors.

After a while the pace of work seemed to speed up. Piles of paper were being shoved into large brown envelopes. It was like a political campaign before an election. Maude stacked them on the desk. Eventually, they tidied everything up, and the Professor picked up the pile of brown envelopes and looked around like someone packing his suitcase before going on holiday. Then, happy that he had left nothing behind, he left the room. The last thing Madigan saw was Maude's hand switching off the light behind her as she shut the door.

A minute later, Madigan saw them emerge onto the courtyard. He slouched back into Rosie's reclining seat. The Professor placed his pile of brown envelopes on the passenger seat of his car before sitting in and reversing out of his parking spot. Maude sat into her red Nissan and did the same. He said something to her out of his open window, but Madigan did not catch what it was.

When they reached the end of the tree-lined avenue, they drove off in different directions.

After they left, Madigan crept into the building. Security was lax, something he had noticed about universities. All you had to do was look scruffy, wear a white coat, or put on the preoccupied look of an academic, and you could walk anywhere in a university. As long as you gave the impression that you knew where you were going, nobody would challenge you.

He turned on the lights and walked decisively in the direction of the Professor's office. A minute later he was standing in front of it. There was nobody about. He slipped his credit card into the door jam and opened the door without difficulty. Once in the office, he shut the blinds, turned on a table lamp and went through the office as carefully as he could. The only unusual thing he found was a large blue plastic bag full of sweets, chocolates, toffee, fudge and every kind of confection imaginable. So the old Prof has a sweet tooth, he thought. No wonder he looked like a bison.

After finding keys in the Professor's desk he searched all the filing cabinets, finding nothing there but loads of unreadable stuff about neurobiology. The office was about as incriminating as a sacristy, he decided, although with the reputation of sacristies of late that might not be an apt metaphor. On the office desk stood a photograph of the Professor and his wife, taken in Italy or Spain or some place where the sun shone.

As he left the building, Madigan noticed a small truck pulled up outside. It was from a company called GAS Gases. Two men in white coats got out and began to push a large shiny metal canister in his direction. It looked like R2D2 or one of the things CNN roll out when they want to imply that some Middle Eastern dictator is about to wage biological warfare.

'What have you got there, lads?' he asked.

'Liquid nitrogen,' one of them said.

'It's a bit late in the day for nitrogen, I'd have thought.'

'It's a late delivery.'

'That's what drives these happy boom times; people working all the hours that God made.' Madigan opened the door for them. 'It's called the programme for competitiveness and work. I hope you're being well paid for it.'

'Thanks, mate,' one of them said.

'You're welcome.'

They went on into the building, shoving the canister of liquid nitrogen before them as if it were a patient about to expire on a hospital trolley.

As he walked out into the car park he noticed the wind had risen. The glow from the city had become more feverish. He picked up a card from the gravel where the Professor and Maude had parked their cars. It was the card for one of the restaurants the Prof seemed fond of visiting, if his expense accounts were to be believed. The Baldy Man is an expensive restaurant frequently listed in the Sunday papers and run by a well-known city businesswoman. Madigan decided it was time for a gourmet experience.

FIVE

Madigan faces the great curse of modern life and likens traffic to a
pestilence in the lives of men. A dead language. An old friend.
His wife phones. Rivers of woe and lamentation.

The following Monday he was awakened by the radio; the weather forecast informed him that the day would be wet and windy. It
was 7.00, which for Madigan was too late; it meant the traffic
would be ferocious. All hell broke loose on the first week of
September each year when the kids went back to school. In summer, the city was comparatively normal. While you would be
stopped every few hundred yards by traffic lights, at least for the
most part, you could actually move between lights.

Once September came, however, cars materialised with the
blinding chaos of snowflakes in the Alps. The main arterial roads
changed into massive car parks, full of nose-picking, tight-veined
men and ill-tempered women with their squalling kids, inching
through traffic in the general direction of school and college.

By the time they reached their offices and sat down at desks,
every last hypertensive one of them was ready to commit mass
murder. And wet days were the worst.

So Madigan sprang out of bed like Michael Johnson out of
the blocks. There was no time for a snooze, no time for a dream

of lovely or lost or brokenhearted women, no time for the first bud of an erection ...

He left the flat at 7.40 and promised himself that that very evening he would visit a motorcycle dealer and put in place his own particular solution to the traffic chaos that was Dublin. As he past Lily Bowen's door, he envied her life of cats and Caruso and the fact that she could sleep all day if she wanted to. He was envious too of the fact that her life was now beyond the need for rushing to the finishing tape.

As it happened, it didn't turn out to be such a bad morning. The traffic was loose, nudging along like wet gravel. Madigan travelled half a mile before hitting the first jam; and then it moved again. Rosie was warmed up by then. He switched the radio on for company. A current affairs programme in Irish was on. He had taken to listening to Irish rather than English because he did not want to know what was going on in the world. Folk on the radio, to borrow Garrison Keillor's phrase, might as well have been talking Urdu, for he didn't understand a single word of it. Dead languages are not without their uses.

He did not get solidly jammed until he reached Rathgar, and there, to his surprise, an old friend of his crossed the road in front of him. He did not recognise her at first. It was Vikki Morgan, whom he had had nicknamed the Mexican, because she reminded him of Salma Hayek in *From Dusk Till Dawn*. He was amazed at how much she had changed. When he first knew her, years earlier, she was a nice girl who never got out of her jeans – for anyone. Now she looked like she was dancing to the tick of the biological clock. She did not see him at first and loomed over his windshield, all style, all thighs, all miniskirt, airing her credentials on high heels with a bracelet around one ankle. Now she was the kind of girl he could very easily take a liking to. She waved at him when he honked his horn. It is always nice, he thought, to be recognised by somebody in a tight miniskirt who can honk your horn and was happy to see you. He decided to give her a call the next time he could find a space in his overcrowded social diary.

When he got to work, his assistant, Ted Plunkett, was waiting in the office. Ted was wearier-looking than a dachshund who has been left out all night in the rain. There had been more trouble in the brewery during the night shift. Ten thousand gallons of beer, enough to keep half a city going for half a week, had been sent into a vessel containing 50 litres of caustic. The caustic knocked the beer out of spec. Ted wanted to know what to do with it.

'Blend it off over the next few days, Ted. Nobody will notice.'

'It's not that far out of spec.'

'I'm afraid out of spec is out of spec, Ted. You'll just have to hold it until we've enough beer brewed to blend it.' Though Madigan looked at Ted, he stared through him, for what he still saw in reality was Vikki's smooth legs walking away from him.

'Does Alan know yet?' Alan was Alan Spratt, Madigan's immediate boss. All the new senior managers in the brewery had names like Alan or Brian or Shaun. These were the clones, the bland men in smooth suits who ran whole corporations; they had taken over the world, though most of the world did not know it.

Spratt had been headhunted from a rival drinks company where he had made a name for himself by mixing blended piss wines and putting a fancy label on the bottle to pull in the up-and-coming young wine drinkers with a big marketing push. This was regarded in the business as a superb marketing stroke. Blue Ridge Mountain, it was called, the favourite tipple of the sucker wine market. That's what past for 'pure genius' in the trade.

Now this boring clone was expecting the likes of Madigan to give 'good example'. Spratt had been sent in by the multinational food company that had taken over the brewery to 'sort out the Irish' in a kind of cultural exchange where Irish managers were packed off overseas, while outsiders were brought in to break up the cosy running of the local operation. 'Increasing shareholder value', it was called. To Madigan, he was a bollox of the highest order and should really have been invested in the order of bolloxhood. He was probably a Freemason anyway.

'Yeah.' The bags under Ted's eyes were a strange puce blackness like bruised turkey neck. 'I told him ten minutes ago.'

'How did he react?'

'Ah, you know. The usual: panicked first, then calmed down, then said that it was not the end of the world.'

'Any calls, Ted, any other stuff?'

'Let's see. Yes. After you left last night, your wife phoned. She said to phone her back. And there was a call just ten minutes ago. I had just put the phone down when I heard you come in. A fellow called Philip Marlowe. He said it was urgent and you should call him back as soon as possible. He sounded serious.'

'Did he say anything else?'

'No, just that it seemed important. He said you had his number.'

Marlowe was now a superintendent at the local police station. In another life he had been a private detective. Now he too had joined up and was in for the pension and the promotion. He and Madigan came from the same type of country and had grown up tired and disillusioned together.

'Anything else, Ted? Anybody else trying to bring half the bloody brewery down around our ears?'

'I don't think so, I suppose the caustic is enough for one night.'

Ted walked out and closed the door behind him. Madigan

sharpened a pencil, something he liked to do every morning before getting stuck into work. The soft grating of wood calmed his nerves.

But Marlowe? What the hell could he want at that hour of the morning? Madigan owed a lot to Marlowe. When Marlowe heard Sally had flown the nest, or at least had forced Madigan out, it was he who suggested there was work for private eyes, that the snooping business could always be used to turn a few bob. He had been in a similar situation himself, so he knew what hard-up was. 'It is, I suppose, a form of prostitution,' he would say, 'but then isn't all employment, except for the few who actually like their work?' So Madigan had taken his advice and ended up trotting after sad cases and watching what they got up to after darkness fell. Now he rang the police station and asked for Superintendent Marlowe.

'Marlowe? Mike Madigan here. What can I do you for?'

'Mike. I'm glad you got back so quickly. I'm afraid I've a bit of bad news for you. You're in a spot of trouble.'

'Go on.'

'I believe you know Professor Crowley, Professor William Crowley?'

'Yeah, well, I don't exactly know him. But I know who he is. Yes. I ... eh ... know his wife a little better.'

'Well, that's something you'd have in common with a lot of people.'

'What are you saying?'

'What I'm saying is, Dr O'Neill Crowley is not exactly a shrinking violet, now is she? But that's beside the point. The fact is the old Professor was found dead last night and we have reason to suspect foul play. It seems your car was spotted around the University last evening, Mike, and that makes you a prime suspect.

You may be one of the last people to have seen him alive.'

'What happened?'

'I can't talk about it on the phone. But you'd better call over to me as soon as possible. We're looking for leads. Do you think you could make it before lunch?'

'Yeah, I guess so. But why would anyone want to kill the Professor?'

'Your guess is as good as mine, Mike.'

'OK, listen, I'll be over around midday.'

'Fine. See you then.'

Madigan put the phone down and shivered a little. It was great to feel wanted, but being wanted like that was not exactly what he had in mind.

He thought to himself: maybe the Professor was not dead, maybe Marlowe was only taking the piss; or maybe he was dead but had died from natural causes. On the other hand, Marlowe was the professional; he did not go in for messing around. Madigan was an amateur after all; murder was simply not on his ledger, at least not most of the time.

And the funny thing was that, though he had never actually met him, he had decided that he liked the Professor. He had noticed a certain kindness in the eyes from the photographs in the office. The Professor might be a glutton, but he did not strike Madigan as being a bad man. He could see similarities between his own life before he and Sally split up and the life of Professor Crowley: the working late, the piles of paper, the perpetual hum of the photocopier. And now the Prof was dead, a huge corpse lying on a bed somewhere, a challenge to whoever would have to lift him.

Madigan picked up the phone and dialled Sally's number. It rang for a long time before it was picked up. Sally was probably still in the nest with her ape, he thought.

'Michael!' Madigan felt the day cave in on him when he heard the familiar sound of her voice. 'I tried to reach you yesterday. You never seem to be at your desk!'

He felt weak, like he was about to come down with the flu. Suddenly he was heavy and empty at the same time, as if he had just been blown up into a sort of emotional, jelly-like Michelin Man.

'I'm here often enough.'

'I need £500, Michael. Liam will need braces after Christmas. And dental work is expensive, you know.'

Madigan took a long deep breath.

'I know, I know, I got your message the other night.'

Liam was the apple of Madigan's eye; he was a great, blue-eyed kid and fruit of another life. Madigan missed him like mad and it was breaking his heart.

'Don't get abusive, Michael. Remember we're supposed to remain on civil terms.'

'Don't say it.'

He was lost for words. Like she was lancing a wound, Sally had the knack of bringing out the worst in him. All the clichés came out of him together, like the Thing in 'Alien', a twisted reptile of anger and predictability.

'Liam needs his teeth fixed and you agreed to foot the bill. You know the terms of our agreement.'

'Oh, all right. We'll meet at the usual place on Saturday?'

'No, that's why I was trying to contact you yesterday. I was hoping you could meet us on Sunday instead. I have to visit the hairdresser's on Saturday.'

'Well, fuck me. That's nice. And what if I've already arranged to go to a football game or go fishing or play a game of golf?'

'Well,' Madigan could almost see her doing her nails at the

other end of the line and blowing on them delicately, 'your football team are not playing on Sunday, and the fishing season is closed and you hate golf.'

'Well, maybe I've taken up golf ...'

'Listen, if you want to see Liam, you turn up, okay?' She slammed down the phone.

The funny thing about Sally, he reflected, was that she was very persuasive. Everybody loved her when they knew her first. They were impressed by her energy, her charm and her get up and go. It was with better acquaintance that these ideas tended to evaporate. Then people began to wonder. He could see it in the quizzical looks they gave him when he and Sally were out together. It made him feel vulnerable, like he was wearing no clothes. Most of their friends took Madigan's side after the separation; that was one of his few consolations and was also oddly gratifying. Then again, he was the one who was being cheated on. He was Mr Cuckold. Most fly over the cuckoo's nest, ignoring what's going on. But in his case it was one of the few situations he could think of where people took the side of the loser.

But Sally moved on and she moved on well; she could shed pasts like so many wasted skins. She had what she wanted now: Liam and her career, and she had an ape to service her. And there wasn't a damned bit Madigan could do about it.

And he blamed Sally for it. Though, of course, he was also to blame, if the truth were known. The world will turn out to be a lot weirder when the current generation of one-parent McDonald-eating families grows up, he thought. We are in the middle of a massive sociological experiment: statistically, the world will be half full of gaiety, while the otherhalf will be fatties who hate men. People are too busy now to care about anybody but themselves.

SIX

A long tradition. The boys in blue. The grim nature of the Public
Service. He ain't heavy, he's my brother. The aromatic weed. Hell's
Angels. A good pen. The plot thickens. Historical perspectives.

The police station was in a corner of the old city, near the cathedral. It was an eighteenth-century building, surrounded by a high
wall and a cobbled courtyard full of crashed cars and stolen bicycles. The air in the reception area was stale as an undertaker's
office; crypts had more life in them. Madigan half expected to see
a hoary monster materialise from behind a dry ledger, or a phan-
tom inkpot to be spilled across the desk. Instead, a red-faced
baboon of a policeman with an expression that suggested he was
well capable of verbal and physical abuse, peered over the counter
at him. Eyes you would hate to meet of a dark night observed him
in the bright of the dusty office.

'Name?' His voice sounded like it was bubbling out of deep
water.

'Madigan, Mike Madigan. I've an appointment with
Superintendent Marlowe for 12.00.'

'Uh,' he grunted, and vanished back into the interior of the
station. While waiting for him to return, Madigan entertained
himself by reading the posters on the noticeboard: one about

rabies, another about foot-and-mouth disease; a notice to voters to make sure they were on the register for elections. He smiled at the thought of his own registration; he had been struck off no fewer than three voting registers by anti-divorce groups before a referendum on divorce. The political is always personal.

'Mishtur Madigan, come this way.'

He followed the simian blue into the interior of the station. It was decorated with more notices on various laws and by-laws on gun licences, dog licences, marijuana growing and HIV risks. All that was missing, he thought, was a wanted list and gangsters with ugly mugs and ladies of the night with good legs and short skirts and tight asses like they always seem to have on television cop programmes. Nothing exotic here though, just the fly-spotted tackiness of small-time crime.

Marlowe was sitting at his desk with his pipe to one side as if it were asleep on the pillow of his ashtray. He looked well. He had lost weight since the last time Madigan had seen him. He wore a well-cut serge suit. Madigan could never understand why he bothered to dress well in a place like this. Perhaps it was some- thing about keeping up standards, even in the face of decay and the shabby nature of working in the Public Service. Marlowe was like the Baptist in bedlam, who prayed while all about him turned into animals. He was in a sordid job, dealt with sordid people and worked on second-rate crime, but he was not sordid himself and he was not second-rate.

'Mike! Long time no see, old son.' Marlowe stood up behind his desk and came around to greet him. He was six inches taller than Madigan and had a handshake as firm as a dentist's on Monday morning.

'Sit down, Mike. Cigar?'

'No thanks, I'm off the weed for the past few weeks.'

'You don't mind if I light up?'

'Fire away,' Madigan said, 'if you'll pardon the pun.'

Marlowe began to light his pipe, sucking the flame down as if he had a small stove stuck to his mouth. Madigan watched the mechanism of pips smoking with the intense concentration of a pervert at a peepshow. Puffs of blue guttered up the air like smoke on clear, frosty days.

'They're going to ban this, you know.'

'What?'

'Smoking.'

'That'll never happen.'

'Wait and see. Anyway, how're things with you, Mike?' Obviously, Marlowe was in an expansive mood. It was time for some small talk.

'Well, you know how it is: trying to find time to shave, worked to the bone, run off my feet, coming out through the arse of my trousers. As for the fuckin' traffic in this town, I'm going to have to get a motorbike.'

'You need a motorbike?'

'I was going to call into a dealer on the way home.'

'What do you need?'

'Something strong and fast that can turn on a sixpence and climb footpaths and go up and down stairs.'

'To get away from life's little unpleasantries?'

'If needs be.'

'How does a twelve-month-old BMW Trial Bike, 1000cc, grab you?'

'It might, except that I wouldn't be able to afford it in a month of Sundays.'

'How much would you say it's worth?'

Madigan knew the type of bike he was talking about. It was

the kind of machine a Hell's Angel might dream of, worth at least ten grand. It was the ultimate drop-the-cops-and-robbers bike.

'Ten Gs.'

'Eleven, if you had to buy it on the market. You could have one for a grand.'

'What?' Madigan gulped. He was thinking more of something along the lines of a Honda 125.

'You heard me. In about two months time you could have one of these machines for £1000, if you can wait that long.'

'Of course I can wait.'

'What's the catch?'

'No catch.'

He went on to explain how one such bike had been sitting in the station for over a year, having been confiscated from a drug dealer, who did not want to claim it for then he would have been nailed. It was brand new. There was good money in crack. The bike, newly registered to avoid its nasty owner trying to reclaim it, would be coming up for auction shortly after Christmas. It was Madigan's if he moved to claim it and came up with £1000. Madigan looked at his options. Christmas was coming; he could use Pamela O'Neill Crowley's money or some of it. It could be spent worse.

'By Jaysus, if it's that easy, I'll take it. Never look a gift horse in the mouth. Would that all my problems could be sorted out so easily.'

'You're going to have to get out of that brewery one of these days, Mike, you know that. A clever and good-looking guy like yourself should be rigged out with a handy office job like this one.'

'The brewery is the least of my problems. I'll get a nice handy office when I win the Lotto or the Sweep Stakes or have a thousand on a winning triple at Newmarket. Anyway, tell me about our friend, the Professor.'

Marlowe sat down again behind his desk, rested his elbows on its smooth green surface, joined his hands in front of his face as if praying and gazed over the tops of his fingers.

'About 6.00 this morning we got a call from the woman who comes to clean the Professor's house.' He tapped his pipe on the edge of the ashtray. Ashes fell slowly, like old rose petals.

'That's early for cleaning. I'm hardly in bed at that time.'

'It appears that Mrs O'Neill Crowley likes to have the house spick and span early. This cleaner comes in once or twice a week. Anyway, she goes inside, finds Professor Crowley stretched at the foot of the stairs ... cold as the clay.'

'So the Professor was dead at the bottom of the stairs. Any marks on the body?'

'None at all, except a bruise on the side of his face where he hit it against the bottom step.' Madigan watched Marlowe as he tamped down the glowing ash in his pipe with his finger, as if his skin had a layer of leather on it or had forgotten the meaning of the word 'burn'.

'You think he was murdered?'

'We suspect he was, though we have no direct evidence of it yet. You see, one of his filing cabinets was left wide open, and a whole cluster of files seemed to be missing. The hall door was left wide open ...'

'What about his wife?'

'No sign of her. She didn't sleep there last night. In fact, their bed was not slept in at all. We've started looking for her. I'm sure she'll turn up and maybe the files with her. That's why I called you in. I thought she might have been with you.'

'What makes you think she'd want to be with me?'

'It's a small town. We've been watching her for some time in connection with something else. We traced her to your office the other evening. We figured that you might be doing something for her,' he hesitated, 'or to her, if you catch my drift.' Marlowe shrugged, pulled a wry smile out of the corner of his mouth and shook it like an ingratiating little spaniel.

'Well, thanks for the compliment, Marlowe, but even I don't move that fast, if I move at all these days.'

Marlowe leaned back on his seat and re-lit his pipe with a golden cigarette lighter. Madigan salivated. Expensive tastes, a gift from his wife, he thought. Happy marriages.

'A gift?'

'Yes, how'd you guess?'

'It's my job.'

'You're only the amateur,' he laughed. 'Listen, I've ordered lunch at The Maker's Name around the corner for 1.00. They do hot and cold, spicy and traditional. That suit you?'

The Maker's Name was a pub halfway between the brewery and the police station. It looked 200 years old, but had just been built in mock-Georgian style.

'That's OK by me.'

'Right. Tell me first what you know about Mrs O'Neill Crowley and the Professor.'

'I will, but first tell me how you knew I was in the University last night.'

'The first thing we did after finding out the Professor was dead was to check with the University to see if he was doing anything unusual last evening.'

'And what did you find out?'

'He was working late. Nothing unusual in that. What was unusual was that one of the porters spotted a car parked under his window. When we checked out the number plates we found it was yours. So here you are now, as prime suspect.'

So there it was, thought Madigan: I walk in off the street, I meet a good-looking woman, now I am a principal suspect in a murder case. It was not the best day of his life, though he'd had worse.

'What'll I do now?'

'Tell me what you know. We'll take it from there.'

He told Marlowe the little he knew about the O'Neill Crowley situation: how Mrs O'Neill Crowley had come to him, how she had suspected her husband of having an affair, how she suspected that the third party was this woman, Maude. Then he told him what he had seen at the University.

'This Maude, do you know anything about her?' Marlowe asked.

'Nothing. Except that my client suspected that something was going on between the Professor and herself. Oh yes, I do have her phone number and address. Mrs O'Neill Crowley gave it to me. I presumed part of my brief was to spy on her as well.'

'Did you see anything that suggested there might be an affair?'

'Not last night, they didn't even kiss. Just parted. Looked to me like she was his secretary and nothing else.'

He took the address down on a memo sheet with an expensive old fountain pen in letters so big they almost spoke.

'Did you notice anything else?'

'Well, they were photocopying like mad, and then he drove off with a pile of files. Oh yes, and I found this.' He searched in his pocket for the card of The Baldy Man.

'Ah, so the bold Professor was a client of The Baldy Man. He had good tastes.'

'He was a bit of a glutton, if you ask me. Oh yes, I nearly forgot. There was a big bag of sweeties in his office. The Professor seemed to like his candies. Or maybe he liked to give them as presents to the little girls, or the little boys. You never know.'

'He was a diabetic, actually. He had a diabetic's card on him when he died. You see that's the problem. He could easily have been murdered by an overdose of insulin. Say somebody tampered with his syringes, or slipped him a double or triple dose of insulin. On the other hand, he could have died from lack of insulin too, and that would also be impossible to pin on anybody.'

'Maybe he heard somebody in the house, came down to investigate, and died of a heart attack. That's just as likely a scenario, judging from the size of him.'

'The autopsy will show that up, hopefully.'

'Anything else odd?'

'Well, my lads are combing the place at the moment. But so far they've come up with nothing other than the fact that certain files are missing.' Marlowe got up and began pacing the room like an executive, one of the Alans, Shauns and Brians, trying to make a decision. After a while he said: 'Mike, I'd like to ask you a favour. You seem to be getting on well with Mrs O'Neill Crowley. Assuming she turns up, and I dare say she will, I would like you to continue to meet her. Tell her you were able to dig up something about this Maude. Say you found evidence of an affair, say anything you like, but try to keep in contact with her. Use your charm. I suppose I'm looking more than anything else for her reactions to what happened to the Professor.'

'I suppose I'm not allowed to ask what this is all in aid of?'

'Not yet. Just try to keep this investigation of yours going. I don't care what you do. Just watch her.'

'Nothing would give me more pleasure. But what's in it for me?'

'Well, you know how it is, Mike, with all the scrapes you get into; it's always nice to have friends in high places. Who knows how many parking fines might be quashed, if nothing else. And remember the bike. You're getting a good deal there. Of course, if you don't want to do it, we would still have to keep you on the list of prime suspects.'

With that he shot Madigan a glance over his glasses – Madigan knew it well – a sort of you-know-the-score-kid kind of glance, a better-do-what-I-tell-you-or-end-up-in-the-shithole glance.

'What if she doesn't show up?'

'Don't worry. She will. You could start by checking out The Baldy Man. Enjoy yourself. Have a good meal. Live it up. We'll foot any bills she doesn't pay.'

'That's precisely what I had planned on doing.'

Madigan felt he should be living in the old days of the British Empire. He would have made a great informer, he mused, a double agent, a creeper to barracks in the dead of night.

SEVEN

Saturday. An obituary. The Baldy Man. Marika. Madigan laments the
passing of youth and mourns his lost opportunities.

Madigan had to call to the brewery for a few hours on the following Saturday morning. It was the fifth weekend in a row he
had to go to work, but as he had had a reasonably good night's
sleep, he did not mind too much. When he woke at 9.00 it was
already light.

To Madigan, Saturday was usually a brutal and lonely day. He
spent most of it in bed with a hangover, or else thinking about
something Sally had said to him, or something he had said to
Sally or just thinking about Sally.

Today looked OK, though. He would not be meeting Sally.
He could work till lunchtime, then ramble into town to take in a
movie, or go for a walk by the sea, assuming the day held up. The
prospect of an afternoon with nothing to do but kick the cans
along the street lifted his spirits no end.

He switched on the radio as he ate his breakfast. There was a
tobacconists' strike in Italy. The country was going crazy and queues
were forming for miles at the borders into Austria, Switzerland and
France as frantic Italians struggled in vain to get supplies of cigarettes. The ferries to Corsica and Greece were overflowing.

It was his own predicament multiplied by millions. When he smoked, he could not bear the idea of being in a house where there were no cigarettes. Even at night, when he had five or six cigarettes to last him till morning, he would sometimes go out to buy some more. After all, he rationalised, you never know when the atomic bomb might go off or the global economy might suddenly grind to a halt, leaving you stranded without cigarettes. This behaviour, of course, did not gain him any brownie points during his life with Sally.

He switched off the radio, went outside and breathed the frosty air. It was fresh and chilled as Bavarian lager. He climbed into Rosie and drove towards work. He found a Steve Earle tape and turned the volume up high. He whizzed down the dual-carriageway that was dry and free of traffic, pumping out Copperhead Road as loud as he liked, one of the advantages of having nobody to answer to.

He bought a newspaper in a small shop near the brewery gate from a man called Sid, one side of whose face was covered with a puce birthmark. He expected to see the Professor's death notice on the back page, but there it was, on page one, between news of a protest about abortion and a trial of a man accused of repeatedly raping his daughters.

NOTED PROFESSOR FOUND DEAD.

World-renowned neurobiologist, Professor W.B. Crowley was found dead at his home in Dartry yesterday. Prof Crowley, who won the Samuel Taylor Memorial Medal for his work on the cerebral cortex, had been known to be diabetic for some time. Ms Dymphna McCarthy, who worked for the Crowley family, found the body when she arrived yesterday morning for her day's work. Police have not ruled out foul play. Dr Ivor Dunne, Chairman of the Society of Clinical

Psychology, said that Prof Crowley's death would be a severe blow to his many friends in the profession. 'I can only extend my sincerest condolences to his wife, Pamela, and family. Prof Crowley will be sadly missed,' Dr Dunne said. Funeral arrangements will be announced later.

So, he thought, the Professor was not your average nobody. When he reached the brewery, its sole inhabitants were the brewery cats, whose job was to keep the brewery mice in check. The sound of heavy-duty motors, of valves and pumps and boiling coppers, whirred at each other across the brewery yard. A broad trail of steam rose into the air, as if it were a factory manufacturing clouds. Madigan's computer had spewed out twenty feet of lab results during the night. It took him two hours to get through them, and another hour to plan the brewing programme for the following week. When he had finished it all, he set off for The Baldy Man. He drove Rosie out of his parking space, opened the boot for the gateman to check that he was not stealing kegs (every car was checked, as whole businesses were once run with goods stolen from the brewery), and inched towards town in the heavy, pre-Christmas traffic.

The streets were full of buskers and girls in frilly skirts. A carnival atmosphere filled the pedestrian areas.

In The Baldy Man he was waiting for a table and reading the newspaper when he felt the silent glide of somebody at his elbow.

'Would you like a table, sir?'

He looked up. It was a vision.

She had calm brown eyes and small jewellery and skin so smooth you wanted to lick it. And her smile ... well ... a man would give his life to gaze upon a smile like that.

She might have been as young as nineteen or as old as 24, but she was no more than that. The accent was odd; American, yet with a tinge of somewhere else, Russian, Eastern European, he could not tell. He read the name-tag pinned to the lapel of her waitress' outfit, Marika.

'Well Marika, I'd love a table, in your own time of course.' He flashed what he hoped was a winning smile.

She led him between the tables and indicated a seat in the corner. He always liked to sit in the corner because it allowed him to survey the room. He hated to have his back to the crowd. It made him nervous. And he hated to have his back to the window in case there was someone outside nursing a grudge, who might want to have a pot shot at him.

The room was full of the quiet tinkle of forks on plates and whispered conversations. Intimacy was everywhere. He had a hunger as big as Black '47 when he sat down and felt as dry as three Saharas. She handed him a menu.

'When you're ready, sir. Would you like a drink in the mean-time?'

'I'll have a glass of Harp, please.'

He watched her walk between the tables. She was of medium height but she looked taller because she was so slight. She had a splendid, elegant figure and the healthy glow and honest face of youth. A student trying to earn extra fees for college, at a guess. She brought him his beer; he smiled up at her and ordered pep-pered steak, well done. The *E.coli* would be dead and he would take his chances with the heterocyclic amines.

In recent weeks he felt new to food, like a starving waif who finds an unopened tin of sweetened condensed milk in a ditch. One of the advantages of having given up smoking was a marked improvement in the ability to taste. The food in The Baldy Man was great, delicate, perfectly cooked with oodles of butter. When

Marika brought him his lunch he thought he would never get enough. He ordered a bottle of red wine to dissolve the cholesterol and bring a smile to his face; his belly could grow in proportion to his expense account.

For the want of something better to do, he watched her go from table to table, checking to see if everybody was satisfied. She moved like a willow between the tables, her hips swaying like she had oiled bearings somewhere in her lower back. Smiles fell from her, like stars from an angel, not that he had ever known too many angels. But one thing was sure; she certainly was not Irish.

When she returned he decided to ask her what she did outside the restaurant job. She said she was a student, studying medicine at, of all places, City University.

'But you're not Irish?'

'No, Moldovan.'

'Moldovan?'

To Madigan, Moldova sounded like one of the nowheres that had a habit of knocking Irish soccer teams out of the World Cup with nil-all draws.

'Moldova? Where's that? Part of Russia?'

'It is not part of Russia. It never was.' She was suddenly serious. He had touched a sore point.

'We hate the Russians. The Russians treat us badly. We are rid of them now. They are barbarians, the Russians.'

'We are all barbarians in our own way,' he said. 'By the way, your English is very good. Where did you learn it?'

'You think so? I learned it at school and from watching reruns of 'Dallas' on TV. English is the world's language. It is important too for medicine. I came here from the UK to study medicine in DCU.'

'That's a coincidence,' said Madigan, spotting the chance to get some background information for nothing. 'I happen to be interested in the subject at the moment. Personal reasons, you know.'

'I hope everything will work out all right.' She gave a sympathetic smile. 'I know how it is.'

'You don't happen to study neurobiology by any chance, do you?'

She did, and what's more, it turned out that Professor Crowley was one of her lecturers. Madigan was laughing all the way to the gossip bank.

'Have you seen this?' he showed her the newspaper report on Professor Crowley's death.

'Yes, it's terrible, isn't it? And he was such a nice man. He used to eat here sometimes, you know. He knew Sylvia very well.'

Sylvia was the businesswoman who ran The Baldy Man. She was glamorous and stylish; unattainable, unless you were loaded.

'Listen, you seem like a nice girl. You could do me a favour.' He scratched his head in search of a plausible reason to have another chat with her.

'As long as it's not personal,' she said, with a laugh.

'No, you see, I work for the *Herald*. I'm currently writing an article on Professor Crowley, you know, human interest kind of stuff, what he was like, that sort of thing. Our readers like to know what's behind the stories. Would you mind if I asked you how he was regarded in the faculty, was there anything unusual about him, that sort of thing?'

Suddenly she laughed.

'What's so funny?'

'I thought ... I thought you were ill. I thought there was something wrong with you, or somebody in your family.'

'There may be things wrong with me, but so far as I know,

they are not physical.'

Then she became serious again.

'You're not a pig, by any chance, are you?'

'Me, a pig? That's funny phraseology for a Moldovan. If I was a cop, would I be eating here at this time of day?'

'You might.'

'Well, I'm not anyway.'

'OK, would your newspaper make it worth my very valuable time to have a chat with you?' she asked with a coquettish toss of her head.

'Well, it might. It would certainly buy several rounds of drink, as much as you wanted. It might even be persuaded to fork out for a decent meal. All out of expenses, you understand.'

'Oh, I understand. But I finish up here now. How about 7.00 outside the Swan in Rathmines? Just for an hour. I don't have the whole night.'

'That's near where Professor Crowley lived?'

'Not too far.'

'That's fine by me.'

As she walked away, she seemed to swing her bottom just that little bit more than she did before, or maybe it was just his imagination. Before she disappeared into the kitchen she gave him a coy smile and a wink. Suddenly, he was in love with all things Moldovan. He would have to get out a map of the world and find out where it was.

As he ate the rest of his meal and drank his coffee and swam to the bottom of the bottle of wine, he wondered about the glibness of people. The Irish were worried about prices, about mortgages and broken marriages and the ever increasing hike in the cost of housing. Moldovans were worried about Russians, decaying nuclear warheads, radioactive water supplies and dying in hospital from the want of antibiotics, not to mention where the next meal was going to come from. It put things in perspective.

And he was too old for someone like Marika, though he did at least have the honesty of failure. He was filled with wine-induced sadness. Not only had he missed the bus, but he had arrived at a time when all the buses had just moved off, one after the other, down the wet streets of the future. It would be a new century and it would not be his and he would not be one of the ones riding the buses to their terminals, or riding the girls either. Oh, to be just ten years younger.

EIGHT

Dublin can be heaven. Madigan shows that he is not blind to the ironies of history and its consequences. Strategies for survival. Lingerie and erectile memory. A lousy trick. Choice. A new religion. A break-in at Madigan's place. Shopping.

When he came out of the restaurant the sun was still shining in the cool, restrained way that it sometimes shines in the middle of December. The Christmas lights were up. He looked for a toy store to buy a Christmas present for Liam. The pedestrianised streets were heaving with people, all rushing to grab what they could of the glitz to supply Santa. Buskers and stylish women filled the streets; a guitarist with a cracked voice attracted colonies of shoppers around him; a ragged man playing two strange-looking pipes reminded him of a spider with half his legs tangled up; a middle-aged hippy with a sad face offered him a copy of *The Socialist Worker*.

'The shipyard workers of Gdansk wanted capitalism,' Madigan couldn't resist informing him. He was not exactly a fan of capitalism himself but it was time to face the facts.

'Socialism has never been tried,' the man said.

'Better luck, next time.'

The hippy shoved his newspaper under the nose of the next

guy who came along. Maybe he would have some luck before the day was out, Madigan thought, though he had his doubts. One thing was sure – the Irish had no time for socialism.

A good-looking, rich woman in a fur coat and shiny black heels came rushing out of a store with an armful of parcels and nearly ran him over.

'Oh, excuse ME' she muttered, and gave Madigan a lipsticked fragile smile.

'Any time,' he said.

He was admiring her ankles as she walked away, when he noticed a badly-dressed man shuffling from foot to foot as if he were on the run from somebody. He had hunted eyes and wore a grubby gabardine mac, with his trousers halfway up his ankles. He had his hands under his coat and looked like he was playing with himself. However, instead of pulling out his pecker, he took a large brick from under the gabardine and slammed it straight through the plate-glass window of the store in front of him. There was a sudden crash and an avalanche of glass fell upon mannequins, expensive gowns and gold lamé dresses. For a second, the ant-like chaos of the street crystallised into passing interest. There were shouts and a security guard from a nearby shop called a police-man. Then, when people could not see who had actually broken the window, they moved on, stepping around the commotion, much as they would had a murder been committed. The man looked like he was going to rob the window display, but instead he sat down on the pavement on a pile of shattered glass, folded his arms across his chest and smiled benignly at any of the passers-by who cared to look at him. Madigan went over to the man.

'Hey, are you OK?' he asked him. 'Attacking windows like that can be bad for the circulation.'

'I never felt better in my life,' he replied. Madigan detected a smell of meths from him, like the smell you get from a dusty old lamp you find in an attic.

'You just smashed that window, do you realise that?' He thought he might be some kind of half-wit, not that Madigan cared, but it was something interesting, a seed of dementia in the milling conformity of the street.

'I know. I wanted to smash it. I love smashing them at this time of year.'

'You get a thrill out of that?'

'I do.'

'Each to his own ... '

Squinting into the sunlight the tramp looked at Madigan with carious teeth and a self-satisfied smile spread across his face, as if he had won the Lotto and Madigan was the loser who had sold him the ticket.

'Come on man, clear off out of here before the cops get you,' Madigan said. 'And rob something before you go. Make your day's work worthwhile.'

'But I don't want anything they have in there. I don't want any of that stuff.'

'Then why don't you run, now that you have the chance? You could lose yourself in a minute in that crowd. The cops will be here in no time and the store's detectives and what not.'

'I don't want to run. I want to get caught. I want to be put in jail for Christmas. People have needs. That's what I need, to have a roof over my head, and a slice of turkey and a bite of pudding and warmth on Christmas Day. Christmas Day is the worst day of the year, it's cold on the arse and hard on the shoes and there's not a bob anywhere. The cops are great lads for the Christmas dinner. I do this every year. I'll even get cranberry sauce. How about that?'

'How much do you expect to get for this?'

'A week. Two if I'm lucky. It'll pass the Christmas and maybe the New Year. Jail is grand and warm. At least I won't freeze. The police know me well at this stage.'

The public service was not in such bad shape, for within two minutes a policeman arrived, accompanied by a group of do-gooders, who pointed their fingers at the man. So somebody had noticed. Madigan stood to one side.

'Are you a friend of this man?' the policeman asked Madigan.

'Never saw him before in my life.'

'Good for you.'

When the policeman moved to arrest him, the man smiled and gave Madigan the thumbs-up sign before sauntering off down the street, arm in arm with the copper.

'Happy Christmas, everyone,' he called over the copper's shoulder.

'Happy Christmas,' Madigan replied. 'And good luck.'

And a happy Christmas is better than dying of the goddamn cold, Madigan thought. Not many down-and-outs would have had the initiative to destroy plate-glass windows and more's the pity. No one should have to freeze to death when there were bricks on every derelict site, and plate-glass windows glinting on all the high streets just begging to be broken. It was a trade with great possibilities. Madigan decided to keep it in mind if things ever got really rough for him.

When he reached Brown Thomas, he went inside. He liked the up-market stores. They reminded him of the old days. As he past the lingerie section, he remembered his better nights with Sally. In the first year of their marriage, before they got on one another's nerves so much that they could hardly sleep together, she was full of surprises, and would appear in all kinds of crotchy gear: bodices, G strings, teddies, stockings, suspenders. He loved her underwear, whether they were on her or not. And he would almost weep over the soft feel of her things in the drawer in the long, drawn out months when their marriage was falling apart.

If only he could have the bits of Sally he wanted and leave all the other bits behind. But that's the problem with men and women: you get either all or nothing. The strange thing was that the sex had never really died between them. Even after they separated he still ached for her. The sex probably kept them together longer than they should have, but he had to admit, it was a small enough raft upon which to build a life.

And that was the way it was with Sally, erectile memories, bad dreams and erotic nightmares. Sex was the closest they got to each other, sexual attraction between completely incompatible people being one of nature's lousiest tricks.

Yet he never past a display of black lingerie without thinking of her and longed to have her all over again and take the bad with the good. In those moments, like an ageing boxer, he was foolish enough to think he could go back into the ring with her. But all he had to do was imagine her voice and her coming-up-in-the-world ambitions and the demands that started like a siren at 6.00 each morning and he was cured of his longing again. Working-class girls wanting a middle-class lifestyle made the worst kind of wife. They were never satisfied. All he had to do to keep his thoughts in check was to block out his visions of Sally in her best lingerie and remember Puddle of Mudd and the song, 'She ******* Hates Me'.

He had little trouble in finding the toy section. If there is a reward for affluence it lay in the standard of children's toys. In the simpler decades, Santa brought one toy, usually a wind-up car made in Taiwan from discarded tins with a flywheel that whizzed across the kitchen floor for two hours until it broke down. Now it was different. Toys talked, laughed, squealed, climbed, rolled over obstacles, dug. The previous Christmas he had bought Liam a complete simulated dashboard for a sports car. It had everything: steering wheel, gear change, indicators, a horn and all the lights that a dashboard needs, including a screen in front of the 'driver' where he saw 'the road' coming up to meet him. Sally, in one of her rare unguarded moments, admitted it was money well spent.

He spent an hour looking at various gadgets without success. Choice is the curse of the better-off. He took the coward's route and decided the best way to get a present for Liam might be to let him choose for himself. Besides, Brown Thomas was too expensive anyway. Besides, this little cheating on the natural order of commerce would give him the opportunity to be with Liam for a little longer than usual.

When he got back to his flat he called on Lily Bowen to see if she wanted anything picked up at the supermarket. Since religion had caved in, the supermarket was the main ritual left to him for weekends. And it was not unlike going to church: he saw the same people, week in, week out, he tossed a coin into a collection for the profit of some distant and nebulous god, he was offered body and blood in the form of free samples of cheese, sausages, salami and low-alcohol wine, he heard prayers in the form of advertising announcements for discounts off various products, which, just like real prayers, past over his head as background noise. Advertisements promise much but they will not be able to save our souls.

When Lily came to the door she was wringing her hands and was pale with fright.

'Oh, Mike, I'm so glad to see you. A young man called, looking for your flat. When I told him where you lived, he just walked past me up the stairs. He never said another word. Oh, the young are so aggressive. I'm very sorry, Mike. I should never have told him, but it just came out before I could stop it. I never thought. He seemed an ignorant type, rough, brutish, common, one of the lower classes. I didn't like the look of him.'

'That's OK, Lily. He'd have found out anyway. What time did this happen?'

'It must have been, what, 11.30. Yes, I remember now, I was pouring breakfast for Keen and Terri and Miss Pretty and Suzy and Arthur. That would have been breakfast time for my little ones.'

'Did you hear him leaving?'

'No, that's a funny thing, now that you mention it. I didn't. Then again, I was playing Enrico later on, so he could have left without my hearing him. It's strange. Is something going on, Mike?'

'Something is always going on, Lily, but don't worry, I can look after myself.'

'Oh, I'm sure you can, Mike, but please be careful.'

'Did anything come for me in the mail? Anybody throwing money at me?'

'Just one bill. Now where did I put it?' She searched the interior of her cat-ridden den. 'Here it is.' It was a final demand from the cable company. Nothing new in that. Still, no news is good news.

'Anybody else call, Lily, like that fine lady you saw a few days ago?'

'No, Mike. You would not be so lucky. You can't expect the ladies to keep coming after you like that, you know. A woman will only go so far. You should make a bit more effort, Mike. I might be only an old dear but I'm thinking of your own good.'

Madigan signalled to Lily to keep talking while he crept up

the stairs as silently as he could. He needn't have bothered. The stairs creaked so loudly that anyone in his room would have heard him a mile away. He slipped his fingers into the knuckleduster in his jacket pocket. It was one of the few weapons he carried. He gave the door a little shove and stood back. It swung open.

There was no one inside, unless he could shrink to the size of the tiny wardrobe, which was unlikely. But he had been there. The place was a mess, like a seagull's nest. To the outsider, it looked no worse than usual. But Madigan knew where everything should be and nothing was where it normally was. The guy was thorough, he would have to hand that to him, more professional than he would have been himself. He had searched drawers, cupboards, wardrobes. He had been through everything. Madigan poked around. There was nothing missing, as far as he could see. Then again, there was little worth stealing. And he left nothing behind him. He was good.

Madigan went down the stairs to Lily, who described the man as small and thin and dark and wearing a leather jacket. Well, that was a help. She might recognise him, she said, but she was not sure.

'Well, there's nothing to be done about it now. No point ringing the cops. They'll do nothing. I'm off to the shop now, Lily. Do you want me to get you anything?'

'Oh, if you would be so kind, Mike, a dozen tins of Kitti Kat.' Every week she said the same thing, the if-you-would-be-so-kind bit. The only bit that changed was the quantity of cat food. Either she was catering for different numbers of cats on different weeks or else she was stockpiling. Madigan suspected it was the latter. Lily was like himself in his cigarette period; she was always afraid of the nuclear holocaust that would do her out of cat food. She poked in her purse for money.

'There's no need to give me anything, Lily. Consider it a commission for keeping an eye on my place.'

'Oh, Mike, you shouldn't. I'm not much of a watcher, now am I?'

'You're great, Lily, You're great.'

And Madigan went off to the local supermarket where he got his bits and pieces, sufficient to ensure he would not have to go near a shop for a week. And he collected the dozen tins of cat food for Lily and four bottles of whiskey to last him till after Christmas. He loaded up Rosie under the lights of the car park, bought some nicotine chewing gum in the pharmacy to feed his craving and ease his mind, and wind him down after the break-in.

When he got back to the flat, the evening was a pale smear lost in the rising smog. The city lights rubbed orange on the undersides of the clouds. The forecast was for sleet and more rain. A car alarm went off somewhere. It could have been a house alarm, or it could have been someone breaking a plate-glass window in a department store. He did not bother to look.

NINE

Rath Maonais. The Late Mike Madigan. Leda and the Swan. Going on a date. Madigan poses as a reporter. Public house banter and speculation. Hate mail. A word in his ear. A definite proposition and some surprising statistics. Whores that he had known.

The funny thing about Rathmines, Madigan thought to himself, was that nobody ever came from there but everybody lived there at one time or another. He had lived there during his early days in Dublin. He had lost his virginity in Rathmines and lost a lot of other things there too, including his heart and an expensive watch. It was that kind of place, within walking distance of the best pubs and pick-up spots, a Mecca for the single. If you wanted to get laid, then Rathmines was a good place to start.

The area was full of decaying Victorian terraces, long turned into flats for its thousands of transient inhabitants. Nothing was ever permanent in Rathmines, not the people, not the love, not the shop signs, not even the names over the doors of the pubs. Madigan felt comfortable there though because, unlike Temple Bar, it was not full of fakes and wankers.

He looked at his watch. Marika was late. He was relieved. It was usually he who was late. He was well aware that he would not have to wait till he was dead before being called the late Mike Madigan.

A pair of swans flew right up the main street between two lines of street lamps in the direction of the canal. They were all wing and wheezed leisurely at the air as if contemptuous of the fact that it was holding them up. The swans looked slow and heavy, like old B52s, in this fantastic invasion of the natural into the man-crazed street.

'They're lovely, aren't they?' He heard her voice behind him and turned. 'Funny, they never seem to move their heads up or down, while the rest of their bodies move with their wings.'

She was right. The swans' heads were like spirit levels, while their bodies rose and fell with the beat of their wings. They seemed to take ages to reach the canal. Then they landed on the water, like a pair of clapped-out cargo planes. He wondered gleefully what they would do if there was ice on the canal but did not say so.

'They mate for life,' he said.

'They remind me of my childhood,' Marika said. 'We used to go to the Black Sea. There were these big marshes filled with geese. My father told me the geese came from the Kola Peninsula, and I had this picture of Archangel as an incredibly rich and fertile land, full of pastures and meadows and larks and geese grazing miles of short grass. Funny the notions you have when you are young.' The accent was more American than on the first day. Perhaps she had been watching more re-runs of 'Dallas'.

'Things are OK when you're young, unless you have the misfortune to be born in the wrong place at the wrong time,' he said. 'And a lot of places are the wrong place and a lot of times are the wrong times.'

'People have to do strange things to survive,' she said.

'Strange enough to be in on a Saturday night?' He pointed to the pub across the road. Is Maguire's okay?'

'Maguire's is wonderful.'

They crossed the road. She was wearing jeans and a light sweater, with thin canvas shoes and no socks. It was not suitable clothing for the middle of December. Then again, December in Dublin compared to Moldova was probably semi-tropical.

They went inside. The bar was half-full of early evening drinkers, middle-aged topers and those afraid to go home. There was a smell of stale smoke from the carpet and wafts of urine when anyone opened the toilet door. The regulars looked at Madigan and his young companion as if they had seen the story a hundred times: the boss trying to have it off with his secretary, the lecturer trying to get into his student's pants, the man from an unhappy marriage falling in love with his best friend's daughter. After a while they turned their attention back to their drinks.

'Listen.' She looked straight at him. She had high, smiling eyebrows that lifted her cheekbones and her face and light appeared to come out of her eyes. Madigan decided there and then that she was beautiful. 'I want to say something before we start. I don't like journalists. I don't trust them. Nothing personal, you understand. I went out with a journalist once. He would sell his grandmother for a story. I agreed to meet you because I liked Professor Crowley. He was a good man. And if there's anything strange about his death, I'll be of any help I can.' She suddenly sounded older than her years and world weary, as if she was in her thirties rather than just 22 or 23.

'Maybe we would all sell our grandmothers if we got enough for it. Or maybe you just met a bad one. One stinker gives the rest a bad name.'

'Will your newspaper give me something for telling you what I know about Professor Crowley, cash in hand?' This seemed a strange request in view of what she had just said about grand-mothers.

'Depends on what you know. Put it like this, if anything you say finds its way into my story then I'll make sure you get something. That OK?'

He bought her a gin and tonic and he had a glass of Harp himself. The barman gave him a knowing wink that signalled complicity in what he supposed was the corruption of a young, beautiful minor.

'I suppose we might as well get started. It's pen picture time.' He took out a note pad and biro and stuck the biro behind his ear, just as he supposed real reporters did. 'Like, what did students think of Professor Crowley? Was he liked, disliked, that type of thing?'

She swirled her G and T in its glass. The ice cubes turned slowly, like icebergs oiled in the Bering Sea.

'Quinine,' she said, 'good for malaria. Yes, well, as I was saying, he was liked, loved even, by many of us. He was the most popular of the academic staff and he was the best lecturer on the course. He knew his area very well, better than anybody else. He was a bit absent-minded though. I remember one day he came into class with a sheaf of notes but had lost his glasses. He couldn't read a word without them. He was all in a flurry. He found them eventually, but everybody was terribly embarrassed for him.'

'So the praise by this Ivor Dunne fellow in the newspaper is a fair reflection of his standing in academic circles, not just phony bullshit?'

'Sure, he was lovable and he brought out the caring instinct in all of us, especially the girls. His occasional mistakes just made people want to help him. Professor Crowley was a gentleman. He was a gentle person, if you know what I mean. He hated failing students, and often nearly gave us the contents of exam papers before we sat them.'

'Surely that's not being very professional?' Madigan had started taking notes, like a real pro.

'Well, I don't know. He used to say he could get a better insight of how well somebody understood something if they all knew that it was going to be on the paper beforehand.'

Madigan thought of his own short-lived career in college, before he failed his way out of the system at the end of first year. In those days many people chose courses for no better reason than that they joined the shortest queue on the first day of term.

'You see, students have the reputation for being lazy. But that is wrong. Nowadays, everybody studies very much right from the beginning of the year. The libraries are full in October. Nothing matters but reports and term exams and assessments and essays all year. It is very hectic.'

Madigan loved the determined way she said 'but that is wrong', as if she were declaiming some high-hidden truth.

'Medical students always worked hard, even in my time,' he said.

'Not as hard as they work now. Anyway, the point is that Professor Crowley always did his best to make life as tolerable as possible for us. I can say no more than that.'

'Did girl students fall for Professor Crowley, I mean in a sexual way?'

'Absolutely, no. He was lovable and kind, but you would not, how would I say, fancy him. I mean he was like a big teddy bear. And he had big soft eyes, but I could not imagine any student getting involved with him.'

'Does that sort of thing go on? I mean students having affairs with lecturers?'

Madigan had often fancied that being a lecturer must be a great job, having all these girls in their prime gazing up at you.

'Oh yes, occasionally. There are one or two girls in every class who will sleep with lecturers. It's power, I guess. And some of the lecturers make the most of their chances.'

He wanted to say 'lucky bastards' but didn't.

'If someone told you Professor Crowley was having affairs, what would you say?'

'I'd say the idea was, what is the word ... ludicrous. In the case of Professor Crowley, I don't think it would come into the equation. I would doubt very much if Professor Crowley would get involved with a student.'

She seemed to be pretty sure of herself in this.

'They're often the most dodgy; the lads who'll put it into unexpected places.'

'I don't think so. Not in this case.'

Madigan laughed. 'When I was your age, I thought people didn't have sex until they were married.'

She too laughed at this, 'Well, you see, my people are different. It's circumstances. Maybe we have to do things that the Irish never have to, sitting cosy as you are on the edge of Europe.'

'Maybe it's better to grow up more slowly.' Though he didn't believe that. 'What's the point of losing one's innocence too young?' In reality, he felt the complete opposite. One of the regrets of his own life was that he had kept his innocence for far too long. Then he was ripe for the plucking when Sally gave him the goods.

'Tell me, what do you know about Mrs O'Neill Crowley?'

'It is not for me to say. I mean I don't know the woman except to see her around the Department.'

'But what is the received wisdom, the general opinion of her?'

'The received wisdom, as you put it, is that, how would you say; is that she is not a nice person. I don't know what that's based on. She never lectured to me, so I never had any direct contact with her. But it is said that she ran around behind the Professor's back. You're not going to print that now are you? I mean this is only rumour. She might be the most faithful woman in Dublin for all I know.'

'No, hearsay is off the record. Besides it's the Professor I'm writing the article on, not his wife.'

'It is said, I don't know how true it is, but she's said to be a bit of a ... according to the technicians in the Department, and they have the gossip on everyone, she regularly had affairs behind his back. I have no idea who with, and if the technicians knew, they were not telling me. But there you have it. That's the gossip about her.'

'Who knows, maybe she had good reason to have them? Maybe something was radically wrong at home. Maybe the good Professor was no good in the hay. Maybe he had a melted crayon in his trousers.'

'Well, I don't know about that. They have a few children, so the sex cannot have been that bad.'

'It strikes me that there's something odd here. I mean, by all accounts, she's a fine-looking woman.' (Madigan didn't want to give the impression he was working for her.) 'And the Professor was not exactly what you would call full of sex appeal. They're a bit Mutt and Jeff-like.'

'Mutt and Jeff?'

'Old cartoon characters, from before your time. What I mean is that they're very different. You wouldn't put them together. I mean, you more or less said that yourself when you said the students never fancied him. What I'm trying to establish, I suppose, is what did she see in him in the first place? Or was he not always such a big couch of a fellow?'

'As far as I know he was always like that. I've seen pictures of him when he was a student, and even then, he was a big man.'

'I wonder why she married him? I mean, with her looks and brains, she could have had anybody.'

'Well again, I'm no judge, but the received wisdom, as you call it, in the Department, is that she married him to further her career. Now maybe she wanted to further her career, but maybe she also loved him. It is, after all, possible for the two to go together. She was a graduate student of his. Did you know that?'

Madigan shook his head.

'She was his PhD student. She was also an officer in the Students Union at the time. She was heavily involved in protesting for contraception, abortion, divorce, all the usual things. This is what I heard. Professor Crowley was just a lecturer then. He seemed to have been a committed bachelor. He was working too hard to be even interested in women. It came as a huge surprise to everyone when he started going out with Pamela. It was said he wrote her PhD thesis for her. I wouldn't believe that though, because she was more than capable of writing it herself. The next thing they were married. It all happened so fast everybody was taken by surprise.'

'When did her affairs start?'

'I don't know, but the impression I got was that they always went on.'

'She still managed to have three children in the middle of all this.'

'Not only that, but she managed to get on the staff at the university as well, right after getting her PhD. The Professor was a help in that, in all probability, but there's no doubt she's a capable woman in her own right.'

'Maybe those rumours are just a load of old jealousy. The begrudgers haven't gone away, even now. She rose faster than anyone else in the place. That must have raised a few hackles. There's nothing like success to call out the knives. I mean, there's every reason for people to be jealous of her: her looks, her success, the way she manages to combine a career with children, her marriage to a world-renowned expert in his field. He is a world-renowned figure, isn't he?'

'Oh, yes, the praise in the newspaper is accurate on that score. He has given lectures all over Europe and the States. I'd say he was one of the biggest names at the University.'

She stopped there, and there was a touch of sadness in her voice, like the first stain on fresh blotting paper. Madigan went up to the bar and ordered another round of drinks. While he was doing this, Marika made a visit to the ladies room.

'This is a good town,' the barman said to him with a wink.

'This is the best town in the world,' Madigan answered.

'I'd say it's only getting better.' Madigan ignored him this time.

When she came out she had fresh make-up on, which gave a little more colour to her cheeks. Her lips were bright and red and new. The smile had returned to her face.

'Listen,' he said, 'all that info' you gave me is very useful. It's worth more than a few drinks.' He handed her a £20 note.

'I'd like to be in a position to turn it down, but I need the money, so I'll take it.' She shoved the note into her jeans pocket. She sat back and sipped her G and T.

'Tell me, what's it like being a reporter for the *Herald*?'

'Oh it's a job, like any other. It has its ups and downs. It pays the mortgage. It's generally pretty boring stuff; court cases, that kind of thing.'

'Still, you see your name in print.'

'I write under a pseudonym, to keep away the hate mail.'

'You get hate mail?'

'In my business you're not doing your job right unless you're getting hate mail. Hating comes easy to people, a lot easier than loving sometimes.'

'You seem unhappy.' There was a slight inflection of curiosity in her voice as she said this.

'I'm as happy as can be expected.'

'But what do you do with it?'

'With what?'

'The hate mail. How do you deal with it?'

'Usually I burn it. Just occasionally it's entertaining. You'd be amazed at the kind of crazy bastards out there. But mostly it's just dumb shite.' He was on a roll now.

'As regards the job, I'd pack it in tomorrow if I did not have to earn a crust just to keep going. And you, what is it like being a student now?'

'Not as easy as it was in your day. We're always strapped for cash, but I get by, one way and another.' Madigan was impressed by her capacity to slip into Irish and Anglo-Saxon cliché. It showed great adaptability.

The bar was beginning to fill up with its late-evening customers, younger couples and single fellows and girls searching for their dreams of love or sex or maybe just dreams. The barman's face had gone down behind the high tide of the sea of people.

'I'll drop you home,' Madigan said to her, his heart breaking. She was a nice girl; demure, charming, innocent yet worldly at the same time, the kind you could take home to your mother, if you had a mother. She was the kind of girl he would marry if he was fifteen years younger or if she was fifteen years older or if he lived on a different planet or could live his life all over again. The permutations of possibility intrigued him. The long hours of the medical profession had not yet killed off her normality.

'There's no need. I live only half a mile up the road. I'm used to going more or less everywhere on my own.'

'No, I insist.'

They went outside. It was now sleeting steadily in diagonal lines, like plastic strips whipping across the light from the stree lamps. Though he climbed into Rosie as fast as he could, Madigan could not stop the sleet fingering its way down the back of his neck. And he was wearing his anorak. She would have got even wetter, for she wore only thin clothes. He turned the engine and switched on the heater to clear the condensation from the window and take the chill out of her nearly bare feet before inching out into the squelching traffic.

'You like music?' she asked when she noticed his few scattered tapes; his Steve Earle, his Warren Zevon, his early Tom Waits, his old tattered 'Moondance' and 'Astral Weeks'.

'It's the only useful thing I can think of doing in traffic.'

'Where did you get the car? It is, wow, so old. I seem to remember seeing cars like this many years ago on television.'

'This,' he said with a flourish and wave of his hand, 'is Rosie, the world's last comfortable travelling apartment.'

'This is a great seat. They don't make cars like this any more.'

Rosie had an old-fashioned column gear-change. This enabled him to put in a wide front seat, the full width of the car. Rosie was to modern cars what stockings are to tights; not merely functional, but adaptable, comfortable, and with easy access to all working parts.

As they drove along, Madigan told her a few things about his life: how he was separated and lived on his own and so on, the loose falling leaves of his life, while still pretending to be a reporter.

When he reached her flat and stopped the car and cut the engine, she leaned over and asked in a teasing whisper:

'What's three inches long and loves oral sex?'

He looked at her in surprise. He had assumed Marika was what is called a 'good girl', and good girls just don't go around asking near-strangers what was three inches long and loved oral sex.

'I don't know,' he said with a smile. 'You tell me.'

She leaned over, as if to whisper the answer, but instead stuck her tongue into his ear and licked him suggestively. Suddenly he felt very sexy and a shot of electricity jack plugged his gear stick.

'Jesus.'

'Well?' She put her hand on his thigh.

'What can I say?'

'You like my little joke?'

'It's a good one. I must use that line the next time I'm out on a date. It might bring a little more success than I usually get.'

She looked amused. 'So what do you actually say, when you are trying to chat somebody up?'

'Well, let me see,' He thought for a moment. He decided to fight fire with fire. 'How about "there's a party in my trousers and you've been invited"?'

She laughed. 'You say this?'

'Sometimes.' The reality was that he used this phrase once or twice and usually got a slap in the kisser for his trouble.

'Success is easily achieved, though.'

'How do you mean?'

'For a fee.'

'What do you mean "for a fee"?'

'I do sex, for a fee. I sleep with men for money.' She had a calm half-smile on her lips as if she was used to getting this reaction from men. 'I won't do it for too long more, but I need to do it now. You might never get an offer as good as this again.'

'You what? You can't be serious?' He nearly coughed up his pint in surprise. 'But, but ... that's so fucking ... sad.'

'Don't be too surprised. I don't do it by choice, you know.'

'I'm sorry. It's just that it's the last thing I would have expected. I would not have thought you to be a wh ... sorry, a prostitute. But, but, why do you do it?'

'I don't have any choice, as I said. I'd go hungry otherwise. I don't exactly love it, but there you go. I was a pole dancer in London for a while. When I came here first there was no dancing like that in Ireland so I ...' She shrugged her shoulders. There was a small sadness in her face like a lone sparrow on a frosty morning.

'Wait a minute now. Let me get this straight. As far as I can see, you're about to enter one of the professions of the privileged. Doctors are treated like gods in this country. I mean you seem like a nice girl, for heaven's sake. What are you doing on the game?'

'Maybe I should give you a few statistics. My college fees are 3000 a year. It's much higher for foreigners, you see. I need at least 300 a week for rent and heating and electricity. I also need to eat, to buy a few clothes, to go out at night when I am not studying. I need to live a little. I am not extravagant. My family sends me as much as they can, but that is very little compared to the standard of living here. I have a small scholarship but it's not enough. I've had to take out bank loans just to keep going, and there's interest to be paid on them as well. My father pays as much of my fees as is possible and he imagines I make up the rest from summer work and the restaurant and other bar work which I tell him I do. But he has no idea of the cost of living in this country.'

'That much I can appreciate.'

'Anyway, my family thinks I earn a lot more in summer work than I actually do. But I have to study too during the summer months, hospital work, that sort of thing, and this limits the amount I could make, even if I went to Germany or France, which I don't. I started studying in England.'

'Do many students have to go on the game?'

'A few, I'd say. Just to survive. I got the idea from a girl in my own class.'

'Christ, that's ... just, well, wow, amazing.'

'Maybe it is. But I'll be able to stop as soon as I'm earning real money.'

'Are you not afraid of being beaten up or abused or something or ... catching something?'

'I don't do it that often, and then only with someone that I think I can trust. I have to get to know somebody a little first.'

'Like me, for instance?'

'Like you.'

'How do you know you can trust me?'

'It's a gut feeling. I kind of like you. At a guess, I'd say there's a decent person lost in there somewhere in all that, how do you say it, misanthropy.'

'Nice word! Would you not be afraid I might turn out to be some sort of dangerous nut?'

'No. If you're a pervert, I'd say you're a fairly harmless one. Most are, anyway. Perverts are mostly harmless. I think I would recognise a real head case. I like to think I'd see it in the eyes. So far I have been lucky, I guess. I've come to see a lot of it as a form of social work.'

'Healing the lonely?'

'You could say that.'

'How much does that healing cost?'

'Oh, I'm expensive. 100 for a hand job, 200 for a blow, and 300 for the works: meaning straight missionary sex. I don't do any perversions, no anal stuff, no rear entry, nothing like that. I like to see somebody's face in front of me. I'm always afraid of being strangled. I heard of a girl who that happened to once. I'm expensive because I'm good, I'm beautiful and I'm worth it. Nobody complains. It also means I don't have to do it too often, and I can keep a low profile.'

'And what about the waitressing; does that not pay enough?'

'Very little but it's a good place to spot potential clients: lonely men; single, separated or married men, men with the grey colour of desperation on their faces.'

'Like me?'

'Perhaps.'

'Well, what can I say?'

'How about it?'

'How about what?'

'Sex.'

'Sorry, but I think I'll pass on the offer. I've never paid for sex, and I hope I'll never have to.'

'You think you never paid for it, but you have. Tell me something; you said you're separated. But you had a wife, yes? Would you say you got it free?'

He looked at her and thought about Sally. 'Right on both counts,' he said. 'Nothing comes free. It's just that I'm more used to trading in kind, barter if you like, than in simple commercial transactions.'

'So what did you trade?'

'My life, I suppose. Until there was nothing left to trade.'

'There you are. Need I say any more?'

She was a smart lass. 'No, I suppose not. I'll still pass on it though. I don't think I could afford "the works" as you call it. Maybe some other time, if I find the pot of gold at the end of the rainbow.'

'Suit yourself. This is your loss.'

Madigan was severely tempted, though. He knew he could shake the trees every day for the rest of his life and something like this might never again fall into his lap. The whores that he knew were worn, sad-faced crones. He searched his infinity of lonely nights for light but could find none. She would indeed brighten up a few. Still, he hadn't the guts and he hadn't the money, so he said, 'So this is it, I guess.' He felt like Bogart at the end of Casablanca. 'Some day we may meet across an operating table. Then you might get the chance to get to know me a little more intimately.'

'OK, that's no problem. If you ever need me, or need my services, you know where I live. I'm usually there, as I spend most of the time studying. But you should catch it now while it's going, for when I qualify and pay back all my bank loans it's bye bye to the game for Marika. And as I said, I'm one of the best.'

'I'm sure you are. I'm sure it's a great offer, Marika, but I think I'll skip it. I take a tip from my buddy, Marlowe: no screwing on the job.'

'The night is young. See you then.' And she climbed out of the car with her indomitable American smile back happily on her Moldovan lips. 'Don't wank too much' she said and she gave him another sly wink as she turned away, swinging her hips as she did earlier in the restaurant.

As he watched her go, Madigan was already regretting that he had turned down her offer. As he drove away, a kind of sadness came over him. The sleet that was filling up the street was now beginning to fill up his heart.

TEN

Smoking and the small change of time. Sex on a scale of one to ten.
Jogging. 'The Unluckiest Woman in Crumlin.'
Cold winds and a sad heart.

Madigan had a lot of thinking to do. In the old days he sat and
smoked and thought. If he had a problem, he blew it around in
the smoke rings that he sent out between his feet as he rested
them on the kitchen table of his flat. Now that he had stopped
smoking, he had also stopped thinking, or at least stopped thinking about anything other than cigarettes. For weeks he could
hardly breathe and saw big, soft, woolly monsters coming out of
corners and climbing all over him, especially at night. Food and
drink made him crave cigarettes and when he could not smoke, he
felt hungry all the time. He was racked by wave after wave of a
pain very like heartache, a feeling like the one he had felt for
months after Sally left. His heart was squeezed and hollowed out,
he had no desire to do anything other than sit and stare at the four
walls and crave, crave, crave.

He got through it by not thinking in large time segments. He
dealt in seconds, minutes, the small change of time. Days, hours
and weeks were for the millionaires of contentment. Every
moment was the moment when he chose not to smoke and there

were two million such moments in every year.

And then there was his sex life, or lack of it. On a scale of one to ten it would merit at best a three or four, and consisted, for the most part, of watching late-night porn and firing the pump action water pistol at everything that moved on screen. It was limited, but then Linda Lips and Christy Canyon were not the worst companions. This was apt in the age of AIDS but then AIDS was not the reason he was having no sex. He was having no sex because nobody would sleep with him. All the reasons for doing so were gone. He had no money and was past the age of attractiveness. He had no monetary pheromones. There was no good reason to be around him. He was drifting, like a smoking log, into middle age, but there was no sign of the fire going out. So, ludicrous as it may sound, he took up jogging in the hope that it would keep him from getting too horny.

It had started in the autumn. First it was excruciating. He would run a few hundred yards, and then, afraid of exploding, he would have to stop. He reckoned he would have got a heart attack if his job in the brewery had not kept him reasonably active with all the running around he had to do. He would cover up in a warm tracksuit, cap and gloves and huff and puff down the concrete pavements like Bob Dylan on one of his never-ending tours, with his heart an angry monster trying to break out of his chest. But again, just like the time after giving up the cigs, the yards became blocks and the blocks became miles, and eventually he could jog three miles without running out of breath, as long as he went slowly enough. His fastest pace was about nine minutes a mile, a little faster than walking, but he was not complaining.

He took on no snooping assignments for two months after giving up the fags. The waiting and watching would have been too much, without the familiar warmth of smoke slaking the insides of his lungs. The Crowley case was only the second since then.

His previous case had involved debunking a compensation claim by a woman known as 'the unluckiest woman in Crumlin'. She and her family had between them been involved in seventeen claims against Dublin Corporation, the gas company, a couple of large stores and a range of insurance firms over five years. When she and her sister fell into the same hole in the pavement on different nights, the Corporation had had enough and called Madigan in to look into the whole area of 'organised accidents'.

He dug up enough to prove that the woman's most recent 'accident' was no accident at all and the case was thrown out of court. However, it whetted his appetite for more business and when the Crowley case came along he was happy to be back in business.

As he sat in his flat he was so busy trying to think that he did not feel like going to bed. He tossed the various possibilities and combinations of possibilities of the case around in his head. He figured he would have to call on Maude in the near future.

For several nights running there had been a terrifying screaming sound heard in the area. Madigan even heard it in his sleep. To Madigan, although he was no believer in the supernatural, it sounded like the banshee. Now he listened out for it but did not hear it again.

As he looked out on to the street, the rain began to ease up. A cold wind whistled down the wet roads from the sea. There were no urchins about. If it froze during the night, a cat would not walk in the morning.

ELEVEN

Lifers. Thoughts on corporate power. A break-in at the cat's cradle. A hatchet job. The Pride of the Coombe. An interrogation. Progress is made. A dirty video shop.

Ted Plunkett already looked worn out by the time Madigan arrived at his office the following morning. Not only were there bags under his eyes, but half his face seemed to have slid into them.

'Morning Ted.'

'Hmmm.'

'Well?'

He gave Madigan a look that suggested he was well on the way to a nervous breakdown. 'I'm in here since 5.00 yesterday morning,' he said. 'Without a break.'

Madigan watched Ted come and go. He was tired, haggard, getting old. Once a man reaches a certain age, he becomes reluctant to change, he thought, he finds it hard to pack up his bags and move on. But he changes from within, though he doesn't notice it. He falls in love with something rotten and moves with all his stuff into the cobwebbed basement of routine. The brewery was full of lifers on a sentence from which only winning the Lotto could save them, and probably that would not save them either, for they would not live six months without the security of routine.

You find them at all ages. There were 25 and 35-year-old geriatrics walking around the brewery. They died in their mid-twenties but continued to exist for another 40 years before being buried after retirement. In a kind of routine of the undead, they did the same job, getting up at the same hour, passing the same lamp post at the same time every morning and seeing the same streets and the same newspaper seller, day in day out. They lived for two weeks' holidays every summer. More men die immediately after retirement than at any other time. This is something the insurance companies understand. Madigan saw them clock off like dead roses at the end of September and it was not a pretty sight. But a man must eat and a man must feed his children.

Ted went on to tell him of the latest disaster, this time involving a work-to-rule by the electricians' union. Madigan put his ears into shutdown and waited till he had finished his story.

'Any calls for me, Ted?'

'Sorry, Mike. No idea. I've been down on the floor all morning.'

If Madigan was doing his job properly, he would be trying to fire Ted with enthusiasm for his work, or at least trying to tell him that things would be better in the future. But the new meanness in the company meant that circumstances were against enthusiasm. To Madigan it felt like he and Ted were pissing against the wind of conglomerates merging, of management structures getting ever more 'streamlined', of computers running entire businesses with a skeleton staff, of people working day and night for a smaller and smaller slice of the corporate cake. This was known as 'sustained growth'.

The real power was in the hands of senior executives like Alan Spratt and anonymous board directors and fund managers and the shareholders of multi-nationals who controlled all the lolly and ruled the country from behind the politicians' backs. Ah well, Madigan thought, you have to accept powerlessness as part of growing up.

It was 5.30 before he had time to read his e-mails. And there it was, a message from Mrs O'Neill Crowley to the effect that, 'for obvious reasons', the assignment was to be called off 'in view of the recent sad happenings' and that payment for his time would be made in full as soon as the funeral arrangements were over. The message went on to say she would be in contact with him in a few weeks. That was good. He didn't care a damn what she did or had to do, as long as he got paid. He was already dreaming of his new motorcycle.

When he got home, he encountered Keen and Terri, two of Lily Bowen's cats, having a good screw in the alley outside his front door. Terri was bent over and screeched with pain as Keen pulled in and out. So Terri was the banshee he had been hearing in his sleep for several nights. He hoped she was getting some pleasure out of it. They seem to scream loudest after you pull out, he thought.

Lily Bowen was waiting for him when he got inside. She had her finger to her lips and signalled in a low feline whisper for him to come into her flat. Terri escaped from Keen's clutches and rubbed her back against Madigan's leg as he past.

'Mike. You remember that young man who searched your flat a week or two back, the one who asked me where you lived?'

'I remember.'

'Yes, well, he's back. I saw him go upstairs about half an hour ago. He has not come down since. I think he must be up there waiting for you.'

'OK, thanks Lily.' Madigan thought for a minute. 'Looks like

I'll have to give him a little surprise.'

'Oh, please be careful, Mike. Don't do anything foolish.'

'Don't worry, Lily. I can look after myself.'

Madigan always kept an axe handle in Rosie's boot in case he ever had to use violence as part of his job description and had trimmed about a foot off it, to make it easier to swing in enclosed spaces. He had done plenty of practice with it and was so fast that only a gun could beat him. Whenever he used it, he went for 100 per cent damage, for the only way to fight was to fight dirty, strike first and break bones if possible. He liked to get his retaliation in first.

And he would smash skulls, if he had to. For there was nothing as disconcerting as the knowledge that the prison system was housing, feeding and clothing some hoodlum who had nothing on his mind but to murder you just as soon as he got out. It did not lead to a good night's sleep.

He took the axe handle from the boot and shut the hatch quietly. The hickory was smooth and hard and balanced nicely in his hands, the perfect weight for cracking skulls. He slipped it under his coat and crept around the back of the house.

He was, of course, a coward, a sheep in wolf's clothing; he knew that, but what had to be done, had to be done. He climbed the fire escape as quietly as he could.

The guy was in his kitchen all right, a small dark fellow in a leather jacket, sitting at the table, picking his nails with a flick-knife. The catch on the bedroom window was undone. The first rule of the professional burglar: always leave an escape route open. Like God, a good burglar never closes one door without opening another. If Madigan had his way, though, he would be in no position to use that flick knife, or the window either.

He slipped back down the fire escape and asked Lily to ring

his phone number in exactly two minutes and to let it ring for as long as possible. Then he climbed back to the window ledge and waited.

The phone rang. While it was ringing, Madigan opened the bedroom window, and as quietly as he could, climbed inside, leaving the window open. He knew the draught would attract the man's attention sooner or later. He slipped behind the open door of the wardrobe where he would be able to swing at the intruder as soon as he came through the door.

The phone kept ringing and ringing. Madigan was lucky. He had disconnected his voice mail to avoid having to pay for other people's phone calls. Eventually, he heard the chair scrape on the lino floor and the sound of footsteps as the man went to the phone. The ringing stopped as soon as he picked up the receiver. He said nothing and Madigan heard the soft click as he put it back into its cradle.

He heard him shuffle quietly around for a few minutes, and then sit back down at the kitchen table. There was silence again.

After what felt like an eternity, while Madigan kept thinking the guy was probably so used to the cold that he never felt a draught, he heard a quiet scrape as the chair moved, and very faint footsteps came to the bedroom door.

Suddenly, he saw Madigan and crouched. The knife flashed like the sun on a windscreen. Madigan parried to the left and to the right, stood back and let him come. Then, as fast and as hard as he could swing, he let him have it.

Madigan caught the man with the full force of the axe handle on the back of the wrist. He knew it would take a surgeon several hours to fix it up and even at that, he might never get the full use of the hand again. The knife went flying across the floor.

Before the man realised what was happening, Madigan had

swung the handle again. This time he got him on the other arm, though too high up to break a bone. He roared with pain and fell forward into the room.

'OK, fucker,' Madigan roared. 'You're brave now, aren't you? You make as much as one attempt to get that knife and I'll break every bone in your fuckin' body.'

He crouched on his knees, holding the more broken of his arms with the other one and whimpered like a slapped child. Madigan poked him in the side with the axe handle.

'Now, you little ball of shit, seeing as you've made yourself at home, you might as well take a seat again. At least now you have the honour of being my guest.'

The young man groaned and clutched at his broken hand and stood up, staggering from side to side. Madigan used the handle to shove him into a chair.

'One move and your knees will feel the same as your arms.' The young man looked up with a frightened stare. Madigan took a bucket from under the bed, which he used occasionally to piss into when he was too lazy or drunk to cross the hall to the toilet. He kicked it under his feet.

'Now, put your feet into that. Go on, both of them, right to the bottom. That's right, all the way, jam 'em in. Just in case you might get it into your head that you lost your vocation as a four-minute miler.'

The young man stuck his feet into the bucket. There was no piss in it, not even a smell. It was a while since Madigan had been drunk.

'Right, buddy. It's time we had a little chat. In fact, I'd say you have a whole lot of chatting to do right now. You could start by telling me what you're doing here, picking nails with a flick knife. And then you could tell me who you are working for.'

'Go fuck yourself.'

'Ah, you know three words, at least. I was afraid I might have had a deaf mute on my hands. Now I'm sure you can do better than just three words, you little bastard.'

Madigan smashed the axe handle down on the sideboard to help him clear his throat.

'Nolan sent me.'

'Nolan? Who's Nolan?'

'How should I know? All I know is that he sent me here to get the files. He said I was not to come away without them, even if I had to work on you to get them.'

'What files?' Madigan hit the sideboard again. An empty fruit bowl, an ashtray and a box of matches did 'Riverdance' around the shelf.

'I don't know. He said they'd be in a large brown paper envelope, and that they'd look like medical reports.'

'Was that what brought you here last week?'

'Yes. But I found nothing, so Nolan sent me back, he said I'd be brown bread if I didn't find the files, he said I would have to get them off you any way I could. Nolan is dangerous. It doesn't do to mess with him.'

'You good with that flick?'

'If I have to be, or at least I was,' he said resignedly.

'You'll not get to use it for a while now. This Nolan, who you say you don't know, has he got something on you?'

The punk nodded. A worried look came into his face.

'What would happen if you went back to him without the files?'

He looked up and stared bleakly into Madigan's eyes.

'Here, let me see.' Madigan rolled up the sleeve of his less battered arm.

'Just as I thought. Nolan's got you hooked on that stuff?'

He nodded again.

'Right, tell me all you know about this Nolan fellow, and we'll get you to detox. Otherwise, I'll send you right back on the streets and if the cops don't get you, then he will.'

The young man spilled all he knew, which wasn't much. Madigan believed him; he knew a defeated man when he saw one. He said he did odd jobs for this Nolan, who seemed to be a gangland boss, though he knew very little about him, other than that he supplied him with heroin and gave him jobs to do and that he owned a wine-coloured Mercedes.

'You HIV positive?'

'Not as far as I know, but maybe I am.'

'You meet this Nolan often?'

'Only once or twice. Usually he sends a note, by bike courier, when he wants a job done.'

'How does he get the works to you?'

'After I've got a job finished. He sends that by courier too.'

'You said you'd be brown bread if you came back without the files?'

'I'd be brown bread for want of a fix, in the first place.'

'OK, let's get back to basics. This Nolan, what does he do?'

'Stuff. He used to do a lot of porn. But the bottom's fallen out of that market now, with the Internet. Though he still does some.'

'Do you know what you pick up and drop off on your errands?'

'Used to be videos. Now it's mostly smack.'

'Where do you make these deliveries?'

He gave Madigan a list of drop-off points for drugs and porn, one of which, AM/PM Videos, was just around the corner from where Madigan lived.

'What did Nolan say about the files he sent you here to get?'

'He said they were important, that you stole them, and that they mightn't be easy to find. What was I supposed to do? I was just following instructions.'

'Now listen to me. I'm going to take you to the police now. It's for your own safety. That way, you can tell Nolan that I busted you, that you told me nothing, and the police will send you to hospital to set your wrist and put you on rehab. If I let you out on the streets now Nolan will have your guts for garters. It's your best hope.'

The youngster thought for a moment.

'Yeah, OK.'

'By the way, what's your name, kid?'

'Benny. Benny Mulligan.'

'Ah, the Pride of the Coombe. Right, Benny, time for a stroll. We're going to take a walk to my car.'

Benny extracted his feet with some trouble from the bucket and staggered upright.

'Now, no heroics, Benny. No point trying to run before you can walk.'

They went down the stairs and into the laneway beside the house. Madigan brought the bucket with him. As he past her door he saw Lily's terrified face in the doorway. He gave her a wink as they past. She did not wink back. Her mouth was open, as if she was catching fish.

Madigan opened Rosie's passenger door and placed the bucket in front of the seat. He ordered the kid to sit in and jam his feet back into it.

He dropped him into the nearest police station, telling the cop that he had apprehended the suspect in the course of breaking and entering his flat, that he had fallen over the fire escape trying to escape and broken his wrist. He told him that Benny was a drug addict in search of cash with which to feed his habit and that the boy had serious problems and would need specialised medical attention for his drug abuse. The policeman looked at him as much as to say; 'who the hell do you think you are, some lefty liberal do-gooder trying to tell me how to do my job?'

When Madigan got back to his flat, the first thing he did was to go around the corner to AM/PM Videos. The store had a stale, sweet smell, the smell of all the lewd visions of everybody who had ever seen a porn movie borrowed from the joint. A pale young man in a goatee beard stood behind the counter watching a film on the monitor on the wall.

'Hi,' Madigan said. 'I was wondering if you have a video I'm looking for. It's called 'Victoria Blue'.'

'Just one moment. I'll check for you now.' The pale man punched a few keys on his computer and watched the flickering titles appear on his screen.

'No, I'm afraid we don't have that one in stock at present. I can have it in a few days, if you're prepared to wait.'

'No. Well, actually what I was really looking for was to buy it rather than rent it out. Do you have any idea where I might get my hands on it?'

'We don't sell videos here. This is just a rental outlet. The big chains do any buying that goes on. But I can give you the names of our suppliers, if that would be any good to you.'

'That would be just fine. I suppose not all suppliers would carry a title like that?'

'No. But here are the names and phone numbers of our three main suppliers. I am sure the one you're looking for will be here. One of these is bound to have it.'

He handed Madigan the piece of paper and looked at him as

if he was at best a pervert or at worst a half-wit for actually wanting to buy a porn movie.

'OK, thanks.'

'You're welcome,' he said, with a knowing leer.

Madigan began looking through the shelves and selected one.
'Deep Nile'. It looked promising.

'I'll take this,' he said.

The man punched a few numbers into his keyboard.

'That'll be £2.'

Madigan paid him and went back out into the streets again.
It had turned cold. A bitter wind had risen from the east, and a
shake of hail came rolling across the crouched roofs like a swarm
of out-of-season bees. He turned his collar up against the wind
and shuffled around the corner to his flat, quietly closing the fan-
lit door behind him.

TWELVE

The following morning Madigan got up at 6.00 to try to get to work before the traffic got heavy. He worked on the assumption that the Professor would have to be buried that day. The funeral would be a convenient opportunity to see who his acquaintances were. He bought the morning paper from the same kid he had bought the *Evening Herald* from the previous evening and read it in his office. There it was.

> CROWLEY. (Silversprings and Dartry) – 2 December. (suddenly). At his residence, William B. (Willie), deeply regretted by his loving wife Pamela, sons Richard and William and daughter Cecily, brothers, sisters, brothers-in-law, sister-in-law, nephews, relatives and friends. R.I.P. Funeral service today, Tuesday at St Damian's Church, at 3.00 pm. Funeral immediately afterwards to Deansgrange Cemetery.

There was also an obituary. It was signed I.D. That would be Ivor Dunne, Chairman of the Society of Clinical Psychology, who had been interviewed in the *Herald* the day after the Professor's death. Then Ted came in with an earful of problems so he had to put off reading it until evening.

For once, the morning went smoothly. They had a meeting with Spratt at 10.30 to discuss the next week's brewing schedule, then he had to deal with a cowboy maltster at 11.00 who had sold the brewery several truck-loads of under-malted grain. After sending the maltster on his way with the information that he would not be paid unless he replaced the dud malt with a better batch, he phoned Marlowe.

'Hallo, Madigan? Is that you? I'm glad you called. By the way, what extension are you at nowadays? I was trying to ring you yesterday, but you never seemed to be at your phone.'

Madigan gave him his mobile number. It occurred to him that police detectives must have a pretty cushy life. They probably sat around all day pushing paper, waiting for something meaty to come up. Then when it did, they had time to give it their all. He himself was a bad detective because he was a brewer and he was a bad brewer because he was a detective. He was a donkey between two haystacks, going hungry through the inability to choose. But Marlowe coasted when something came up. He was the pro. No man can serve two masters. Madigan envied Marlowe.

'You were wasting your time trying to find me yesterday,' Madigan said. 'I was busy beating people up.'

'What kind of mess are you in now, Madigan?'

'Nothing serious. The reason I'm ringing you is to see if you are interested in going to the Professor's funeral today?'

'I am. But I need to see you before the funeral. There are a few things I'd like to clear up. The funeral may throw up more questions. But I think we should answer the first questions first.'

'What questions?'

'I think we'd do better to discuss this over lunch.'

They arranged to meet in The Maker's Name at 1.00. It served good roast beef on Tuesdays.

Madigan took the afternoon off in lieu of overtime and left instructions to Ted and the shift staff to cover any eventualities.

Marlowe was waiting for him in The Maker's Name. He had swapped his blue serge suit for a smart grey one. Even his shoes shone – not bad for a policeman in the middle of a working day. Madigan hoped he appreciated the care his wife took of him.

The bar was full of lunch-time customers, mostly couples in their thirties and forties, illicit couples from offices and business-es, well-dressed women and smooth men running to flesh.

He found Marlowe in the last smoking area of the pub.

'Well, have you heard from Mrs O'Neill Crowley since last we spoke?' he asked, as Madigan sat down.

'She left a message yesterday, saying I was to consider the case closed.'

'Fair enough, I suppose. Your case is indeed closed. No dead man ever had an affair.'

'It's not closed for me, Marlowe.' Madigan told him about his nocturnal visitor, while toning down the details of the less than hospitable reception he had given him.

'Looks like you're a popular man, Mike.'

'Maybe I should just take the money and run.'

'You're deep in the Marmite now, Mike. And Marmite is sticky stuff.'

'You know anything about this Nolan guy?'

'He could be any of a number of gangland bosses around here. That's if Nolan is his real name. I'll run a check on him when I get back to the office. I'd watch my back, if I were you. He'll prob-ably attempt to get those files again.'

'I wish I had them. He could have them. I've no desire for martyrdom.'

'I suggest you move out for a while. When word gets back of what you did to Benny, you might have some more callers.'

Madigan ordered lasagne and salad at the bar and a glass of lager for both of them.

'What did you make of her message?'

'She sounded pretty much in control. Not that you could tell an awful lot from an e-mail.'

Marlowe lit his pipe. Aromatic notes filled the smoking area, like Bach on dope. Madigan salivated. Non-smokers gave them barbed looks, as if they were some new branch of the SS.

'Did you make any attempt to contact this Maude woman?' Marlowe asked between puffs.

'No, I thought I'd wait to see if she turned up at the funeral first and see her reaction. I didn't like to go barging in, under the circumstances.'

'The coroner's initial report says he died of natural causes. There was no sign of poisoning, or injury or internal or external bleeding, except where he hit his head as he fell. He died of a cardiac arrest, a good old-fashioned heart attack.'

'Not surprising, when you consider the size of him. So everybody's in the clear?'

'Technically yes, and that's the story we've released. Nothing of interest on the body, nothing indicating anything unusual.'

'So you're happy he died from natural causes,' Madigan said, 'and I've been like a fly walking up a mirror, looking at the underside of my balls for the past week?'

'That's the official verdict anyway.' He tapped the ashtray with his pipe.

Madigan's lunch arrived. It was flat and dead and layered, like something found at the bottom of the sea, concrete for the filling in of arteries. Not that he cared much. We all have to die one way or another.

'But you're not sure?'

He shook his head.

'The fact that there were no syringes found in the house of a diabetic is in itself suspicious, wouldn't you agree? In all probability the wife has the files that are missing from the filing cabinet in the house. Those are popular files, whatever is in them. It appears she was in London on the night the Professor died, giving a paper at some conference. I've been on to Scotland Yard to check that one out. They should get back to me in the next day or two.'

'She doesn't strike me as somebody who'd leave a filing cabinet wide open after removing files, especially if the stuff was important information,' Madigan said.

'Precisely the thought that occurred to me.' He took a big mouthful of smoke and let it out like a furnace cranking up on a frosty morning. 'I'm in this game for longer than I'd care to remember and when I think something stinks, I'm usually right. And there's another thing too: the Commissioner has been on to me to drop the case. He says there are far more important cases to be followed. And I don't doubt he's right; there are important cases on the books. But he's intervening too early in this thing, if you ask me.'

'Do I detect the dry crinkling skin of a cover-up?'

'I don't know, but don't be surprised if I'm taken off the case. Similar things have happened before.'

Marlowe put his pipe down and took a long drink of his beer. He looked out the window thoughtfully.

'We've a dead fat man and if we don't get to the bottom of what's going on pretty quickly, the trail will go even deader than it is and nothing will ever come of it. You know that, don't you?'

'Yes.'

'And somebody in a senior position on my side would like nothing more than for precisely that to happen. If I'm squeezed off this case, I'd like you to continue snooping around. I'll not be able to give you any overt help, but I'll do what I can behind the scenes. I have a kitty, a slush fund for this sort of thing. I use it for paying for information from all kinds of sources.' Marlowe looked at Madigan carefully and picked up his pipe. It had gone out. He put it down again. 'I think the Professor had stumbled on something big. It might have been connected to his work or it might not. I think whatever it was, it was worth a lot of money to somebody, and I think the bottom line was that he was killed for it. That is a mere hunch, of course, but you know as well as I do that my hunches have a habit of turning out to be true.'

'And I'll tell you something else. I'll not leave a stone unturned until I've got to the bottom of this. Of course, he might just have died. After all, it will happen to all of us.'

'When did the wife show up?'

'The evening after he was found dead. A few hours after we met here last Friday. She said she was on the last flight from Heathrow. We checked it out. She was on it all right.'

'Does she know there was an investigation going on?'

'Not to my knowledge. Or at least if she does, she didn't hear it from me, or from any of my lads. I explained to her that it was standard police procedure to look into any unexplained death.'

Marlowe went up to the bar to pay for the food. The police department was picking up the tab for both of them. Madigan went to the loo. When he came out, the crowd in the bar was beginning to thin out, the lovers and the romantically inclined having to go back to work.

'Listen, Mike,' Marlowe said, 'it'd be better if we weren't seen together at the funeral. We should certainly not be seen arriving together.'

'That's grand by me. I'm used to doing things alone.' Madigan smiled.

They walked out into the weak winter sunshine. Three workmen were digging up the road outside the pub with power tools. The ground vibrated under their feet. As they drove away, Madigan switched on the news. It turned out that a young man, collecting money from a cash point, was kicked to death by a gang of youngsters only half a street from where they had eaten.

We live in tough times, he thought.

Thirteen

Madigan, full of last things, imagines his own death and speculates on the passing of the Greater Death. He attends a funeral and sees the Black Widow. A large coffin. Ivor Dunne. A heavyset stranger. Offering condolences.

Madigan had strong opinions on the subject of graveyards. He imagined his own grave: quiet, with a sprinkle of marble chips, a few plastic flowers and the sound of birdsong every spring and autumn. He saw the weeds growing there in the summer and was quite happy with the notion of becoming a bright little weed, a part of the earth. The ground did not seem such a bad place to be in, all in all, compared to some of the places he found himself on a day-to-day basis. The peace and quiet would have a lot going for it.

His ideal graveyard would be on the side of a hill, somewhere in the countryside, preferably facing east so as to catch the morning sun. Someone would be burning nettles there in the corner to keep him company, and the smell of burning leaves would remind him of being alive. He liked the anonymity of graveyards, for a graveyard is a city in the ground, a choir whose only music is silence. You are there with thousands of others; millions possibly, if you add them all up. It is like being in the bass section of a brass band: nobody hears your individual sound, yet if it were not for all the individuals there would be no sound at all.

These thoughts kept him company as he parked Rosie among the Mercedes and BMWs outside the graveyard in Deansgrange. The cemetery seemed miles across, a plain of death, a million tombstones of all shapes and sizes, a huge shanty town in stone. In the far corner he could see a little group of mourners gathered, like a herd of animals cowering from the wind in the corner of a field. But the sun was shining. It was a good morning for a funeral, considering the time of year.

He spotted Marlowe standing on his own at the edge of the group. In his Burberry trenchcoat, he looked every inch the private eye, despite his decision to take the pensionable scenic route. Madigan decided to ignore his advice and stood beside him. He needed to put names on faces and faces on names, and there was nobody else in the gathering who could help him. Marlowe looked at him once and looked away again without changing his expression of gloomy solemnity suitable for the occasion.

A priest stood over the grave in a black habit and purple stole and shook water over a coffin as big as a garden shed. Beside him stood Pamela O'Neill Crowley, looking resplendent in a black suit and fine high shoes which seemed to have picked up no mud from the yard. On her head she wore a small black hat and lace mantilla that fell across her face in a freckled shadow that made her look striking and mysterious. By her side were her three children, sad-faced little mites choking back tears. One of them was a round fat youngster who looked like a smaller version of his father.

She was sniffing softly, practiced Kleenex tears. In the beauty of her sorrow, whether real or false, she could turn whole battalions into crowds of gibbering idiots. She reminded him of certain film stars who shed small passions in small doses, on stage, at films, at Oscars and times of high drama, but who when it comes to real passion are as divorced from it as mountain tops are from the sea.

Or was he being harsh on her, he wondered. Maybe she was capable of grief and love, and life did beat under those magnificently calm breasts. Perhaps she had discovered that there was more to life than crawling her way to the top of some stinking academic pile.

He looked towards the grave that was big enough to bury a small car. Two fellows in bowler hats, like Laurel and Hardy, removed a mat of plastic grass from over the mouth of the grave and the coffin was lowered by at least a dozen men. The priest made a few more incantations, shook a little water and started saying repetitious prayers on his beads. Those in the congregation who knew the responses joined in. Madigan smelled the earth when the mat came off. It made him feel good and reminded him of childhood, and the thought occurred to him that, even in the suburbs, the earth itself is real, even if little else is.

As the ceremony was finishing, and the green plastic mat was replaced over the grave, a tall, distinguished-looking man in a black suit put his arm around Pamela O'Neill Crowley to comfort her.

Madigan nudged Marlowe. 'Who's the big guy?'

Without looking, he replied; 'Ivor Dunne, Fellow of the Royal Society and Chairman of the Society of Clinical Psychology, an old friend of the Professor's.' Marlowe spoke under his breath; his breath went up, his words went down. 'They trained together. My information is that their friendship was greater than any rivalry there might have been between them.'

Madigan doubted that. If he knew anything about academics it was that they would cut one another's throats over the dimensions of a gust of wind. He looked around at the crowd.

'Where's Maude?' he asked.

Marlowe pointed. She stood only two rows in front of them. Madigan could only see her coat and her head buried deep in her hunched shoulders. She was shaking with grief; deep sobs were coming through her as if she were a steam engine of middle-aged lamentation. She moaned quietly and swayed from side to side, like a tree on a storm. Yet she was far away from the centre of things. Nobody seemed to be paying any attention to her. For mistresses, if indeed she was a mistress, must always grieve alone.

The tall grey man, Ivor Dunne, seemed to be taking a central role in the proceedings and ushered the children away from the graveside.

Looking around, Madigan noticed another solidly-built man standing on his own near a yew tree at the far edge of the crowd. There was something vaguely familiar about him, but the clock-works of his brain were not working well enough for Madigan to remember where he had seen him before. The stranger watched the ceremony with his hands joined across his ample stomach. He had the build of a cardinal or a successful businessman. He exuded canonical authority and looked like he could put away a fair sized meal.

Madigan turned around to ask Marlowe who he was, only to find that Marlowe had gone across to the other side of the crowd and was talking to Pamela O'Neill Crowley, offering his hand in condolence. She took it and shook it without really looking at him.

Madigan decided it was time to do the same himself. He jostled among the crowd who were queuing to shake her hand. They were as big and heavy and red-faced as Muscovites with winter woollies and raw with cold. It was like joining the queue for McDonalds in Moscow. When she spotted him she seemed a little surprised. Her tear-stained face slipped for a moment into the ditch of a grimace. Then she managed to get the wheels back on the road and fixed it up again, like an election agent straightening a fallen poster after a storm.

'So good of you to come,' she said in a slightly forced voice. 'But there was no need; you didn't have to worry about the outcome of our little transaction. You will be paid.'

She shook his hand, then pushed it quickly away, as if it were a crow's foot that had been extended to her.

'I decided I had to come. Duty, etiquette, you know,' he said.

As he listened to her inappropriate words, Madigan gazed into her veil and gazed into the heart of her night. He felt he had learned what he had come to find out.

'There was no need,' she repeated the words again and fixed up her face of mourning for the next person in the queue to shake her hand. Madigan smiled and left her to the rows of mourners who were lining up behind him.

When he looked around for Marlowe, he was nowhere to be seen. Then he saw the blue unmarked police car pull out onto the road and head off between the rows of respectable houses. The tired old sun had taken the afternoon off, as it liked to do in the run-up to Christmas. The sky had become grey and overcast and there were no leaves and no wind. There was nothing for Madigan but the cold air and the gathering gloom.

FOURTEEN

After the rain, the celestial light. Eating humble pie. A fable. Madigan is forced to find alternative accommodation. *Un film bleu*. Things sure ain't what they used to be. Further instructions. Pay day at last. Tears of joy.

By the time he got back into town, the rain had started again. It hammered irregularly off the gutters like a dicky heart, though not enough to wash the grime off Rosie's windscreen. He had to drive half-blind, peering Magoo-like through the smeared windscreen into the darkened streets. Someone had spilled a bin full of papers along the canal. The wind was now rolling them along the dirt, their print slowly seeping down the drains.

The lights were on at the all-weather hockey pitch behind Madigan's flat. In his youth, only middle-class girls played hockey. When he needed cheering up in the days after he became a grass-widower, he often went to watch the girls train on the all-weather hockey pitch. It helped fill in the long evenings after Sally left him and before he had taken up snooping to help pay the bills. It allowed him to dream of all the possible lives he could have had, if he was not who he was or had not made the choices he had made.

When he got back to his flat he poked around till he found

the flick knife. He picked it up with a piece of tissue and popped it into a plastic bag to give to Marlowe to take a set of prints to see if he had anything on Benny Mulligan.

He thought he heard a noise and looked out. But it was just the orange glow of a shaking street lamp and the trees fighting with the wind. The shadows of the bare branches crept across his walls like skeletons. The city was easing down from its demented rush-hour.

He would have to do something about his accommodation. Marlowe was right: he was no longer safe in the flat. If this Nolan character believed Madigan had the files he was interested in, he was sure to send someone else looking for them and the outcome might not be as fortuitous as it had been the last time.

He decided he would have to seek alternative lodgings for the time being. His parents were dead and his one brother had emigrated. He thought of moving in with Lily for a week or two, but it was too close to home. Besides, the thought of living in a cat menagerie almost asphyxiated him. Finally he reached for the phone. He would have to fork deep into a large helping of humble pie to sort himself out.

'Sally, Mike here. I need a favour.'

'Who do you think you are, phoning in the middle of the week looking for a favour? What favour? No! No! No! You know the arrangement. You have more than enough contact with Liam as it is.'

'No, Sally. It's not about Liam this time, it's about me.'

'Are you in some sort of trouble?'

She sounded as if she was gagging, as if he had caught her in the middle of doing something really important, like giving Steve a blow job.

'Well, if you are, don't come to me looking for help.'

Sally was passionate. She was all heart.

'We're through, Michael, finished, and you know that as well as I do. To me you are past, P-A-fada-S-T, do you hear me. I don't want you messing up my life again, just get that into your head.'

'No, Sally. I'm not trying to resurrect the past. Will you just listen to me, for God's sake?'

'I have listened to you for half a lifetime, Michael. I am tired of your weakness, your promises, your indecision. I am sick to death of your habits; your drinking, your laziness, your nose-picking, your snoring, your smoking, your farting and your general disregard for everyone around you.'

'I've given up smoking,' he said.

'That's probably only going to make you worse.'

'You know, Sal, you're like the wife who put the rat's tail into her husband's dinner. When he refused to eat it, she threw away the tail and offered him his dinner back. "You don't expect me to eat that?" he said. "He doesn't want it with it," says she, "and he doesn't want it without it." That's what you're like Sal, full of logic.'

'More bloody stories. People like you don't know whether you're coming or going. I know you and I know you'll never amount to anything more than a bundle of contradictions. You can fool yourself, Michael, but you don't fool me.'

'Well fuck you too, Sally,' Madigan said and slammed the receiver down. He felt sick. Vertigo. Of course, he admitted she was right in many ways. Sally had a lot of things going for her; she was sexy as hell and she was dynamite in bed, and she could be charming when it suited her. But by Christ, did she make you pay.

What irritated him most was that he had let himself down. He had almost begged her for a place to stay. Though he had long since decided his days of masochism were over, he had shown he was still tied to her, still thinking of her, still liable to turn to her in times of crisis. The city was full of boarding houses, guest houses, one-night cheap hotels and bed and breakfasts. He could afford one for a week or two, yet the thought had not even occurred to him. She was right. He was a fool. He was guilty of the most banal forms of dependency.

He opened the yellow pages and picked a boarding house at random, one in the inner city, near Connolly Station and within walking distance of the brewery. He phoned up. There were rooms available. He booked one for a week. It was in a run-down part of town that he liked to call the Combat Zone, after his time in Boston. But rates were cheap. It would be rough but he would carry little on him, just a change of clothes, so there would be nothing for anybody to steal. He would leave Rosie outside his own place, to give the impression that he still lived there. He would walk the streets and use public transport. It would be like taking a holiday without leaving town.

Madigan turned on the gas ring and cooked himself a feed of baked beans. Then he went out for a walk around the floodlit hockey pitch. There were no girls training, just a few po-faced athletes doing sprints around the track, like prancing horses.

When he got back to his flat he plugged in the electric bar heater and slipped 'Deep Nile' into the video player. He watched it through; it was fairly routine American tits and bums stuff, well-proportioned Californian nubiles being shafted from various angles by studs who kept their eyes on the ceiling to avoid coming too quickly. This was part of the American Dream, the wet part, that involves all the profits finding their way back to the San Fernando Valley.

Madigan was nostalgic for the old days of porn when girls with big hair who looked like Loretta Lynn actually seemed to be enjoying the sex. Now they were all shaved and smooth and pumped with silicone; they all looked the same and they all looked bored. At least Christy Canyon and Chaisey Laine gave the illusion of being real.

He watched the whole thing through and replayed the best bits. Then he went to bed, and had, all told, a good night's sleep.

The following morning he caught the bus to work. He phoned Marlowe and met him in The Maker's Name for lunch to give him the bag with Benny Mulligan's flick knife and asked him if there were any new developments on the Crowley case.

'The only new development, if that's the word for it, is that the case is closed, as far as the police are concerned,' he muttered sourly. 'The Commissioner officially took me off the case this morning. A certain amount of it is due to pressure of work. I've been moved on to another case.'

'Where does that leave us?'

'Well, you know I have my suspicions. But as far as the Gardai are concerned, this was nothing more unusual than death by misadventure.'

'What do we do now?'

'I don't know, quite honestly. Common sense would say to lay off, forget about Mrs What's-her-name and her dead professor. But this searching of your flat by guys with knives puts a somewhat different perspective on it. I could put a tail on you, or put somebody watching your flat on a 24-hour basis. That would be just routine protection. But other than that, I can't be of much more help to you at the moment.'

'What about Nolan?'

'A well-known racketeer. Drugs, pornography, contraband; take your pick. Anything that turns a few bob. He runs his rackets from a distance. All these guys do. They live in cosy suburban homes, with dolled-up wives, and send their kids to fee-paying schools. These are wealthy people, and as you know, cash calls the shots around here. They get unfortunates like your Benny Mulligan to do their dirty work for them. This Nolan could have a dozen Benny Mulligans working for him, but you can be sure of one thing; he'll always keep his own hands clean.' He struck a match and lit his pipe. 'We have a file on these characters. We call it the Teflon File. We've never been able to make anything stick to any of them for ten years. We know exactly who runs most of the racketeering in this city, but we can never pin anything on any of them.'

'Will you be able to find out anything else about Nolan or Benny Mulligan for me?'

'I'll put the word out. That's all I can promise. And my slush fund is still open if you turn up any info' on Mrs O'Neill Crowley. The case might be closed, but I don't think it should be allowed to go to sleep entirely. The only difference now is that I'll no longer be able to help you, at least not officially. You're on your own.'

'Thanks.'

Madigan was getting tired of the case. He was thinking of cutting his losses, sending Pamela O'Neill Crowley his bill and using the money as an early down payment on the bike and have a good night out on the town. He no longer cared a damn about her and her fat dead husband, or whether she killed him or not. He no longer cared about whether she slept with half the city. He felt he had earned a rest.

He did not have long to wait for his Lotto dreams to be fulfilled. When he went back to work, the afternoon's post had been delivered. There, among progress reports and unreadable trade journals, was a plain white envelope containing a cheque for

£2,500. Well, that was the bike taken care of, as long as Sally did not get to hear of the windfall. There was a short note attached.

> Mr Madigan, I'm sure the enclosed cheque is more than sufficient to cover your fees and any expenses that might have accrued from the work you did for us. Needless to say, recent circumstances have made anything you found completely irrelevant. So I trust this is the end of the matter.
>
> Yours sincerely,
> Pamela O'Neill Crowley

'Yes,' he said out loud and clapped his hands in the quiet of his office. At least he was back in the black again. Once he got this guy Nolan off his back he would wash his hands completely of the whole affair.

Madigan sat back and put his feet up and began to contemplate the possibility of having a good time. On his new bike he would be a cowboy around town, getting to work in a fraction of the time it took him now. And when it came to chasing cars or getting away from them he would be Serpico, king of the urban jungle, solving the world's problems on his horse of steel.

The £2,500 was the biggest pay-off he had ever had and for the least amount of work. It amounted to bribery, but Madigan no longer cared. If the police did not think the case worth following up then he sure as hell didn't. He would have Sally paid off in the short term and the bill for her mortgage was not due for another two weeks, by which time his brewery cheque would have arrived. If he had anything to do with it, Sally would not see a shilling of that two and a half grand. It was Robocop time, less than two weeks to Christmas, and he was as rich as a sultan.

FIFTEEN

Madigan sees the broader picture. The big issue. The Little People.
Madigan in the Underworld. The Holy Father.

That evening, Madigan made his way to his new lodgings through
eerie derelict streets. The city was divided into two by the river, as
dramatic a barrier to affluence as the Berlin Wall ever was. Most
of the wealth had drained south, the middle class acting as a giant
Hoover sucking all the goodies away from the rest of town. One
half built cages around itself to keep the other half out. It was
First and Third World economies, global issues on a small scale.

He was going to live now in a land of faded doorways and
cracked windows and thin-faced, blue-skinned inhabitants. This
was the republic of the wretched, the land where the Little People
had finally come to rest. The only life forms here were glue-sniff-
ing, heroin-crazed kids and the occasional meths-soaked bum
rooting through the rubbish bins or lying on the steps of crum-
bling tenements in pools of puke. This was caring Ireland. He
gave £1 to a toothless tramp who said he would pray for him. Pray
for yourself first, Madigan thought.

It was a long time since he had walked the streets of the inner
city, where high railings and locked-down shutters were the order
of the day and the necessity of the night. People did not walk

these streets after dark. Muggings were hourly happenings to feed the living dead of heroin addiction. These were streets where the police did not venture out and the dogs went around in pairs. Madigan was reminded of his first job, as an apprentice fitter in a tannery at the edge of this Combat Zone.

He was eighteen and had just moved up from the country. It had been the finest summer in living memory and he had spent much of it lounging by the sea in an old boathouse owned by a friend's parents. He had spent the summer months painting shop fronts and falling in love with a publican's daughter. He was innocent then. He remembered how the sea rose and fell with his dreams every day, and every night those dreams rose and fell on the publican's daughter. He could have stayed there at a push, but he wanted to experience life, which he believed then existed only in big cities. He wanted the bright bright lights. He was not yet ready for the death-tempting limitations of quiet places, so when the job in the tannery came up he grabbed it and left his publican's daughter crying into the pints she pulled for the sad-faced farmers of the village. The devil was never happy when he was in heaven.

He thought he was heading for glamour. Instead of glamour, he got the stink of the tannery, which hung from his clothes and hair for days like rotting flesh. The dust, the dirt, the used condoms and needles, the streets of litter and yesterday's papers blowing in the breeze all made him think he had entered into a new phase in the history of decay. The seasons were not renewable, the days were not really days, but rather grey extensions of the night, the whole year was persistently and relentlessly the same. There was nothing here but concrete and no place for even weeds to grow. Cars were burned out on a nightly basis, crashed against street lamps by fifteen-year-olds robbing them for kicks. Barbed wire ran along the tops of every wall as if war were about to break out any minute. He paid for his wanderlust with long nights alone, nights that he dreamt of the publican's daughter.

This was welfare world, where the only shop doing business was the labour exchange, and the only time you would see a crowd larger than a gang of youths at a corner was when it opened. Kids sinking needles into their arms and feet and girls injecting themselves in the groin in dilapidated toilets were the order of the day.

But then the boom time came. And during the boom times when employment began to grow, the proportion of Irish nationals among Simon Community volunteers dropped from 90 per cent to fourteen per cent in the space of twelve months. For a while Dublin was European City of Culture, where beggars were sprawled across the bridges with their hands out, mendicants in the most freezing gales of winter. The poor are always with us just as the rich are always with us, though the rich are always somewhere else. And no one really gave a damn for anybody but themselves.

As he walked down the quay towards the boarding house, a skinning gale came up the river. The buildings by the quays were falling into dereliction, smashed up by youngsters who were paid to do this by developers who bought them cheap and made a small fortune by building office blocks and car parks in their place. He turned away from the lettuce-coloured river and headed past the bus station up a dingy street towards his lodgings.

Just as he had pronounced despair on the whole situation, he saw redemption walk towards him in the only form it ever took in the Combat Zone. Father Peter, a six-foot-six Catholic priest with grey hair and a great handsome head, came around the corner like a Pied Piper followed by a crowd of urchins. He had not changed a bit in the ten years Madigan had been out of the place.

Father Peter was the only hero Madigan knew during his early years in the city. He worked, with little help, among the derelict creatures of the street. This man saved lives on a daily basis and never got a penny for it, or made the headlines. He got no free golf-club membership, no high-powered Porches, nor did he keep a small yacht in Dún Laoghaire Harbour. Madigan could not understand why he did not become disillusioned with the deluge of despair and alienation and give the whole business up. Maybe that was why he was a priest and Madigan a second-rate private eye.

'Hiya, Father Peter,' he said.

The priest looked at him for a second or two, as if he could not remember who he was – which was perfectly understandable after ten years. He was wearing civilian clothes and would pass as a steward at the US Open. He would be surprised at a stranger knowing he was a priest. Then he laughed. He had a strange country accent, half northern, Monaghan maybe, thought Madigan.

'Good God, it's Mike, isn't it? Mike ... Mike ... Mike Madigan, the guy from the tannery who went up in the world. Good God, I remember you now. You were always in a hurry when you were around here. And you were a bit of an angry young man, if I remember correctly.'

'Was I? Maybe I was, I can't remember. I'm too tired to be angry now.'

'That happens to all of us, Mike.'

It was strange for Madigan to be taken back into a previous life, to a time when he was less disillusioned, less compromised, less exhausted. In those days he still had a future, he was the heart and soul of the party in the tannery. The world was still expanding, instead of contracting as it had done later to one flat, several

119

set of traffic lights and a brewery.

'You're still on the old job, Father Peter?'

'Still slogging away at it Mike, you know, still slogging away. And how are things with you up in the brewery? You must have a handy number there now.' Priests always talk in clichés – they have to be nice to so many people; and even more so now, Madigan thought, with the media implying that every priest had his hands in the young lads' trousers.

'Well, we're still making beer anyway. The advantages of working in a recession-proof industry that does even better in boom times.'

'Like myself, Mike, like myself. A recession-proof industry. That's the best of it, hah! There's always jobs for the likes of us, what!' And he roared out laughing while a small boy with an 80-year-old face surveyed Madigan from behind his back, as if wondering if he might have anything worth stealing.

Still, Madigan had to admit the priest cheered him up as he bid farewell to him and his snotty-nosed cohorts and climbed the steps of the dump he was to call home for the next few weeks.

The lodging house was run by a stunted fellow who smoked so much that his left hand was yellow from cigarette smoke. It went well with the wallpaper, Madigan thought. He craved a cigarette again, like he had done in the old days, and began counting to wait for the craving to go away. He went inside.

The Combat Zone boasted a railway station as well as a bus station, and the room shuddered like a nightmare every time a train past through. The mainline diesels roared and shook the walls and rattled the window frames and caused flakes of plaster to quietly depart the ceiling for the floor.

Madigan sat in the room for half an hour before deciding that if he stayed there, he would not get a wink of sleep. He collected his coat and went downstairs to demand a room away from the railway line. The man with the yellow hand nodded morosely and gave him one, this time towards the front, from which he could see out onto the street below. The traffic was noisy but it was not as bad as the trains, so he took the room. He could entertain himself by watching the goings-on in the street outside.

He slept very little that night. The darkness had that unexpected quality that you get after the passing of a locomotive, a silence that is not quite the absence of sound. Cold rain hurled itself against the windows. He had brought his radio with him. He turned it on. Traditional music wheezed without emotion like an old petrol engine pulling on three pistons. He turned it off again.

He finally fell asleep and woke to a winter sun coming in the windows, catching motes of dust like spiders in the air. It was time for business and another day at the brewery.

Sixteen

Night in Hades. Sexual preferences. The Siren's Call. Aphrodite at the
end of a phone. Joy. A bacchanalian reveller. Locked out of his mind.
Benny Mulligan's house. The wine-coloured Mercedes. Nolan.

About a week later, Madigan was sitting in his lodgings watching
the world go by. It was early evening, 7.00. The sky was as black
as the bottom of a burnt pot. Things were quiet in the Combat
Zone. He saw only one or two drunks lying in the gutter in their
own vomit. Even the teenage gangs seemed to have deserted the
place. The wind was rising and set off a few alarms. They began
to sing to each other across the centre of town like pairs of
demented songbirds.

He was thinking of how his life had the near-perfect isolation
of a lighthouse keeper when the sight of a young woman walking
the pavement outside caused him to suddenly take notice. She was
a young tart, hungry, desperate and raw. She had a bruise under
one eye and a very short skirt and he could see the pale flash of
her thighs above the top of her stockings. Wasn't he the lucky
lighthouse keeper who could look at sights like that? Lucky and
unlucky, for he stood on the outside of the world of women, looking in; partly out of choice and partly out of necessity. He was for-
ever staring, like a man at a peepshow, at all the women who past

by his window in the rain.

He watched her legs. They were very fine, tapering to slim ankles, like the legs of East African girls. She was very slight, no heavier than six or seven stone, more delicate than emaciated. She could have been as old as twenty or as young as fifteen. She could be a trip to heaven or a trip to jail or a trip to ten years of retro-virus therapy before you died of 'complications'.

Madigan was a leg man. And that was what was wrong with the world, he thought. Since the proliferation of sexual images, men fall in love with the bits of women and do not hit the buffers of trouble till they try to love the whole caboodle. Still, we make the world we want.

He would have to get himself sorted out though, he thought, as he watched the shivering strumpet in the street below rummage through her handbag and close it again. He would have to find himself a good woman, if such a creature could still be found. Someone he did not hate and preferably one who did not hate him back, though he regarded the latter as the icing on the cake rather than the cake itself. He had always wanted sex rather than a relationship. It was far easier. Men wanted sex. Women wanted a whole lifetime in exchange for the sex. It was a lousy deal, he had always thought. Now he wasn't so sure. Now, if a relationship came as part of the package, he was determined to do his best to go with the flow, one day at a time, sweet Jesus.

The girl outside, with her cheap earrings and gaudy make-up, noticed him looking at her and smiled, her leg cocked to one side. For an instant her sad questioning face came alive. The chances were ten to one that she was both a drug addict and HIV positive, yet when she smiled he knew he wanted to have her that very instant, right there on the side of the street, up against a doorway or against a wall. It didn't matter. Nothing mattered except the desire to go straight in there, between those cold blue thighs. The whole world was concentrated into a pit of longing in his stomach.

He thought of a condom. He was not yet at the stage of running after kamikaze sex, though he knew he was not far from it. He ran downstairs.

By the time he reached the street, the girl had already been picked up by a fellow in a blue Ford. She looked at Madigan as she was driven past, her face a blank screen of resignation.

Then he thought of the money he had received from Pamela O'Neill Crowley and instantly thought of a solution. The solution had but one word tagged on the end of it like a label on a high street shopping rack: Marika. He could spend a grand or half a grand far worse, he thought, especially with Christmas coming up.

And what was the big deal about paying for sex anyway? He paid for drink, he paid for clothes, he paid for food, he even paid for water charges and bin collection now. Why should he not have to pay for sex? After all, sex was a commodity like everything else. Marika herself had no problem in selling it, so why should he have a problem in buying it? He would be doing a good deed. He would be helping put her through medical school. What philanthropist could turn down such an opportunity for doing good?

Madigan went into a payphone and rang her up. The phone went beep beep three times, four times, five times. Just as he decided she was out, it was picked up. A voice answered, hesitatingly, as if trying to swim up slowly from the deep shadows of sleep.

'Yes, who is it?' The Moldovan accent was stronger than it was the night he had met her. It was now more Moldovan than American.

'This is Mike Madigan, you remember?'

'Who?'

'Mike Madigan. The guy from the *Herald*. You remember?' He spoke more slowly – English would not be the language of her dreams.

'Oh, yes. I remember now. What do you want? I have been asleep.'

'I know. I'm sorry I woke you up. I was wondering – you know that little offer you made me – I was wondering if I could take you up on it some time.'

'Oh, yes. That offer, yeah, sure.' The American accent was taking over now. 'I hope you don't mean now? I was asleep.'

'No, not at all. Any time that suits you will suit me. I think I can find a space in my diary.'

'Well, not the next three or four nights. I have to work and study. Say Friday, at 8.00?'

'That's perfect. You won't change your mind?'

'Why should I?'

'You're not annoyed I phoned you at this hour?'

'Just maybe a little.'

'Is that OK so?'

'That's OK.'

'See you Friday then.'

'See ya.'

And she hung up. Madigan put the phone down delicately, as if it was a rose of inestimable beauty. He almost wanted to kiss the receiver but the thought of the kind of people who used public phones in the Combat Zone put him off. When he stepped out of the phone box, he felt a sudden spring in his step and wanted to run up the street, singing at the top of his voice.

It had stopped raining. There was a light breeze coming in off the sea and the air had the sudden freshness you sometimes get against all the odds in Dublin. He was light-headed from the phone call and smiled like a lobotomised half-wit. Dead leaves winked at him, marvellous in the yellow of the street lamps. He was filled with a kind of wild and irrepressible joy. Walking along the quays to the station, he dreamed he was in Amsterdam, where beautiful whores sat in windows in fancy underwear waiting for fellows like him. Except that he did not need them now.

What he needed was a party, some human contact to give vent to his joy.

A man in a suit, looking much the worse for wear, staggered out of a pub just in front of him. His tie was loose and the bars of an old song were getting snagged in his slurring exhalations. This is my man, Madigan thought, instantly recognising a potential drinking companion as he lurched into him.

'Where's the party, me old flower?'

'The party? There's no fuckin' party. The cunts just threw me out on the street,' he slurred, 'the fuckin' cunts.'

Then he went on singing, like Shane McGowan on one of his better nights, as he staggered off down the street: 'They were only a bunch of violets, a bunch of violets fair, fresh and fair and dainty ... fuck 'em anyway ...'

Madigan knocked on the pub door but there was no reply, though there was the sound of singing inside, peals of warm laughter. There was a large crowd in there and they were having a good time. Madigan moved on and wished them well.

Happy as a child who manages his first steps, Madigan walked along two or three deserted streets, watching his shadow shrink under him and lengthen again as he went from street lamp to street lamp. He wished he could run so fast that he could leave it all behind: the night city, the shadow Ireland. He wished he could fly way up high over Dublin and then, like a pigeon, drop

custard on everything below. Then he thought he would rather be
a crow, for crows are such clever fellows and he imagined himself
picking crusts out of bins and flying away with them in his beak,
cawing with his mates in crow-speak, using his talons to balance
on telegraph wires. Why waste your talons? He laughed at his own
witticism as he watched the traffic below.

Suddenly he realised he was in the street where Benny
Mulligan said he came from: McBride Street. Number 12
McBride Street, to be precise, named after a patriot. (Poor areas
were named after patriots. Middle-class areas had fancy names
like Larchfield or the Willows or Trafalgar Crescent. Rich areas
had no names: they were just places with high walls where rich
people lived as quietly as possible.)

As Madigan counted the numbers backwards along the street
from 128 down, he noticed there was a car parked outside
Number 12. It was a wine-coloured Mercedes.

He was out of his reverie in an instant. He sauntered by the
car and touched the hood. It was still warm. The owner was not
gone long.

Madigan decided he would watch the house. It could be any
length of time before the owner reappeared but Madigan knew he
might never again get such an opportunity to see what this man
looked like. He turned his collar up against the biting wind and
walked up and down the street to keep warm. He could not decide
whether to shuffle or hide. So he hid.

It was starting to turn cold. Madigan was sorry now he did
not have Rosie to sit in. He was sorry he did not have a bottle of
whiskey. A shine of black frost polished the paths where the roofs
drained onto the street. The air almost tinkled with little bits of
cold like fine china. A tin can rolled along the pavement.

Madigan hid in a doorway, as much to keep in from the cold

as the danger. Not a dog moved. He waited and waited, stamping his feet on the ground to keep the circulation going and looking at his watch every few minutes. He dreamt of furry slippers and a warm fire. Then a couple came up the road, arm in arm, and kissed in one doorway before going in through another. He wished he lived in a warm country where people loved each other more.

When he finally heard the door of Benny's house opening, he slipped around the corner into an alleyway and watched a middle-aged woman say goodbye to a stocky man in a grey suit. The stocky man sat into the wine-coloured Mercedes. Madigan hugged closer to the wall till he felt he was breathing in the smell of granite. As the Mercedes drove past, he got a good look at the face of the stranger in the light of the street lights. It was the kind of face that bad dreams are made of. But Madigan knew him. It was the heavy-set stranger he had seen at the funeral.

So this was Nolan. He had found him himself. Not a bad night's work for an amateur detective. Missing out on the streetwalker was even a bit of luck in itself. And he had Marika to look forward to as well. He strolled back to his lodging house quite pleased with himself. It was a cold night in the city, a cold night to be poor and selling your ass for a few shillings. It could be as cold again but Madigan felt as if he had just moved out of Dublin and had set up camp in El Dorado – the place, not the movie.

SEVENTEEN

The little life of Miss Brady. Beacons in a bog. Lines of enquiry. No
fund-raiser. The sadness of bereavement. Neurotransmitters. A cocktail
of drugs. The scientific method.

Madigan decided it was time to call up Maude Brady. He phoned
her and asked if he could see her. She sounded distraught at the
other end of the line. After assuring her in his most sincere voice,
reserved for older women, that he was not a newspaperman or a
policeman or some kind of nut, she agreed to meet him.

So that evening he drove to what in spring would be a leafy
suburb but was now just a suburb without leaves and found the
apartment block called Ashleigh Court in an exclusive rise that
oozed with respectability. Nice people lived in these places, he
thought, nice people like the Professor and his nice wife and people like Nolan who managed to sieve the dirt out of the other side
of their lifestyles.

Madigan would be prepared to lay a wager that Nolan played
tennis and golf and went to church each Sunday. He would be a
pillar of the local community, involved in Lions clubs and Rotary
and the like. One thing he had learned about the smoother gangster type was that, in contrast to their rougher rivals, they were
always good at making contacts and were masters of the art of

spring-cleaning. By their suits thou shalt know them. The fund-raiser could often be the biggest bastard of them all.

Maude reminded Madigan of what in the brewery used to be called a 'brewery nun', a sexist term for single women in their forties or fifties who never married because they could never meet a man good enough. Brewery nuns came in three forms: harridans, red-faced semi-alcoholics and gentle creatures. Maude was one of the latter. She was in her mid-fifties, with small feet and hands and soft hair. He recognised the type the moment he saw her; they always liked him. He had a way with older women.

Here was a good woman perplexed by the unexpected death of her friend and boss. How the Professor's wife could even contemplate that there might be an affair going on between them was a puzzle to Madigan. It did not take an awful lot of probing to get her to talk about the Professor. She had the wish of the recently bereaved to speak about the dead loved one.

It turned out she had worked for the Professor for over ten years and thought the sun and all the sun's cousins shone out of him. When Madigan mentioned about him being a diabetic, she said he was ever so careful about his lifestyle and his insulin injections. It was extremely unlikely that he would have accidentally injected himself with the wrong dose, or no dose at all. After all, trained medics simply do not make mistakes about such things. Madigan agreed they might make mistakes and kill other people but surely not themselves.

'Just suppose, for argument's sake, that the Professor was murdered. Can you think of any possible motives?'

'You're not saying that Willie was murdered, are you, Mr Madigan? I mean, who would want to murder poor Willie? Everybody thought the world of him. No, that theory could not possibly be right. Willie had no enemies, so far as I know.'

'I'm not saying anything like that. I'm just looking for explanations for an unexpected death, just like yourself. OK, let's try another approach: what was the Professor working on before he died?'

'For the last five or six years he was working on a drug related to cyclocon, a drug for treating depression. He was working on the genes that controlled the illness. He was doing great work, poor Willie. You've no idea of the number of people who would have been cured, or at least have their symptoms alleviated, if his work had come to a successful conclusion.'

'And how far would you say he was from a successful conclusion?'

'Well, I'm not a technical person, Mr Madigan, but I'd say there was a few more years work needed, clinical trials, all that kind of thing.'

'All of which costs money?'

'All of which costs a lot of money.'

'But the rewards would be great?'

'Yes, I suppose they would, but only if the Professor's work could be carried on to its logical conclusion. You see, Mr Madigan, Willie's work, the Professor's work, was highly specialised. There are only half a dozen people in the world who could finish it.'

'Do you think you could give me a list of their names?'

'I think so. I'll write them out for you before you go.'

'Would anybody in this country be able to duplicate his work?'

'In his own lab? I don't know. Maybe. I suppose, if they had access to all his documents.'

'What about his wife?'

'Yes, I suppose she could. Though she has not worked directly in that area, her work is related in some ways. She has worked a lot in the area of neurotransmitters.'

'Neuro what?'

'Neurotransmitters. They are responsible for passing on messages in the brain.'

'This cyclocon stuff, where is that got from?'

'It's a natural substance. It's synthesised using GMOs.'

'GMOs?'

'Genetically modified organisms. Several big drug companies make cyclocon. It's sold under several trade names; Sonoverol, Meridianol, Lillipol. It's extremely expensive. A course of the stuff costs several thousand pounds. Doctors only prescribe it as a last resort.'

'And the Professor worked on this drug?'

'For several years. But the important thing is that he worked on related drugs as well. More effective ones.'

'More effective ones?'

'Yes, drugs which would have similar clinical effects, only better, faster and with fewer side effects.'

'Curing depression?'

'Yes. I know for a fact he had done quite a lot of work on one in particular.'

'What was it called?'

'Well, he called it MDC, methyl diethyl cyclocon, related to cyclocon but not the same.'

'Do you know what were the results of his work on this MDC?'

'The results were encouraging, very encouraging. He was in tremendously good spirits for the few months before he died. He knew he had stumbled on something very big but I'm fuzzy on the details.'

'Was that what you were working on in the Department on

the night before he died?'

'How did you know that?'

'I was outside in the car park watching you.'

'You were what?'

'Just as I said. I was watching you. All part of another job I was doing.'

'What other job? You've lost me now, Mr Madigan.' She appeared to be in some distress at the thought of being watched.

'All will be revealed in due course, Miss Brady.' In reality he was afraid that nothing would be revealed, even to himself. This case was sticky stuff, viscous: knowledge as treacle.

'Who could give me more background on this cyclocon and the MD whatdoyoucallit?'

'Only two people in this country, by my guess. The Professor's wife, Pamela, and Dr Ivor Dunne of the SCP, the Society of Clinical Psychology. You could contact Dr Dunne at the SCP, his number is in the phone book.'

'You never answered my question, Miss Brady.'

'Which question?'

'About what you were doing on the night before he died.'

'I'm sorry, Mr Madigan, I'm a little upset. You must understand, Willie was like a brother to me. I miss him terribly. I can't believe he's gone.'

She took a tissue from her sleeve. Madigan felt for a moment that she was going to break down. She was like a balloon filled with water but she managed not to burst.

'That night, Mr Madigan,' she sniffed, 'we were photocopying the drafts of some papers he had written. Working late was nothing new with Willie. In fact, he always seemed to work late, as far as I could see. I only worked late with him if there was some deadline to meet, say when he was preparing for a high-level conference or when he was preparing something for publication. That week he was working on two papers he had written, which he was going to send off to the States for publication in the *Journal of Clinical Psychology*. He had put a lot of work into them and I knew he was very enthusiastic about them. I think he believed he was onto something very important.'

'Do you know what the papers were about?'

'Well, I'm not a technical person, Mr Madigan, nor am I a scientist, so I don't know what the findings were or what were their implications. But what I can tell you was that MDC was in the title of both papers. I guess that it was better than cyclocon, something like that.'

'Do you think the Professor was onto something that he did not wish to share with his colleagues?'

'Well, the nature of scientific work is that you share your results with the rest of the scientific community. And Willie always operated in this way. The very fact he had written papers on the topic shows he wanted to share the results of the work, though he could be secretive until he was first to get into print with some finding. He would, like anyone, want to be given credit for something he had discovered himself.'

'Wouldn't we all.'

'When scientists make discoveries they try to get to print as fast as possible in case somebody else beats them to it. You see, at any one time, if there is something waiting to be discovered, the chances are there are several groups working on it and it's a race as to gets there first. Science is funny that way, it requires collaboration, or at least sharing of information, yet at the same time it's highly competitive.'

'Where are the drafts now?'

'I suppose they're at Willie's home. He certainly took them

home with him that night.'

'If I told you they were missing, what would you say?'

'Are they missing?'

'Well, I don't know for sure, but I'd be willing to bet a good night's sleep they are. Call it an educated guess, though I don't regard myself as an educated man. Let's assume for a moment that they are missing. Who would you think might want them, and what would you want with them?'

'It's a highly specialised area. I cannot imagine what anyone would want with them.'

'I'm sorry to have had to bother you like this, Miss Brady, but what you have told me may turn out to be very useful, though to tell you the truth, I can't exactly tell how useful as yet. If you think of anything else that might be of value to me, any little incidents or patterns of behaviour that you remember being unusual or odd, please don't hesitate to call me. I can be contacted at this number all day.'

Madigan gave her his mobile number. As he walked out into the night, his eyes were blind to the street lamps and to the occasional frosty star. He drove his car back to the brewery yard for safe keeping and walked through the Combat Zone to his lodgings. There was no car parked at Benny Mulligan's as he walked past. When he lay in his bed he did not sleep for hours with all the thinking he was doing. He rifled the drawers of every speculation in his mind, but came up with nothing worthwhile. Eventually he fell asleep.

EIGHTEEN

The lecture. Giving a stalk to a dead man. Reptiles he had known.
We come from the same ancestor. A debate on creationism.
The flat earth and scientific imperialism.

Dr Ivor Dunne stood at the dusty lectern with his half-glasses propped like a thin bird on the end of his nose and his eyes twinkling inquisitively at his audience. It was a public lecture in Trinity on the Evolution of the Human Brain. Madigan needed to know about the evolution of the human brain. Some things were very important.

The audience consisted mostly of students, male and female, badly-dressed, tired from study, and the occasional glamorous girl who came to college to find a doctor or a solicitor to marry. The hall had the air of a dry old box which had not been opened in years. It made Madigan feel like he wanted to be a juvenile delinquent again.

Madigan crept quietly into the back row of the lecture hall as befits someone who, in his time, had flunked all his own exams. He was old enough to be the father of almost everyone in the room. He looked around and speculated about all the creepy old codgers who must have taught there over the years. The place was encrusted with decayed knowledge.

Dr Ivor fiddled with the computer in front of him and waited for the projector to heat up. Madigan noticed he had a habit of swaying on the balls of his feet as if he were a fat man, which he was not. He wore tweeds and what looked from the back row like slippers on his feet. Just before he started, the door opened and in walked Pamela O'Neill Crowley. She was dressed in a knee-length black dress and black tights and had a shiny black bag hanging from her shoulder – Gucci, he thought, at a guess. She sat down in the front row, crossed her legs, smoothed her dress and placed the bag on the desk in front of her. She did not notice Madigan perched in the high recesses at the back of the hall. Old Ivor would get a good view.

Professor Ivor Dunne turned his back briefly to his audience and wrote one word on the blackboard. DARWIN. Then he turned around, cleared his throat and began to speak in a voice that was tired from overuse.

'Good evening, ladies and gentlemen, and welcome to our little talk on the Evolution of the Human Brain. I will begin my lecture with a quotation from Darwin who provided, I suppose, the point from which all this work, we could say, evolved.' He shuffled his papers in front of him. Tentative laughter went around the room.

'No one, I presume, doubts that the large proportion which the size of man's brain bears to his body, compared to the same proportion in the gorilla or orang-utan, is closely connected with his mental powers?'

Madigan looked down at Pamela below him in the front row. Her black hair was tied back in a style that coiffed her tresses into a kind of high mane which made her look at least three inches taller than she was. She had such pretty ears, he thought; the little wisps of hair around the back of her neck were so erotic. It was hard to focus on gorillas and orangs with her sitting there just below him. It was enough to give a stalk to a dead man.

'Today, ladies and gentlemen, we would still agree with that statement, for when differences in body size are taken into account, the human brain is at least a hundred times the size of any of the earliest reptilian or amphibian brains and three times the size of a chimpanzee's brain.'

Madigan could think of some people for whom that might not be true. Still, the doctor's talk was interesting.

'If you take reptiles and plot brain size relative to body size, you get a straight line. In other words, the bigger the reptile, the bigger its brain. And yet, compared to mammals, reptiles are small brained.'

That was true enough, Madigan thought. The reptiles he knew were all small brained.

The lights dimmed. Dunne flashed pictures of reptiles and monkey brains on the screen over his head.

'The early mammals, small nocturnal creatures, were four or five times brainier than the average reptile, an increase that can largely be accounted for by the appearance of the cerebral cortex, which is unique to mammals. The mammalian brain, once established, remained the same relative size for about 100 million years. Then, as modern mammals evolved some 64 million years ago, it began to expand rapidly, coinciding with the evolution of ungulates, carnivores and primates.'

Dr Dunne went on in this vein for over an hour and Madigan, to his surprise, was able to follow most of it. He showed at least two dozen slides on the screen behind him. The gist of what he seemed to be saying was that the brain's development involved long periods of constancy punctuated by bursts of rapid evolution. But one thing was true: 'size isn't everything', he said. My own feelings entirely, thought Madigan, though it helps. And he also concluded that the human brain was not at the pinnacle of any evolutionary tree. Also true.

'It's a common fallacy to think of the human as the end to which all evolution has been aimed. But it must be kept in mind that the human brain, though highly complex, is, from an evolutionary point of view, an adaptation of no more significance than the fin of a whale or the ability of a flower to show colour to attract insects. And it's also worth keeping in mind, if we should trigger a nuclear holocaust, that we would be survived by those self same insects, who along with bacteria and some fungi and grasses, would inherit the world. What a lot of good our highly specialised brain would be to us then! I leave you, ladies and gentlemen, with that humbling thought.'

An outbreak of clapping started in the darkened room like bats being disturbed in a chimney. Then the lights came on, to find Ivor Dunne fiddling with his computer at the table beside the lectern. He did not smile or look up as the clapping continued. Gradually it subsided and Pamela O'Neill Crowley stood up to give a short address of appreciation.

Madigan did not want her to see him if it could be avoided, so he pretended to be writing.

'Thank you very much, Dr Dunne, for that excellent and I'm sure you'll all agree, very interesting talk. Now if there are any questions from the floor, I'm sure Dr Dunne would only be too willing to answer them.'

Madigan watched her through his fingers. She was smiling at Dunne and holding a little note pad in her hand.

A pimply male student sitting near Madigan asked an irrelevant question, indicating that he must have been asleep during the talk. Then a scruffy alternative type with a Christ-like beard said that he had to disagree with much of what the doctor had said.

Madigan could imagine him working in an organic food store, his toes sticking out of his worn sandals, selling oat and nut cakes that looked like dried horse turds.

'Am I right in assuming that what you are saying, Dr Dunne, is that man is descended from the monkeys?'

'Well, not from the monkeys exactly, for they followed a somewhat different evolutionary pattern to what man did. But from a common primate ancestor, yes. All the evidence suggests that we came from a common ancestor.'

'Then you believe that you are descended from an ape?'

'Me personally? Of course I am. All the evidence from Darwin right up to ...'

But the Christ figure was not to be denied, certainly not for the third time.

'Therefore, you think God was an ape?' he said with triumphant finality. The neat scientific consensus became suddenly confused and uncomfortable. But Ivor Dunne was up to the task.

'I'm afraid you have me there, my good sir. Unfortunately, I'm not qualified to discuss theology and I think I'd rather leave the matter to those who can.'

'I know that what I'm saying might sound irrelevant, Dr Dunne, but ...'

'Yes, you're absolutely right,' Pamela O'Neill Crowley cut in, 'it is irrelevant. Thank you. Now I know Dr Dunne is in a hurry, and I know this room has to be vacated in the next ten minutes. We have time for just one other question. Anyone?'

There was a coughing silence in the room as if quietness had grown feet and crept around uncomfortably without socks. Then the Christ-like creationist cried out, pointing a finger at Dr Dunne:

'This is just another example of scientific imperialism. You people think you know everything. Well, I'm telling you, you don't. There are far more things in heaven and on earth than can be accounted for by your theories.'

'I'm sure you are right there, sir,' she shot back. 'Now, if there are no more questions, I'd like, on behalf of the Society, to thank Dr Dunne for taking the trouble of coming here and giving us an insight into this very interesting aspect of brain function. I'd like you to put your hands together for Dr Dunne.'

There was another outbreak of clapping and a shuffling of bags and desks as 50 people stood up to go. Madigan kept his head down, still pretending to be writing. He noticed Pamela going up to the podium and having a few smiling words with Dunne. Then she went out into the hall in the midst of the crowd of students. She had not seen him.

He watched as Mr Sandal-man traipsed after them with a defeated expression and what looked like a bag made out of yak skins hanging over his shoulder. When he was sure Pamela was out of the way, he walked down the steps of the hall. Dunne was still rearranging his papers on the stand.

'Dr Dunne, my name is Madigan, Mike Madigan. I'm a private investigator. I've been hired to look into the circumstances of Professor Crowley's death. I need to talk to you, in private if possible, if you don't mind.'

He looked surprised, bemused to have to change his thought processes. Then, as if something struck him suddenly, he rearranged his expression like Lego blocks and looking around, said 'Good God, man. I thought you people were supposed to be circumspect about these things. I can't be seen talking to you here. Do you think you could call by my office, say in an hour's time? I should be free then.'

Madigan noted his rapid West Brit accent; at least he seemed willing to talk. What is more, his sudden interest surprised him.

'Your office?'

'Top floor, end of corridor, last entrance on left. You can't miss it. My name's on the door.'

'I'll be there,' Madigan said and walked back up the high steps and out the door he had come in.

In the house of knowledge there are many mansions, and it was not hard to find corridors where he was unlikely to run into Pamela O'Neill Crowley. He found a deserted common room with a pool table and a tiled floor, which had been pitted, like rain-spattered concrete, by a million cigarette butts. Smoke hibernated in the half-ripped padded furniture. He slipped a coin into the slot and the stomach of the table churned to cough up a set of balls. Craving the drag of a cigarette, he found a cue with a battered tip and began cracking pool balls into the pockets.

A frightening spectacle. It's all in the hands. Madigan discusses philosophy with the professor. Lonely as a planet. Does the Deity exist?
Genetic engineering. Playing God. Keeping an eye on patent literature.

The walls of Dunne's room were covered with shelves full of box
files, books and theses of PhD students who had long since
departed the life of the university. On one wall hung a large chart
of the human brain, with illustrated diagrams of all its functions.
It was a complex cartoon show with little men in various segments
of the brain doing whatever job was carried out there.

On his desk stood a homunculus as ugly as anything Madigan
had seen in his worst, smoke-deprived nightmares. It had huge
hands, a big thick mouth and lips, and a small shrunken body like
a partially decomposed corpse.

'What the hell is that?' he asked, reluctant to sit near such a
specimen.

'That, Mr Madigan, is Fred. I bring Fred into my first lecture
with new classes every year. Look closely at Fred, Mr Madigan.
See his huge hands and his tiny frame. Fred's proportions repre-
sent the amount of brain space devoted to different parts of the
body. The somatosensory cortex, Mr Madigan, is the part of the
brain devoted to sensations of touch and pain. As you can see,

there is more sensory space given over to the hands and mouth than to all of the rest of the body put together. I use this to illustrate how important the hands were to the development of the brain. The hands, Mr Madigan, were the cart that came before the horse of the brain, if you follow me.'

'I suppose I do. Where I come from, carts have a habit of coming before horses.'

'Yes, quite. It's an interesting field, Mr Madigan, fascinating in fact. But, of course, we are not here to discuss the origins of the brain.'

'Do you often get clowns like Mr Hairyface in there?'

'You mean the young man who seemed to think we were turning God into an ape? Yes, we get an odd one. It's worse in the States, of course. The creationist lobby there is claiming equality on many campuses.'

'I have no problem with the ape theory, myself. It fits in with my own findings.'

'Oh, you are acquainted with our field, Mr Madigan?'

'Not in so many words, just bits and pieces, you know, observations of the general run of things.'

'But to get back to the creationists, it's politics, Mr Madigan. Politics and, I suppose, a philosophy of a kind.' He looked out the window. 'People need comforts. Science carries no comforts. Life is hard enough, Mr Madigan, without the thought that there is nothing at the end of it but the grave and a box of maggots.'

'That's true enough. Life can be ... lonely as a planet.'

'Yes, that's a good image, Mr Madigan. Lonely as a planet, indeed. Anyway, I don't believe we are here to discuss planets. You said you wanted to talk to me about Willie's death?'

'Yes, well, it's a long story, and I don't have time to bore you with the details. Put it like this; I've been asked by persons whose identity I'd rather not disclose to look into the late Professor's death. My clients are not convinced that he died of entirely natural causes.'

'I've had my own suspicions, to tell you the truth. You see, Willie was always a very careful man. OK, he was not in the best of health but he looked after himself reasonably well. I think it inconceivable that he could have made a mistake in his insulin dosage. Willie was one of the most methodical people I've ever met. I have to say I was surprised to hear the police had called off their investigation. It seemed premature, to say the least.'

'Well, call it off they did, which is where I come in. Not everything is adding up and I'd like to find out why. What I really want to ask you is this: can you think of a motive why anybody would want to take the Professor out of circulation?'

'That thought occurred to me too but I just couldn't see why anyone would want to do such a thing.'

'What's your understanding of the Professor's work?'

'Well, he had spent several years working on variants of cyclo-con, a cure for depression. Then, more recently, he began working on MDC, a new, more promising, drug for the same condition. He told me a few weeks ago that he had made a significant breakthrough, but when I asked him what it was, he couldn't tell me. He said I could read it in two papers which he was about to submit to the *Journal of Clinical Psychology*.'

'Do you think he was hiding anything?'

'No. The distinct impression I got was that he did not want to steal the thunder of the papers by telling anyone in advance. I got the impression I would be suitably impressed when the papers came out.'

'Surely he was not working on his own?'

'No. He had a post-doctoral research fellow called Simon

Callaghan working on the project. He was the only one who knew in detail what was going on. I could phone the lab now. He's likely to be still working. Those research fellows work all the hours God made.'

'Though God doesn't exist?' Madigan said, smiling.

'Maybe He makes time for us all to exist, Mr Madigan. And no doubt He exists for those who want Him to exist.'

Dr Dunne picked up the receiver and dialled a number. After a few inquiries he put the phone down again.

'You're out of luck, I'm afraid. Simon Callaghan left last week for two weeks holidays in the Canaries. Looks like life may not be as hard for post docs as I had thought. He's not due back for another week. He should be able to fill you in on all the information you need.'

'If Professor Crowley had made a major advance in the treatment of depression, who would stand to lose?'

'Well, at present it's treated with a whole range of antidepressants, most of which are called tricyclics. But what Willie was working on was quite different. He was approaching the illness from a genetic perspective. I suppose the drug companies who make the drugs would lose a considerable amount, if he were to be successful, though I would assume they are doing similar work themselves. It is not inconceivable that he was about to go public with something which one of them had discovered themselves independently. You see, if Willie published his results, his work would be in the public domain and anyone could use it. It would not be protected by patent.

'Now, if some drug company had spent many millions in R&D to develop a drug, and Willie had just beaten them to it, it would be very much in their interests to keep him quiet. I would not be surprised at what some people might do if the stakes were high enough.'

'I think the first thing you should do, Mr Madigan, if you'll pardon me telling you your job, would be to contact the *Journal of Clinical Psychology* to see if they received the two papers as submissions for publication. Then I'd keep my eye on the patent literature to see who has published patents in the area in the last few years and I'd be especially watchful over the next few months to see if anything new appears from any of the major drug companies – use the Internet.'

He stood up. Madigan's audience was over.

'Let me know if you hear anything,' he said. 'I'm afraid I'll have to let you go now, much and all as I'd like to keep this speculation up all night. I have two lectures to write for tomorrow. You know where to find me if you need more help. Sorry I could not be of more use to you. I trust you'll find your own way out?'

'Well, I found my own way in. And thanks for the philosophical speculation. It's as rare as hens' teeth where I come from.'

'You're welcome, Mr Madigan.'

'Bye, Fred,' Madigan tapped the homocunculus on the head on the way out. 'Keep up the good work.'

Madigan wandered out into the dusty corridors, thinking of what to do next. The building was full of the echoes of all the students who had past through over several hundred years. He could hear their weanling voices in the hollow clanking of the radiators and was glad for once that he was no longer young.

TWENTY

A long distance phone call. Clinical psychology and missing files. Are
Larry Kelly and Nolan one and the same person? Can a swim duck?
Corporate matters. The relationship between wealth, power and
adipose tissue. Free to be a slave. Two deaths.

The first thing Madigan did the following day was to contact the
Journal of Clinical Psychology to see if it had received the Professor's
two papers. When he finally got through to the New York office
of the company who published the journal, he spoke to a helpful
girl who told him the journal had received no papers from him,
though they had his name on their files from previous papers.

Then he phoned Marlowe to let him know what he had
found. He told him Dr Dunne's theories about the papers and the
fact that they had not been sent for publication. He told him how
he had seen the Mercedes outside Benny Mulligan's place and
went on to describe Nolan, where he was standing at the funeral
and so on.

'Could be the same guy, Mike.'

Madigan had the registration number of the Mercedes. He
could hear Marlowe typing it into his computer.

'That car is registered to a fellow called Larry Kelly. Let's see.
Lives in a quiet cul de sac in the suburbs. Yes, yes, it's coming up

now. No convictions for anything. There you go.'

'Maybe Nolan and Larry Kelly are one and the same person?' Madigan said. 'Do you have anything on Benny Mulligan, anything on the prints from the flick knife?'

'Yes, Benny was more or less what he said he was. We have a record on him. He's a heroin addict, no worse or no better than a thousand others. Like every heroin addict he'd do anything for a fix. He drives a motorcycle and does courier runs around town, though I doubt if that would earn him enough to feed his habit. He has been implicated in a number of small-time breaking-and-entering cases, grabbing a hundred pounds here, snatching a handbag there. He once held up a petrol station with a water pistol. That's the worst thing he's done. He got three months for that. By the way, you smashed him up pretty thoroughly, whatever you used.'

'Me? Smashed him up? He fell off the fire escape trying to get away from me.'

'Come on, don't give me that shit. We checked up on him. His wrist was broken like a matchstick. That couldn't happen in a fall. According to the surgeon who operated on him, the wrist bone was in smithereens. That could only happen from a hard blow from a blunt instrument. How do you explain that?'

'He fell down two flights of stairs.'

'Then how come nothing else was broken and not another inch of his skin was even marked? Do you mean to tell me that a fellow could fall two floors, break his wrist, and yet not even graze his knee?'

'Maybe he landed on his wrist, you know, kung-fu style?'

'Yeah, can a swim duck? Is a pie bald? Is the Pope a Catholic? Don't expect me to swallow that story, Madigan. If Benny Mulligan wanted to, he could have you up for assault. I'd watch my step if I were you. You're saved by the fact that Benny says it was a fall too and doesn't seem in any hurry to go back on his story. You're lucky that he's afraid of someone. But lads like Benny just love the compo'. So don't push it too far, Mike. Things might backfire.'

'I'm still left with the problem of getting this Nolan or Larry Kelly, or whatever his name is, off my back.'

'Get him the files.'

'Get him the files! Christ, how am I going to get him the files?'

'Why don't you ask Pamela O'Neill Crowley for them?' Madigan could imagine Marlowe at the other end of the line, smiling as enigmatically as any Mona Lisa.

'Ask her? And you think she'd give them to me?'

'Well, if you don't ask her, then you'll never know, will you?'

Marlowe laughed softly – Madigan actually heard it – bland as a marshmallow down the line at him.

'OK. Let me get this straight? I call her up in her fancy mansion, right? And I say; Pammy, I mean Pamela, would you please give me the files your husband was working on the night before he died. You see, dear Pammy, there are guys breaking into my flat and they're going to beat the living shit out of me if I don't hand them over to them? Is that it?'

'That's it, a watertight argument if ever I heard one.'

'That's a load of bollox.'

'Think about it. You might turn up something if you keep your eyes open.'

Madigan heard the door open behind him. 'Listen, Marlowe, I'll have to hang up.'

Alan Spratt came in just as Madigan was putting the receiver down. Madigan remembered he had promised Spratt he would go with him to the Company's Annual Presentation. This was a lark devised by the MD to get across gee-up type messages to the staff. Spratt was in great form, clapping his hands and rubbing them with enthusiasm. He gave Madigan a hail-fellow-well-met clap on the back.

'Things are looking up, eh, Mick? What do you think? Have you seen the share price? Up 30 pence since the half-yearly results were announced! This division is up by fifteen per cent in a market that's shrinking. We're screwing the opposition to the wall. How about that now? Excellent isn't it?'

Big fucking deal, Madigan said to himself, but to Spratt he said, 'Yes, that sounds pretty good.'

'Pretty good! It's excellent, my dear man, excellent.'

They walked across the brewing yard to the MD's presentation in the Sir Edmond Campbell Memorial Hall. Not that the Company gave a damn for Sir Edmond Campbell now, thought Madigan. He reluctantly sat through the usual drivel about share prices and margins and competitiveness and endless, endless growth. Afterwards, Spratt called him into his office. He stuck his fingers into the waistband of his trousers and shoved out his big belly. He was bigger and bulkier than usual, thought Madigan, probably thanks to the share price.

Madigan reckoned that, for people like Spratt, their power was in direct proportion to their waistband. You could tell the number of lives a senior executive controlled from the volume of his adipose tissue. Every fat cell represented a worker, a worrier, a Ted Plunkett, a family whose very future owed its existence to decisions made by him. Capitalism was the control of the many by the few. We put democracy in place to protect it, a nice little irony.

'The future is looking splendid for us, isn't it, Mick?'

'Yeah, great.' Madigan agreed.

Yes, Madigan thought, the fat rule the world and the only justice comes in the form of cardiovascular disease. He looked at Spratt's expanding girth, Citizen Kane playing Orson Wells. The big executive lunches, the expense account dining was paid for in the long run by the exorbitant fees charged by private health clinics to scour clotted arteries and plumb by-pass tubing around the saturated valves of sclerotic hearts. It also came in the form of dead marriages that grow like weeds around such men as years of neglect took their toll on wives and families. The manager is the ultimate factotum, for when the buck stops, it stops with him.

'Mike,' he said with a smile. Usually he called Madigan 'Mick' when he wanted to keep him in his place. Now that he was calling him Mike it meant he was either looking for a favour or else he was going to be shot of him for good.

'Mike, we've been watching you for some time now.'

Who were 'we', for Christ's sake? So this was it, the endgame, thought Madigan. He was about to be fired for sleeping on the job, or using the company phone lines for his snooping work or the company computers for accessing porn. But he was wrong again.

'We think you're doing a very fine job here, Mike. We're creating a new post in the brewhouse after Christmas. We think you're ideal for it. It's to be called Brewing and Fermentation Supervisor.'

Madigan knew all about the new post. It came about because of the amalgamation of two previous posts. Brewing supervisor and fermentation supervisor were to be rolled into one. The brewery was dumping a whole layer of middle management and this was where one post was to be lost. The 'lucky' incumbent would get to do two men's work, with double the hours, double the amount of hassle with unions and plant breakdowns. He would get an extra grand or two a year, of which the tax man would take half, and he would be burnt out by 50 and probably dead by 55. Madigan already knew he would not accept the job. But he had to buy time.

'Well, that comes as a bit of a shock, Alan. I wasn't expecting it, you know.' That much was true. He did not think he was in line for anything. 'I appreciate the offer. I'll have to give the matter some thought. I'll get back to you on it.'

Madigan was good management material. His marriage, having been on the rocks, was now long since sunk. There was no conflict of interest between having to get home to change nappies or take the kids to ballet or do the shopping, and the brewery's requirements for his time. He was free to be a slave. Sometimes, he thought, the brewery turned a blind eye to affairs at work so that fun and play would be in-house and so much more work could be done. Wives and children just got in the way.

'You do that, Mike.' He clapped Madigan on the shoulder and smiled benignly. 'You do that.' Only for knowing what an old bastard he was and what the brewery was up to, Madigan would have fallen for it. But once bitten, twice shy. He had just got back to his own office when the phone rang. It was Marlowe again.

'Mike? I just got a call from the Drug Squad. Your friend Benny died this morning with 300 Ecstasy tablets up his ass.'

'What?'

'He was running mule on the ferry from Holyhead – overnight trip, over and back – but it turned into a bigger trip for him, unfortunately. Condom leakage. He was in a coma for an hour before the ship docked. He was still alive when the ambulance got there, but he was as dead as a door nail by the time he reached the hospital.'

'Poor Benny, at least he died happy,' Madigan said.

'It was the only bit of happiness the poor bastard ever had. The Drug Squad will be looking into all his contacts. They will probably be along to question you too, seeing as you eh, met him recently.'

'Shit. I keep running into people before they get killed. I think I'd better become a recluse.'

'Might not be such a bad idea.' He hung up.

Madigan looked at the pile of papers in his in-tray and tried to concentrate. But catching his thoughts now, he felt, was as easy as picking up tomato seeds with a fork.

He looked out the window. The one stunted cherry tree in the brewery yard was waving its limbs like a tick-tack man at the racecourse. The wind was up, ripping rain off the corners of the gutters. Madigan thought of Benny winding up in spaced-out death on the high seas. There were worse ways to die but there were better ways to live, not that they would ever be in the range of someone like Benny. In retrospect, Madigan was sorry he had given him such a beating but then, retrospect was always a flaky and unrewarding science.

He had parked Rosie in the brewery yard and as he had to call to his flat to see if there were any telephone messages or mail waiting for him, he decided to drive home before returning to the Combat Zone.

As he sat in traffic by the canal he bought a copy of the evening paper. A hundred yards later, still stuck in traffic, he spotted the small headline:

LOCAL YOUTH DROWNED IN CANARIES

A 24-year-old research fellow, Simon Callaghan, was drowned during the weekend in a freak accident in Puerto Rico, Gran Canaria. Mr Callaghan, who was on two weeks holidays with his girlfriend, fell overboard from a yacht on which he was attending a late night party. There was no question of foul play, local police said yesterday.

This is not my lucky day, Madigan thought. That morning he had three solid leads. Now he had none and the corpses were accumulating at a rate he was not used to. But there were people who were having a far unluckier day than Madigan was.

It started to rain more heavily and the beating on the cold slate of the tenements mixed with the wailing of the wind. Madigan thought of the smallness of a life like Benny's in a city of a million souls and the smallness of the column inches given to the death of Simon Callaghan, and he wondered how far the sound of one raindrop could travel through all the other drops of rain.

Twenty-One

White musk and the raiments of beauty. Methods of payment. A piece
of cake. A theatrical event. Rick O'Shea and his bad jokes. A man of
easy virtue. Fear of the Melting Man. Orlando di Lasso. Miracles
happen. His Mighty Sword. Madigan finds redemption. A happy bird.

Madigan was singing 'Happiness is a Warm Gun' as he pulled up
outside Marika's place the following Friday night. It was raining
again, wet curtains draped from the sky. He had found a bottle of
body lotion that Sally had once given him and so was coming up
roses and anything else that came up.

Marika opened the door. She was wearing an orange top,
freshly washed jeans and open-toed sandals, even though it was
now the middle of November. The mild Irish winter was nothing
to a Moldovan one.

He stepped into the hall and shook the rain out of his hood.
The air had the cardboard smell of flatland, the carpet on the
stairs was faded, looking as though it had not been replaced since
the days of the British Empire. Marika wore cheap perfume,
White Musk at a guess, though Madigan was not good on per-
fumes. But White Musk turned him on. It was sexy, dirty sexy,
cheap sexy, sweaty sexy; it took him back to early 'poor but happy'
relationships – a reflection, he supposed, of his own inability to

156

outgrow his past.

She smiled beautifully though, her eyes full of practised charm of the kind you got in air hostesses and shop assistants before the new ugliness of the boom knocked the time and the smile out of everyone.

'Do you want to go out, or get down to business straight away?' This could mean anything, he thought, from a hand job to Burt Lancaster and Deborah Kerr on the beach in 'From Here To Eternity'.

'Well, I was thinking that maybe we could do a bit of both.'

'OK. Let me get Sam first.'

'Who's Sam?' For a moment Madigan thought with horror that Sam might be Kelly or Nolan turned up by strange coincidence to haunt every last corner of his life. Then he thought Sam might be a pimp. He thought of 'Mona Lisa' and had visions of a big black guy with muscles like a racehorse's arse.

'Sam's my fur coat.'

She went back inside and ran up the stairs. Madigan was admiring her ass when a mouse came out of a hole under the lower stair and looked up as well. He twitched his whiskers, sniffed the air, watched Marika's departing rump, then trotted back in home.

'You have good taste, Mr Mouse,' Madigan said.

'What did you say?' Marika called from the landing.

'Oh, nothing, just admiring the view.' He did not mention the mouse. Women are squeamish about sharing their homes with small furry mammals. Something like that might ruin the entire evening.

Five minutes later she was back down. She had changed into a black miniskirt over which she wore a large brown fur coat that looked like it had recently been ripped off a young bear cub.

'You won't catch cold in that,' he said, 'whatever else you might catch.'

'It belonged to my mother. She gave it to me before she died.'

'I'm sorry to hear that. I didn't know.'

'She died of pneumonia in a hospital back home, because they couldn't afford to buy antibiotics for her when the whole system fell apart after the end of Communism.'

'That's terrible.' Madigan did not know what to say when the matter of death came up, so to change the subject he asked, 'Were you happy to see the collapse of Communism?'

'At the start, yes. Communism was very limiting, no freedom, no lightness, no colour, dull flat lives. The Russians looked down on us. Then, it just ended, I don't know, and things got worse and worse all the time. A lot of people back home now think Communism was not such a bad thing after all. At least it looked after those who couldn't look after themselves. There was also, I don't know, an idealism that's no longer there. There wasn't as much greed as now. Anyway, let's change the subject. I find the memories of my home too painful.' And she shivered in her fur coat as if the past was a gale of wind blowing suddenly from Siberia.

'People around here must find the coat unusual,' he said. 'Are you not afraid that some anti-furry type might attack you for wearing it?' The animal welfare people had been attacking women for wearing furs in the streets of Dublin and throwing paint on them.

'Well, they haven't attacked me yet. And if they do they'd have something else coming to them. I am a black belt. I was Moldovan junior karate champion; I had hopes to make the Olympics when the country fell apart. Anyway, I love Sam, his fur keeps me nice and cosy.'

'Is the karate the reason you feel safe doing what you do?'

'That, and other things.'

The more he got to know this girl, the more he liked her and wondered what she would look like naked. OK, he would be paying for it but he would be paying for it in cash only and somebody else's cash at that. As Marika herself had said, he'd paid for it with Sally too but he had paid with his life, not to mention his sanity. He had come to realise that with Sally you got the works but you paid for it every minute of every day, with sweat and tears and blood and guts, with every pore in your skin and every nerve in your body, and for the rest of your life, every waking moment and most of the sleeping ones. And you paid for it in the embarrassed smiles of your friends who felt pity for you but did not know how to break the news to you, when they came to realise that what looked like happiness might in fact be a death sentence. But this was very different, a straight, direct transaction with all the cards on the table. Who says the best things in life are free?

Madigan must have betrayed his thoughts because she asked, 'What are you thinking?'

'I was thinking that relationships are a piece of cake.'

'Do you really believe that?'

'No, of course not, but it's a nice idea. It makes the notion of living seem somehow more, how shall I put it, feasible.' Of course, what he really believed was that you don't get over things, you just do your best to get around them.

'That's a good word. I believe life is feasible, but not in the way I think you're living it. You just exist; you don't really live. I mean, I've never seen your place but I can imagine what it's like.'

'OK, what's it like?'

'Let me see now. I bet it's full of opened, half-empty milk bottles and jars of jam and let's see, half-eaten packets of biscuits, a typical bachelor pad. Am I right?'

'You seem familiar with bachelor pads?'

'I am.'

'Well, you're not far wrong but I like it that way. I'm like an old dog, happy in the midst of the familiar. Everything has its place.'

'You're complacent. That's dangerous.'

'The fur-lined mousetrap?'

'Right.'

'Where do we go from here?'

'That's up to you,' she smiled.

'You call the shots. You're the guest.'

'Right. I'd like to go to the theatre,' she said.

'The theatre? The theatre is where the assholes go. Theatre is a load of snobby bollox. One of the advantages of growing up is that you no longer feel you're missing something if you never see the inside of a theatre. By definition, it's not the kind of place I want to be.'

'Come on, Mike. Theatre tickets are so expensive I never get the chance to go. Look on it as a treat to me.'

'If you want to spend an evening in the company of wankers watching self-important drivel, then be my guest.'

'I intend to be.'

They went to the Gate, where Madigan had heard that some modern classic thing was on but they could not get in, as all the seats had been pre-booked. Eventually, they got seats at the Abbey, where against all the odds – Madigan regarded Abbey productions as exercises in national navel gazing – *Miss Julie* was on. Madigan had a soft spot for Strindberg ever since he had seen a television production of *Miss Julie* just as his marriage was falling apart. After years in the university of misogyny, the teachers did not come any better than that twisted Swede. Strindberg's heroes could not handle women; there was lots of seething hate around. It was great stuff. Strindberg was the prophet of our times.

'What did you think?' she asked when they came out.

'Well, fuck a duck, I'll have to say I liked it.' Madigan liked it so much in fact that he had the urge to run up to everyone in the street urging them to go to see the play, though while actually watching the play, he had been more interested in the crossing and uncrossing of Marika's legs on the seat beside him. He was surprised at how much he liked the play and how it managed to overcame his antipathy to theatre. But then, it was about the sheer misunderstanding that is life. What could be more natural?

'Did you not think it was a little over the top?' she asked. 'A little hysterical?'

'Not at all; it was just about right, I'd say.'

He watched her little dress riding up as she moved her ass and sliding down again then as she pulled at it. That was one of the things he noticed about women; when they wear short skirts they're always pulling down at the hem, as if they wanted to cover up for some previous mistake in their life. But it made no sense; if you're worried about showing your bottom, then why wear short skirts in the first place? The same applied to midriffs and cleavages. If you show, you show, it's a bit late in the day to get nervous about it afterwards. Still it was one of the divine mysteries. He wanted so much to go down on her and eat whatever he could find.

They decided to go for a drink in Rick's on the Green after the show. Ricks was owned by Patrick (Rick) O'Shea, an old friend of Madigan's and a major league sleazeball player. The place was packed. Madigan was wondering if he should tell her he was not, after all, a reporter for the *Herald* and that in reality he was a burnt out brewer down on his luck. But she beat him to it, for when they sat down she asked,

'I was wondering ...' she hesitated. '... I was wondering if maybe with your contacts, you could get me a spot, maybe a photograph in the *Herald*.'

The newspapers liked to carry photographs of pretty young things to liven up the news of genocide and rape and the intractability of Northern Irish politics.

'I'm surprised you'd want that, being a medical student and all.'

'Well, you know how it is, beggars can't be choosers. Besides it might lead to a modelling stint. I have the looks. All I need is the exposure. If I could make a few hundred, I could stop this job for a while. Who knows, if it was regular enough, maybe I could stop it altogether.'

Madigan had been wondering how it had all been so easy. So this was it. He was to be her contact to fame and fortune.

'What if I were to tell you I don't work for the *Evening Herald*?'

She threw him a hard look that skidded along his surface, making him feel like he was a pond that had just frozen over. There was toughness there; the toughness that knew it was tough.

'What? You mean all that business about Professor Crowley was a lie! You mean you've been fooling me all along? What are you, a pig or a pervert or both?'

'If I was a pig, as you call them, then I would have reported you for what you told me the last time we met. I mean what you are up to is not exactly legal, now, is it? And if I'm a pervert I'm a pretty harmless kind, as you'll find out if you ever get to know me better.'

'Listen, Mr Smartass, I took you at your word. I told you everything I knew about the Professor and too much about myself. What are you playing at? How do I know you will not go to the police with this story.'

'Because I want to wake up and find my shoes under your bed tomorrow morning, if that's possible at this stage. Because I would give everything I have just to touch you, just to be with you. And because I am prepared to pay for it.'

'Men never stop to surprise me.' He was touched by the occasional inaccuracies in her English. 'I thought you were Mr Principle. I never pay for it, you said.'

'Yes, but then I realised it's no different to having to pay for anything else. I'm a man of easy virtue.'

'Listen, I know what I have is worth paying for. I know men who pay a lot for what I can do for them. That's why I don't have to go on the job too often. In one weekend I can make enough to keep me for a month in College. I don't come cheap.'

'I know all about what it takes to make ends meet.'

'Well, you're no use to me then, are you?'

'Except that I've come upon a sudden unexpected windfall.'

'Oh, have you?' Suddenly she seemed interested again. This was Lotto syndrome, he thought, people getting suddenly interested in you when they learn you have money. He had seen it many times, ever since he went into the brewery and shot suddenly up in the attractiveness stakes because of having a prestigious job. That was before he met Sally. Sally suffered from a bad dose of Lotto syndrome – before she discovered he had a lot less than she had originally thought.

'So what do you do?' Marika asked.

'I'm a foreman in the brewery.'

'My father was a foreman in a pharmaceutical plant in Moldova. Do you have to work all night too?'

'Some of the time.'

'If you're a foreman in the brewery, why are you so interested in Professor Crowley? Is he your cousin or something?'

'No, that's the whole point, you see. Remember I told you about my wife and how I was married but we're separated now? We've lived apart for the last few years. But I still pay her an allowance for her upkeep and the raising of our son, and I still pay the mortgage on her house.'

'That does not seem to be very fair.'

'Well, maybe it's not, but that's the way the judge saw it. She'll keep possession of the house until the young lad is eighteen. Then maybe I'll own part of it, I don't know. Anyway, to make a long story short, I do a bit of private investigating on the side. Just to make ends meet, the same as yourself and your forays into ... well, into prostitution. We're not that different, you and I. We both sell what's left of our souls.'

She became angry at this.

'Not true. We're different. You're old, well not exactly old, but you're almost middle aged. I'm young and attractive and I still have my dreams. I'll get out of this business just as soon as I'm qualified. Then I'll be able to support myself. And who knows maybe then I'll get married. I'm not sure yet.'

'Why did you do medicine?'

'Because I wanted to help people.'

'Well, that's something, at least. Most people get into medicine because there's lots of lol in it.'

Just then Madigan heard his name being called out. The voice was as familiar and as unwanted as the smell of his own underarms. It was Rick O'Shea. He wore a short, grey ponytail and a loud shirt that suggested he had just come off a surfboard in Hawaii, and a face that tried to look young but failed. The last time Madigan laid eyes on him was about a month earlier when he was in the midst of the DTs after giving up the cigarettes.

'Well, if it isn't the old brewing private eye himself! Madigan, me auld flower! Still off the fags?' This was O'Shea in normal mode, slimeball mode, Madigan thought.

O'Shea used to fancy himself as a comedian. Madigan remembered their first week at university. O'Shea stood up in a lecture room in the old engineering building at UCD, caught himself in the crotch and brought an entire freshers class to its knees with: 'See this lads: Certified Seed!'

Now he was circulating like a king surveying his kingdom, watching everything that moved while chatting up girls and pretending to prop up different corners of the bar. Madigan was surprised he had not seen him earlier. He had not changed; the tan was as fake as ever.

'What did the Polo mint say when he was asked to go into space?'

'This better be good, O'Shea.'

'I will in me hole!' Rick O'Shea slapped his knee as if it were the funniest thing since the day he decided to try engineering at UCD because it was the shortest queue.

'Rick, this is Marika. Marika, this is Rick, Rick O'Shea. We go back a long way.'

Rick put on his most serenely false face.

'Back is right, boy. Back to the days when men were men,' he laughed his loud, forceful laugh, 'and sheep were nervous.'

Madigan knew from many years of observing O'Shea that beautiful women always brought out the essential greaseball in him; the sincerity, the earnestness, was enough to make Madigan puke.

'Hi Marika,' Rick said, lashing on the slime mayonnaise, 'and how are you?' He was about as sincere as a fairground pickpocket.

He began by asking Marika what she did, and when she told him she was a medical student, Madigan had to calm himself while O'Shea held forth on their college days and how great they were and how he almost did medicine but then decided that arts might be better for a broad education, dropping engineering for arts, not that there was anything wrong with engineering or medicine, for that matter, from an educational point of view, you understand, but that was just his judgement at the time. Doctors were super people, Rick averred, super people altogether. It's a super calling. That was one of Rick's words, super. Pukesville super, Madigan thought. Whenever Rick began to fling around the word 'super' it meant a load of brown stuff was about to come out his mouth to impress somebody.

'I was thinking of going out to Somalia myself,' he said.

'You were what?' Madigan spluttered into his pint.

'You know, go out to Africa, do something to help the starving. There must be something the likes of me could do.'

'Yeah, chase after black girls and get AIDS. You'd be about as useful in Africa as an ice machine on the North Pole. Are you out of your mind? What do you think you could actually do? I mean what could starving Somalis do with an arts-graduate nightclub owner who never did a decent day's work in his life?'

'Now, now, Mike. Do I detect that we're getting a little ratty?'

'They could eat you, of course. Pop you into the pot with a little seasoning. There's enough meat on you to feed a whole tribe.'

'PC, Mike, PC. That's racial prejudice. A pigment of the imagination, so to speak.' He laughed at his own joke.

Marika smiled. For an instant Madigan could have killed her.

'It was just an idea of mine. I saw those pictures on telly the other night and they just looked so awful. I mean, it's dreadful, isn't it, Marika?' He looked deeply, so it seemed to Madigan, so soulfully, so fake-seriously into her eyes. 'Those unfortunate people.'

Marika nodded her assent.

'Well, a lot of good you'd do. That's all I can say,' Madigan said.

Suddenly Rick stood up and looked at his watch. Rick, with his low boredom threshold, never had an attention span of longer than five minutes. It was time to move on to someone more important than Madigan and Marika.

'Well, I'd better be going, folks. I'm expecting to meet somebody in a few minutes. Nice meeting you, Marika.' He stuck out his paw.

Madigan was thinking of the number of crotches he must have groped, and winced.

She took it and smiled.

'Get me the sick bucket,' Madigan said.

'See you around some time, Mike. Keep in touch.' He gave Marika a sly smile and one of his sleazy winks before going around to the other side of the bar. Five minutes later he was joined by a big blonde, wearing tight black leather trousers. Madigan watched his face change from neutral to sincere to soulful again as soon as the girl sat down. Rick would always be an utter bollox, he thought.

'What was that!' Marika exclaimed.

'As you no doubt noticed, Rick and I go back a long way,' Madigan said resignedly. 'We were in school together and then in college. It's amazing what you can tolerate in someone you've known since childhood.'

'You must be very tolerant,' she said, shaking her head.

'More lazy than tolerant. I don't see much of him nowadays. He's some kind of agent, as well as owning this joint. He handles pop stars, girl groups, boy bands. They think he's cool and let him mind their money. It's a great trick when you can get away with it.'

'Well, I wouldn't trust a man like him. He's the type of fellow who'd go through your underwear as soon as you'd turn your back.'

'He'd go through more than your underwear as soon as you'd turn your back.'

'Yes, I know.'

Later, as we drove home to her place, Madigan finally thought it only fair to explain to her what he was doing, that he was investigating Professor Crowley's murder on behalf of his widow.

'Now I understand.'

'It was her money I spent there tonight and there's lots more. I'd be broke otherwise. I could never afford you in a month of Sundays. I can pass this off as expenses.'

Certainly he could not afford Marika on the normal run of his salary, even with the additional money he made from snooping. He thought of the whores near the docks and up the park where he sometimes jogged from work. They were rough enough to turn off the greatest stud that ever lived. And yet they had a market. Madigan's mind teetered over the verge of the weirdness of humanity and hoped he would never have to resort to them. Then he remembered the girl on the Combat Zone and realised he was too near that bracket himself to judge her. He looked at Marika and realised he was in the middle of a miracle.

'She must be very rich,' she said, 'the Professor's wife, to be able to pay you that kind of money.'

'I think we should make hay while the sun shines, don't you? Go out together, maybe go off somewhere for a few days, have some good meals, go to nightclubs, live it up. I could pretend I was having real dates and you'd make enough to keep you in college at least until Easter. It would save you from three months on the game at least.'

'Are you trying to save my soul?'

'Save your soul? I'd never be so presumptuous as to want to save anybody's soul. I doubt very much I could save my own, even if I believed I had one.'

'We'll see. Miracles happen.'

But Madigan's idea of a miracle happened when they got back to Marika's flat.

'I suppose you want to come in for a cup of coffee?' she asked, finding a surprising familiarity with Irish cliché.

'Yes, I thought you'd never ask.'

'Ask? This is business. I've given you a lot of my time. If I give a little more, I may not have to do this again for ages. Hey, don't worry about it. I'll give you the time of your life. I'm the best. You'll see.'

'Do you end up hating all men like me, all clients, I mean?'

'No, I like quite a lot of them, especially some of the regulars. Obviously, I get an odd creep who would try to make me do things I would not want to do. But most are just lonely, looking for what they should get at home. A few are screwed up.'

'Am I screwed up?'

'Oh, you are, but no worse than a lot of others. I like you. You're probably too old for me but I like you. I really do. I like your smile. You're not afraid to laugh at yourself. You have a sense of humour. You're good company. I enjoyed tonight, you see, and I'd like you to enjoy the rest of it.'

Madigan followed her long legs up the stairs, his own legs weak with anticipation.

'I presume you don't want any actual real coffee?' she said as she inserted three or four keys in the various locks of her door.

'Not really. I avoid it at this hour. It keeps me awake all night.'

'Well, you shouldn't need anything to keep you awake tonight.' She smiled again. 'I'll be your human caffeine.'

It was an unusual room, Madigan thought, L-shaped like the one in the book. In the corner stood a table covered with folders and medical textbooks. A mug full of pens sat on the table as if daring anybody to use it for anything except study. In the toe of the L was a little cooker and a kitchen table and two chairs. The rest of the room was taken up by an air of tidiness and a single bed. A door in the middle of the L presumably led into the bathroom.

'You run a pretty tight ship here,' he said.

'I have to be tidy when there's so little room. I always need to move things around. The bed is often the store where I dump things. Then I have to dump them all off again when I want to go to bed. It's often musical chairs around here or at least musical rubbish.'

'And it's like Fort Knox.'

'I know. I've been robbed several times. I don't know what they thought they'd find here. Some cutlery and blankets vanished one night. I presumed they were down-and-outs. The police said to forget about it and they were right. I hope the blankets keep somebody warm.'

'You don't need many blankets here,' he said.

Madigan looked at the bed. It was so little girly, so pristine; it was hard to imagine that she brought clients into it. It was hard to imagine that a large number of different men had had sex with her there. It was hard to imagine ... Madigan thought, and that was about it.

'Is this where you usually do it, with clients, I mean?'

'Usually it's their own places or hotel bedrooms, mostly in hotel bedrooms.'

'So I get special treatment?'

She smiled. 'Yes, you get special treatment.'

'But why?'

'There's something ... I don't know. I like your reluctance. You don't treat me like a piece of meat.'

'And the hotels?'

'I have a good arrangement with the management of some of them. They like pretty girls to hang around the bar area and they turn a blind eye when they see me with visitors. Most of my clients are foreign businessmen, over here on business trips. They often want no more than company or to talk about their wives or how their marriages are all messed up.'

'What if something nasty happens?'

'What I do is guerilla warfare. I make sudden swoops on the enemy. Then I vanish into the woods again. I fight only when I want to, and on my own terms. Perhaps I am naïve.'

'So you see men as the enemy?'

'Of course I do. It's gone that way, isn't it? Men are all bachelors at heart.'

'You're painting everybody with the same brush.'

'Well, that's my experience. Men are naturally polygamous. Women are monogamous, I guess, for the most part. The whore caters for that side of men. I probably help keep marriages together, prevent men having affairs. Sometimes I think it's a wonder men and women can ever live under the same roof – like in that play tonight, especially for a whole lifetime. The expectations are too much. Take yourself, for instance, your marriage cannot have been a bed of roses.'

'Our marriage should never have happened in all probability; we lived on two different planets, our expectations were so different. It's hard to explain. Sally and I, well, Sally wanted to be married to a successful businessman, she wanted a big house, two cars, that sort of thing. Sally wanted to show me off to her friends. Whereas I had no ambition. All I wanted was a quiet life; some place to go home to in the evenings where I could be myself. But I could never be myself with Sally around and Sally could never be herself with me around, I guess. We were both pretending to be other than what we were. It was bad enough having to act in the brewery all day without having to act when I came home as well. There's only so much acting a person can take. Sooner or later you have to be yourself. Otherwise we'd all be raving loonies.'

'Maybe we are.'

'Yes, maybe we are. Do you want your money now?' Madigan thought he'd get the business end of the deal out of the way first.

'Usually I take it beforehand. But I think tonight, later on will do. I think I can trust you.' She smiled. Either she was a true pro or she actually liked him or best of all, he hoped, a combination of the two.

Suddenly she came into his arms and began kissing him, her tongue and fingers busy as serpents around his mouth. (Women who know what they want, in Madigan's view, will tell you what they want by doing it to you.) A bolt of erotic electricity shot straight to his balls and made his toes curl.

'Why don't we do this in bed?' she said, pulling suddenly away from him.

'OK,' he agreed, and walked awkwardly towards the bed like a pole-vaulter on the runway. (That's the disadvantage of wearing boxer shorts, he thought; when you get an erection it jags out against the leg of your trousers, like a stick wedged in the mouth of a drain. There's only one place where an erection is comfortable and it's not in boxer shorts.)

'Make yourself at home. If you want to play some music,

help yourself.'

She showed him a box of CDs in the corner of the room beside the latest in sophisticated Japanese audio technology. Madigan looked at her disc collection. Lots of pre-baroque stuff, madrigals, Palestrina, Monteverdi, choral and church music.

'You like choral music?' he shouted into the next room.

'I love it. It's very restful after study, when I'm tired of reading. I love the sound of the human voice. I used to sing in choirs while at school. I keep those pieces. They remind me of what life could be like.'

'You're beginning to sound like me.'

'Oh no, I'm not. The difference between you and me is that I believe it can be like that.'

Madigan searched through the discs and selected a piece by Orlando di Lasso. Though he had no idea who Orlando di Lasso was, he just liked the name. It sounded Italian and suitably romantic. The room was suddenly filled with the sinister churchy sound of choirboys, its late medieval, male-dominated world gave Madigan the creeps. It did not seem at all in keeping with what he was about to do. Still he took off his clothes and climbed into her bed. He found a women's magazine beside it and began reading it, or at least scanning through it for the pictures of women in their underwear.

It felt weird getting into her bed – the smell of somebody new, the whole geography of bedclothes, pillows, covers, duvets. The hollow in the middle of another's bed is a whole new foreign country; beautiful, a bit like Switzerland when you've never been there before. And then there was all the pretty, feminine paraphernalia on the bedside table. Madigan realised he had become unfamiliar with the world of female things since the days of his marriage; tubes of lotion, hand cream, hair conditioner, mousse, packets of tights and tampax, small trinkets of discarded jewellery of questionable value gathered into little boxes of Ainsley china.

He felt a brief shudder go through him, not so much from the cold of the sheets as from the memory that all the feminine odds and ends evoked in him of Sally. Memories of Sally were not on his agenda right now but they came back for all that. They came back and his erection went down and he stared at the ceiling with a growing sense of unease. The thought suddenly crossed his mind that the whole thing could turn out to be a disaster. Maybe the fuse had blown and there would be no resurrection and his dick would never again do a Lazarus. Maybe he was so out of practice he couldn't do it anymore. With all the wanking and the thinking about women, perhaps his capacity to make love to a real, live woman might have deserted him. He began to feel miserable all of a sudden, like a small boy who is suddenly deprived of his mother.

Then Marika came out of the bathroom and the whole room suddenly shrank to the shape of her naked body. She was perfect, smooth as the ballerina in Swan Lake on Christmas Eve. Madigan was stunned; he was not used to seeing such beauty outside of quality wank mags. She was delicate, pink, pale and majestic. His pupils, he was sure, had dilated into hub-caps. Apart from a small mole on her shoulder, she was, as they used to say in religious tracts, without blemish. This was human perfection, rare in the flesh, a singular honour for a man like Madigan, a sort of a once-in-lifetime view of eternity. It filled him with wondrous humility.

She reminded him of the first woman he ever fell in love with: Patti McGuire. He was fourteen. Patti was a *Playboy* centrefold and he wore down his youthful penis before her big, luscious, American smile. Patti was perfection and though he never tired of her, she fell to pieces in his pocket after a few weeks, leaving only squares of paper, cubes of flesh, metaphors for his subsequent life with women.

And then she married Jimmy Connors. Lucky Jimmy.

Marika was right up with her on the angel stakes. He was amazed that all the strange, lost longings of his life could lead to this. We pass this way but once and every man deserves to sleep with at least one truly beautiful woman. But how many do? Not as many as you might think, he decided.

He watched her walk to the edge of the bed with that now familiar wiggle of her bottom. Her breasts were smallish but then, more than a mouthful is waste. He felt a weakness in the pit of his stomach for her as she pulled back the bedclothes.

'Wow, that's big,' she said. 'Bigger than I expected.'

'Well, Huge is my middle name,' he said.

She climbed into bed and he felt her snuggle into his arms, all warm and womanly and smelling of perfume and roses and faint deodorising compounds. The last thing he saw before she switched off the bedside lamp was the soft line of her depilated pubes, shaved and trim for the world to see.

It was the best sex he had ever had. She was an expert, with the body of an eel and hands and thighs like a vice. She was wet, yet strangely cool and odourless, like a mollusc taken freshly from the sea. He felt her body and when she was ready she ensheathed him with a condom, slipped him inside her and grasped his buttocks hard to hold him tight. She curled her legs around his back and began to rock and roll. It was high seas and a good swell on the boat of love. Then, just as he was about to climax, she jabbed him hard in the underarms with her fingernails. He came in a spasm, screaming and rigid like a frozen child who has been out in the cold too long. To help him along she moaned herself, though he wondered if she was only acting.

'Christ, that was the best ever,' he finally managed to mutter after ten minutes of trying to catch his breath. His voice sounded trapped in the darkness, as if it came from a mouth other than his own. He assumed she had faked her orgasm, for he remembered reading somewhere that prostitutes never have orgasms with clients. Still, he had to hand it to her; she was the best actress since Dietrich.

'Did you like it?' he asked. 'I was too blinded to know what you were doing.'

'Sure. That big thing of yours filled me up good.' The American accent was back.

'Size is everything,' he said, remembering the past. 'But size is no good without money.'

'Here, give me a kiss.'

And she put her arms around him and held him close and he could just make out her teeth smiling in the dark. He stretched his hand over the curves of her waist and hips and it struck him that her body was as precise a definition of eternity as he would ever need. Then they slept, a great, deep dive of a sleep, the two of them stuck together in the single bed. They seemed to have the same metabolism, a sort of biochemical compatibility, which for Madigan was unusual, for he hated sharing a single bed. But because she was so slim, they fitted easily together and every time one of them turned the other did so too. And four arms and legs were found when they were awoken by church bells at 9.00 the following morning, with the winter light filtering lazily through the dusty windowpane.

They made love a few more times whilst listening to the cars of the early Saturday shoppers, grabbing hold of Santa before he got crowded out. Then they got up and she cooked scrambled eggs and toast. As he gave her the money he had promised, he was more than a little sad, not over the money, but that such a transaction had to happen in the first place. She took it without speaking. Then he told her that he had to get going, that he had to meet Liam that afternoon.

'Do you think I could see you again?' he asked.

'If you want to.' She smiled.

'Of course I want to.'

'OK, I'll phone you at the brewery.'

Madigan gave her his extension number and his mobile number, and his e-mail address for good measure.

'I'll contact you,' she said, 'when I have a free evening.'

'Any time. You know where I am.'

And Madigan knew she would. And the world was suddenly wonderful.

She came down to the door to see him off. As he sat into his car she leaned in the window and gave him another kiss.

'The next time you come, you will not have to pay,' she whispered into his ear and Madigan, bitter, hardened, isolated old Madigan nearly wept with joy.

He left her smiling and drove up the Saturday-morning street. The sun peeped out between the houses and searched for the small change of frost in winter gardens. He put Warren Zevon on the stereo and waved at the sun and bought a Sunday newspaper. A crowd of gulls fought over the rubbish from well-pecked plastic bags. The houses were bare against the sky, the streets unfamiliar without their usual distortion of traffic. He had spent nearly two hundred quid, all told. He had only a tenner in his pocket. As he drove across the bridge over the canal, he saw a swan float towards the rising dawn.

'If you're as happy as I am, old son,' he said to the swan, 'then you're one hell of a happy bird.'

TWENTY-TWO

A Great House. Message in a bottle. Brazen banter with a tough lady. Searching for the missing files. *Hasta là vista*, baby. A car chase through the leafy suburbs. The Boss' boss. An invitation to a party.

It was rubbish collection day in the leafy suburbs, though because it was December there were no leaves, only rubbish. Every mansion guarded by a black wheelie bin looked much the same. Piles of plastic bags stuffed with trash neatly propped up every gateway, as if rubbish too was a form of décor, junk as modern art, not an outrageous concept. It was the kind of neighbourhood that made Madigan want to stand in the middle of the street and yell four-letter words at the top of his voice.

Madigan drove up and down the tree-lined avenue several times until he found the Crowley house, wedged between the embassies of two banana-state dictatorships.

A 'For Sale' sign leaned drunkenly over the front gate like a tipsy gossip at a midnight party. Madigan was surprised that Pamela would want to sell the house so quickly. This was prime property in a prime location, worth at least a million. With the way house prices were going, in a year it would be worth double that.

He parked Rosie a hundred yards beyond the house and walked back. There was a sign which said 'Beware of Dog', though there seemed to be no dogs about, only the lawn which was as clipped as a poodle's bottom. The drive swung around in a long curve between trees. Madigan strolled up the short-cut cobble block path across the lawn as if he owned the place.

The house itself was a large Victorian stone mansion with cast-iron guttering and a flight of steps leading to the front door. Four fluted limestone columns supported the portico over the steps. Madigan had checked the city's housing files and found that the house had been in the Professor's family for several generations. This was old money – old in a country where most of the money was new. Four or five large Scotch pines grew in the garden that seemed to be at least an acre in size. It was a perfect property for a developer to get his hands on, Madigan thought. He could cut down the trees, rent out the big house as apartments, build two or three apartment blocks in the garden and wank money out of it for as long as he wanted.

Madigan pressed the doorbell and heard a cathedral chime in the hollow of the house. He expected it to set dogs barking but the only thing that barked was the deep and dusty silence of the house. He looked through the glass panels by the side of the hall door and pressed the bell again and cracked the monkey-faced knocker against the door but still there was no sign of life. And there was no sign of Christmas lights or decorations in the hallway either. One thing was sure: this house would not be celebrating any Nativity.

Somebody had been doing some renovating, however, and a skip, half-filled with planks and broken pieces of mortar and plasterboard, stood by the gable end. There were several bags of domestic rubbish tossed in the skip. Madigan thought of the sycophants who root through the garbage of rock stars as he climbed into the skip to do a little rooting of his own. He ripped the plastic bags and scattered the rubbish around in the skip. It was the usual domestic stuff: eggshells, tins of dried out beans, half-eaten take-away food, empty loo-roll cylinders, plastic bags filled with ashes.

It was then that he spotted it, lurking in a small, half-opened cardboard box: a brown 100ml medical bottle sealed with a rubber septum and still containing a small quantity of clear liquid. The label had been washed off it. There was one hole in the septum. Madigan took a tissue from his pocket, picked up the little bottle, dropped it into a plastic bag and pocketed it.

He was clambering out of the skip when he heard a car coming up the drive. It was the black BMW convertible, low and sleek as a lizard's tail. He got out and hid behind the skip. The car came to halt in a shower of gravel. Pamela O'Neill Crowley got out. She was wearing similar clothes to those she wore at Dr Dunne's talk. Black. Widow's weeds. Grieving in glamour for her Professor. Madigan hid behind the skip.

She fished a large bunch of keys out of her handbag and went inside. Madigan gave her two minutes, then he walked back to the front door and rang the bell again.

When she opened the door she looked annoyed, as if Madigan's appearance was interrupting something very important.

'What are you doing here?' She threw him a hard look, like small pebbles at the side of a country road. 'I thought this business was finished?'

Madigan put his foot in the door in case she slammed it in his face. He decided to play for time.

'That's what I was hoping to ask you about. I got your cheque and all that. I was surprised with it quite frankly. Over £2,000, though I didn't actually find anything that could be of use to you.

So I was passing and I decided to call by to thank you for your generosity.'

'Well, I'm glad you're happy. Now if you'll excuse me, I have a thousand things to do.' She put her hand on the door as if to close it. Madigan flexed his foot to be ready to take the weight of it.

'In fact, I was so surprised by your contribution I felt in all conscience that I had to go to the police with it.'

'You what?'

He shoved in the door. Suddenly he was standing in the hall. It was a nice hall, high, with expensive wallpaper. It was a little too civilised for what he was doing now. But he knew he had one major advantage: he knew that for as long as she believed he had gone to the police she could do little about him.

'I think it's time we had a little chat, Mrs Crowley.'

'I don't see what we have to chat about.'

'No? Then I'll tell you. But first let's get away from the door. You don't let a guest in your house stand in the doorway, now do you, Mrs Crowley? It's very bad manners. I'm sure we'd both be more comfortable inside.'

'Look' she said. She was getting worried now. 'I don't know what brought you here. But you can't stay. My children will be home from school any minute.'

'I'm sure my presence will not disturb them, Mrs Crowley. In fact, I rather like children, sometimes at least. I have a son, you know.'

'Well, I'm expecting other guests too.'

'I'm sure this will not take too long. I am house trained, after all.'

'I'd never have guessed.' Once more, Madigan thought how much he'd like to have her over a couch. But he knew that was the born masochist in him, the vixen lover.

'Now, what can I do for you, Mr Madigan? Was the payment I gave you not enough?'

'Oh, it was more than adequate. I'd even go so far as to say it was generous, over-generous even, a good present coming up to Christmas. And don't get me wrong, I am grateful for it. Ours is a shabby little business, Mrs Crowley, and a cheque like that will keep me from having to do more of it until well into the new year.'

'Well, I'm glad I did good for someone for the festive season.'

'Well, it hasn't been all good, which is why I'm here. You see, Mrs Crowley, ever since I took this case, things have not been running exactly smoothly for me. People have acquired the habit of breaking into my flat, turning the whole place upside down and threatening me with knives and I'm sure it's only a matter of time before they begin to use guns. I'm not used to that, you see. I'm a gentle man. It's a little upsetting. Maybe I'm too soft for the job I'm in. Maybe I should expect these things in the type of work I do, but you see, it's affecting my sleep, and I don't function well when I don't get enough sleep. I keep thinking all kinds of different things, to be honest. I keep having the weirdest dreams and having all sorts of strange suspicions.'

'Are you trying to blackmail me?'

'Now why would I want to do that, Mrs Crowley? I'm sure you have done nothing that I could use for blackmail. No, my main interest at present is to find out why people want to beat me up and why they've only started to want to beat me up recently. I'd also like to find some way to stop them wanting to do so. You follow my drift?'

'Why come to me with your problems, Mr Madigan? I fail to see any connection between the insignificant little job I gave you to do and the fact that your flat has been broken into. We're not exactly living in a safe city and nobody should know that better than you. Every place gets broken into every so often. This house, for instance ...'

'Not by people who want to steal nothing and come searching for things I don't even have or ever had, for that matter. Things that vanished out of this house on the night your husband died.'

'What are you saying, Mr Madigan?' The colour vanished from her cheeks as if some incompetent GP had syringed it out of the back of her skull. Madigan decided to press on.

'The files containing the papers your husband was working on before his death. They disappeared out of this house on the night he died. Now the problem is that, for some reason, people think I have them and they're prepared to go to a lot of trouble to find them and get them back. And their means of persuasion are not exactly out of the "Boys Own" school of ethics.'

'What files?' she spat.

'That's what I'd like to know. And I'm sure you're about the only one who can tell me.'

'What makes you think there were files missing after Willie died?' Now she was rattled.

'I'm not a private investigator for nothing.'

'Well, you're welcome to look through Willie's filing cabinets if you think that will do you any good. Some files were missing on the night he died. That was because I had them for a conference I was attending in London. You can check that if you like.'

'I believe you. I'd like to see those files though, Mrs Crowley.'

'I don't see how it would do you any good, but if you insist. There's nothing secret in them, just routine scientific papers. You're welcome to go through them.'

She led him around the back of the house to the Professor's teak-panelled office. Madigan looked around for bags of sweets or chocolates but there were none.

Much of the furniture had already been cleared out; there were marks along the walls where they had stood. In the corner there were still two filing cabinets, old wooden ones of good oak, from the days before the hard drive.

'You're doing a little spring cleaning?'

'Just trying to sort the place out.'

'This is a fine house. I'm surprised you're selling it.'

'I just put it on the market, more to see what it was worth than to actually sell it.'

'Yes, it's nice to know what assets you have, I suppose.'

She opened one of the drawers of the nearest filing cabinet. It was not locked. She pulled out a thick beige folder.

'This contains all the files that Willie was working on before he died. It also contains the files I took to London that week.'

'Do you think I could copy them?'

'There's nothing in here of interest to anyone but specialists in the area. But you can, if you want to.'

'I think I'd like to go through all the files here,' I said.

'Help yourself. I have some things to do. And I am expecting visitors.'

This was going far too easily.

'And your children?'

'OK, that was a ruse to try to get you to leave. If you must know, they've started in boarding school. I felt they'd get a better education that way.'

'Clongowes I suppose, or Newbridge College?'

'Gonzaga.'

'Ah well, the Jesuits in any case. They will, of course, be back for Christmas?'

'They will, Mr Madigan. Now, any more questions about how I rear my children?'

'No. I'm sure you're right. People learn the most amazing things in boarding schools.'

She let the comment pass, which surprised Madigan. Maybe she did not care too much about her children, he thought.

'Now, if you don't mind, Mr Madigan, I have other things to attend to. I'll be in the kitchen.'

Madigan knew already that he would get nothing of value in the files. If there was ever anything of interest, there had been adequate time to weed it out. Still, he took the papers that were dated from the two weeks before the Professor died and stuffed them under his shirt. If nothing else, he might be able to use them to get the hoodlums off his back.

He noticed her mobile phone sitting on the hall table and popped it into his pocket when she turned her back.

'Can I use your toilet?'

'It's under the stairs.'

He went into the toilet and as quickly as he could copied down all the most recent phone numbers in her mailbox. For good measure, he took the battery out before replacing the phone where he'd found it.

As he was coming out of the toilet he had noticed something that surprised him: under the stairs stood a liquid-nitrogen canister, similar to the one he had seen being delivered to the university the night before the Professor died.

'You were a long time in there,' she said as she came out of the kitchen.

'Don't ask. Too much low fibre food, the McDonalds way. By the way, that's an unusual choice for a domestic freezer, Mrs Crowley, if I may say so?' he said, pointing to the liquid-nitrogen cylinder. 'You're not trying to preserve anybody in there, by any chance?'

'You're very observant, Mr Madigan, I'll give you that. That's my culture collection. It's part of my work. I keep vials of all my cultures here as well as in the university, as a back-up. One cannot be too careful.'

'Too true,' Madigan said. 'Nobody can ever be too careful. Anyway, to get back to the files; I've gone through them, and I'll have to say I agree with you. The stuff looks horribly scientific and at least at first glance it does not look like anything that anyone would want. However, someone thinks there's something of value in them.'

'I cannot see how Willie's work could be of interest to anyone. It's pure academic work. There can only be half a dozen people in the world who are sufficiently well up in the area to even care about what he was doing.'

'Well, my information is that his work on depression may be of more than academic interest.'

'So you've become something of a biochemist of late, Mr Madigan. Quite an achievement for someone like you, I should imagine. Now, if you don't mind, could you see yourself to the door? I'm expecting guests at any moment.'

'Thanks for your help, Mrs Crowley. *Hasta là vista*, baby, as they say.'

Madigan gave her his most charming smile and headed for the door. He closed it quietly behind him. The evening was already dark, as if the soot had fallen down too early.

He slipped around the corner of the house where he had noticed earlier that the telephone cable was connected and cut it with his penknife. Then he sauntered out the front gate to where he had parked Rosie and waited for the fun to start.

He did not have long to wait. Five minutes later the lights of the BMW came down the drive and out the gates. The Beamer went off down the road, low and fast, as if there was a rocket in the exhaust. Madigan spun Rosie around and followed her as closely as he could.

The good lady, he quickly realised, was made for Formula One. She ran three orange lights, which were red by the time he ran them. She hit the ramps as if they were not there. It was all he could do to keep the little BMW from shrinking into the early evening smog. He prayed for turbo charge and fuel injection as they cut through the suburban glades between the overhanging cherry trees of Milltown golf course that gave the false impression they were in the middle of the countryside.

Eventually she pulled into the winding drive of a big house in Rathfarnham. She quickly got out of her car and, with her own key, let herself in the front door. Madigan pulled into the gateway and noted the address.

Madigan, if he were a betting man, would have expected to find a wine-coloured Mercedes somewhere around the place. But when he was a betting man all he ever did was lose on the horses and on the stock market, so, being the bookie's friend, he made no predictions. Rather he sat in the car and waited.

Nothing happened. No one came or went. Eventually he decided to have a snoop around. The house was big, an old mansion, with a long drive and tall Lebanon cedars. The side gate was locked but he could look over it. Again there was a 'Beware of the Dog' sign and this time it meant something, for a big Rottweiler came snarling around the corner of the house as Madigan approached. As he was fresh out of strychnine lamb chops, he decided to go no further. He took one look around the corner. There was only the BMW in the drive. There was no Merc or, if there was, it was in the garage.

Madigan went back to Rosie and waited again. After a while the hound stopped barking. He looked at his watch. It was 9.00.

He decided to sit it out. He checked the radio. There was a programme about incest on. Madigan was bored with incest, so he
put a Warren Zevon tape on instead.

Warren Zevon was Madigan's man. Springsteen wasn't even
trotting after him. He was The Boss' boss; he sang about heroin
and sadness and the various ways you can destroy your life; he
sang about mercenaries and the consolations of listening to the
radio in the middle of the night. Zevon was great for long car
journeys and Madigan took him everywhere with him as much for
the pain as the West Coast sound of the piano ... the piano ... the
piano ... Madigan dozed before the tape finished.

In his dreams he was in doggy heaven with Marika. When he
woke up, he was tingling with pins and needles and as cold as a leg
of lamb. It took him five minutes to shake some life into his limbs.

He waited a while longer but she never came out. Eventually,
he got tired of waiting and drove back to his own flat. He figured
there was unlikely to be anyone waiting for him at that hour of
night. He was happy with himself. He had done a good evening's
work.

When he got in there was an unexpected note waiting for him.
It was from Vikki Morgan, the girl he had seen going to work the
first week he was on the case and who had nearly caused him to
crash into the car in front of him. She said she now worked at a
pharmacy just down the road from his flat; she was throwing a
party and Madigan was invited. Nothing would give him more
pleasure. It never rained but it poured. He got into bed – it had got
only a little damp in his absence – and dreamt about Marika again.

TWENTY-THREE

Apothecary. Vikki Morgan. Neurology revisited. Madigan discovers that
the femme fatale is not who she appears to be. Going down on history.
Hoolihanism. The Professor's plasmids. A crucial clue. Sally phones.

A travelling woman was sitting on a dirty blanket outside the
pharmacy with a plastic milk container held out looking for
money. She looked like an Indian squaw, with a nose as cold as he
imagined her backside was. Madigan expected to see a peace pipe.
Instead he got a kind of grunt when he gave her a coin.

When he opened the pharmacy door, he was suddenly hit by
the air of the shop which was redolent of women and the rooms
of women. Madigan loved pharmacies. They were so full of the
feminine and he did his best never to think of the people with bad
feet who visited the chiropodist working at the back of the shop.

Vikki smiled, high and busty from behind a tall counter covered with bottles of perfume, arch supports, prophylactics and
pregnancy kits. Cardboard roses and Christmas decorations gild-
ed the counter and pictures of perfect women in Santa swimsuits
advertised everything from tampons to various methods for the
depilation of legs.

'Hi Mike. You look happy.'

'Happy is what happy does, Vikks,' he said.

'What can I do for you?'

'A packet of condoms and maybe a bit of information.'

Condoms had always been bad juju with Madigan, though they could also be construed as good advertising. Being in possession of a condom had always been inversely proportional to his chances of getting laid. Now he suddenly felt different about these cute little rubber things. That's what love does to you, he thought.

'Got something going?' She handed him the prophylactics over the counter. 'Who's the lucky girl?'

'Naw. I'm just being on the safe side. You'd never know when the Good Lord would see fit to put a bit of action under my nose. If He does, I don't want to be seen going into combat without a helmet.'

'Oh, you're an awful man, Mike.'

He figured there was no point in telling Vikki about Marika. Women tended to respect one another's patch. Things might not work out with Marika. By keeping his mouth shut about her, he might hit the jackpot some time with Vikki, for you never knew when luck and desperation might combine to land the goodies. It's the poor mouse that depends on only one hole. Besides, she was unlikely to approve of his having liaisons with hookers.

'And another thing, I was just wondering if you'd know what are the best money-spinning illnesses for the drug companies? How would depression rate on the list?'

She smiled. Her perfectly made-up lips were etched on a canvas by Lancôme. 'Well, in terms of prescription drugs, the treatment of heart disease and depression lead the way.'

'So, if a cure could be found for depression then the drug companies would stand to lose a lot of money?'

'They'd lose a fortune, I'd say, except for the company who made that drug, of course.'

'What is your best-selling treatment for depression?'

'Cyclocon. It's sold under the brand name Simeverol.'

'How much of it would you sell every week?'

'We'd clear £1,000 worth of it in a week, and we're only a small outlet. A big branch of one of the chain pharmacies might sell ten times that.'

Madigan whistled. 'That's a lot of dough when you multiply it up.'

'Is that all you want?'

'That's all I want. I'm always an easy bloke to please.'

'Come to my party,' she said. 'There'll be lots of interesting people there.'

Well, how about that, Madigan thought. All people are interesting or nobody is interesting, depending on your point of view. However, Vikki looked like she was game for a bit of fun. It never rained but it brought the cats and dogs down as well. It was obvious he did not look desperate any more. If he was, he would never get asked to a party like that. Desperation stinks like the skunks that visit American gardens every night to root for garbage. Desperation turns women off like the smell of rotting flesh. Now, rather than desperation, Madigan had Marika-induced pheromones. We are nothing if not nasal gazers.

'I just might do that,' he said.

Wishing Vikki a 'Happy Christmas', he went out into the street again. A queue of cars was lined up behind a pair of traveller kids on a cart pulled by a piebald nag. They sat on a bale of hay and acted as if they owned the street. Fifty furious faces glared but nobody honked their horns in case the boys would fling stones through their windows. This was peacekeeping. The UN take note. They called to the woman who was still sitting outside the pharmacy. She told them to 'fuck off'. A mother's love! You'll never miss her till she's gone.

For the second time, Madigan went shopping for a Christmas present for Liam. He knew he would have to face it sooner or later. Eventually, he found something: a computer game that simulated the operation of an entire building site. It came complete with sand and JCBs and dumper trucks, and walls and roofs went up or could be dismantled depending on the controls. 'Bob the Builder' eat your heart out. He tried it out himself in the shop. Virtual reality. Better than the real thing. Live in dream worlds. Everyone's at it. Not a bad option.

He then called to see Dr Dunne at the university and showed him the papers he had nicked from the Professor's house. Dr Dunne said they were old work the Professor had done years earlier.

'The *Journal of Clinical Psychology* has no record of receiving any papers from the Professor,' Madigan said.

'There's a cover-up going on, old man,' he said. 'Pamela's behind all this, you know.'

'It's too early to say that yet. There's no evidence to incriminate her in any way.'

'You keep digging, Mr Madigan. Eventually, you'll come up with something. I know a lot about Pamela that might interest you.'

'Shoot.'

'Well, for a start, did you know she has connections with the Hoolihan family?'

The Hoolihan family was a politico-criminal outfit that caused mayhem in the country for as long as Madigan could remember. They were worse than Al Capone, Dutch Schultz and Pretty Boy Floyd all put together. They liked to think they were the owners of history and struck at random, murdering, robbing banks and railways and post offices. There were times when they were quiet, when they seemed to vanish into the woodwork, times indeed when people thought the country was cured of them. Then, just when everyone thought they were safe, the gang would emerge again from the shadows of normality and start their round of bombings and shootings again. It was believed they ran much of the racketeering in the city, among other things.

'Her original name was Hoolihan, Kathleen ní Hoolihan. Did you know that? Of course she keeps changing, with the prevailing wind, as it were.'

'I would have thought she was a little too middle class for that kind of thing?'

'Her ancestors were peasants. It took just one generation to elevate the peasant to the centre of things. That said she still has many of the qualities of the peasant, namely cunning and avariciousness. Of course, Hoolihanism was originally a middle-class phenomenon, though it has to move with the times.'

'That would make her the daughter of Hoolihan, I suppose?'

'She changed her name to O'Neill when she first came to town. The name Hoolihan was not fancy enough. Maybe she was trying to hide her roots. The double-barrelled name would always go down well. You know how it is, the nouveau riche moving up in the world.'

'New money?'

'You could say she's the epitome of bourgeois self-interest, to put it mildly. Of course, she was never anything else. Largely influenced by the American model, I should think. And it has to be said that in the old days much of the funding for the Hoolihans came from America. Still does. It is, of course, her corruption that makes her interesting to people like you and me, Mr Madigan. The space between what she says and what she does, the difference between rhetoric and reality, if you catch my drift.'

'The peninsula of greed jutting into the sea of her being?'

'Another splendid image, Mr Madigan, if I may say so.'

'Thank you.'

'Respectability, it's called.'

'But you gave no hint of any of this stuff the other night. You seemed to get on quite well with her.'

'I keep on the right side of her, Mr Madigan. We all do around here. We have to. The woman carries the Hoolihan flag; we have to be careful. Of course, it's the friends she still has from the old days that you have to worry about.'

'The friends?'

Ivor Dunne smiled.

'Let's just hope you don't have to meet any of them.'

'Who, exactly?'

'The embarrassment of the past, Mr Madigan, the embarrassment of the past, the people she would like to get away from but cannot. You see, people like her need to be ruthless to get where they are today. And when you're ruthless, you need henchmen, followers, sycophants, psychopaths in many instances. She uses them, she moves on, but they are still there. She'll never be able to walk away from them. Our oldest friends stay with us the longest, Mr Madigan; most of us will never be anything more than the shadows of the street we grew up in.'

Madigan was slowly beginning to see the implications of what he was saying. This added a whole new dimension to everything.

'If what you say is true, then I'm surprised she's got away with it for so long.'

'We are not a thinking race, Mr Madigan, we are not given to self analysis, except of the most banal kind. We fail, in many cases, to see what is under our noses. We are easily fooled, in other words. Of late, we have been very given to self-congratulation. This blinds us, I would say, most profoundly. The worst form of ignorance, Mr Madigan, is the ignorance that does not know it is ignorant. You need only look at the fat girls in the streets, showing off their midriffs. They think they're beautiful.'

'Some of them are sexy.'

'We fought a revolution to be bourgeois, Mr Madigan. Ironic, isn't it?'

'And what about the Professor? Did he know of this?'

'If he did, he certainly didn't mention it to me. Willie would have been naïve, you see. He may have suspected something but I'm sure he would have been persuaded that all that was in her past. He wouldn't have known what he was getting into. Love is blind, I suppose.'

'Very true. I'm surprised she did not try to seduce me.'

'She did not need to, Mr Madigan. If she had wanted to, she would have seduced you long ago. And you would have been seduced, believe me.'

'I don't doubt that,' Madigan said.

'She seduced many a good man before you, Mr Madigan. Many were led down paths which were not exactly good for their health.'

'*C'est la vie.*'

'Quite the contrary, Mr Madigan. Indeed, *c'est la mort* would be more like it in many cases. Young men led to their deaths and for what?'

'But where does all that leave the missing papers and the Professor's death?'

'You have me there, Mr Madigan. But you're the private eye around here.' Dr Dunne pushed his glasses to the end of his nose and peered out over them as if he were trying to look at Madigan over a high wardrobe.

'Do you think there might be a connection between Nolan and the Hoolihan gang?' Madigan told him about the break-ins and Benny Mulligan and the search for the files.

'Well, I'm not an expert on the gangland and little splinter group politics of this town, Mr Madigan, but at a guess, I'd say they're either all part of the one operation or else they're rivals looking for the same thing. Willie's work is obviously important to the whole lot of them. It's big money and running a big outfit, like the Hoolihans do, bringing in guns and what not, costs a lot. It comes with the territory. I think we can take it as read that the work is worth a lot to somebody.'

'Would you be surprised to find a liquid-nitrogen freezer in the Professor's house?'

'Well, all I can say is that I never saw one there and I was a frequent visitor before Willie's death.'

'There's one there now. Pammy says she keeps her culture collection in it, whatever that is.'

'That's interesting.' He stroked his chin and looked out the window. 'That would normally be at the university,' he said, slowly.

'She said it was a back up.'

'Maybe it is. Maybe, on the other hand, it contains Willie's own gene bank.'

'The genes Willie was working on, or Willie's genes, if you get my drift?'

'The genes for MDC. It's cloned in the form of plasmids, into bacterial strains. They are stored in liquid nitrogen, to keep them viable.'

'Viable?'

'Another word for alive, Mr Madigan, just like you and me,

for the moment anyway.'

'These plasmids. What do they do?'

'They are needed to make the drug – they contain the genetic information – but the files are also needed in order to know which gene is where and so on. One without the other is like a gun without bullets. They're also likely to be on disc somewhere.'

'Could somebody who knew their stuff do it without the files?'

'They could, but it would be very tedious and take several years.'

'It's a funny thing, you know. The only reason I knew it was liquid nitrogen was that I met two guys delivering a consignment of the stuff to the university the night before the Professor died.'

'Do you remember what time that was?'

'It must have been 9.30, 10.00.'

'That's very late to be delivering liquid nitrogen.'

'That's what I said to them. They said it was a late delivery.'

'What did they look like?'

'They were wearing white coats, for a start and ...'

'White coats? It's unlikely that men working for gas delivery companies would wear white coats. Dungarees maybe, but I've never seen them wear white coats.'

'Well, they were, and they were rolling in one of those R2D2 things.'

'A flask – we call them flasks. You sure it was the same type, exactly the same type?'

'Quite sure. I wouldn't have recognised the one in the Professor's house otherwise.'

'That's very interesting, because liquid nitrogen is normally filled from a hose off the back of a truck, into a flask admittedly, but a very different shaped one from those used to store cultures.

I'd be willing to bet, Mr Madigan, that you'll find that those men, whoever they were, were in the process of stealing the Professor's plasmids.'

'And why did the police not notice they were missing?'

'Why should they? They would have no reason to search the department and even if they did, the two men obviously replaced it with the one you saw being delivered. Check it out. I bet you won't find the cultures in it – not the ones with the MDC genes anyway.'

'Who else would know if it were missing?'

'Pamela, I suppose, and Simon Callaghan.'

'Did you know, Doctor, that Simon Callaghan drowned during his holidays in the Canaries?'

He showed the kind of shock that Madigan normally associated with Batman when he's just heard that someone's put a hydrogen bomb under Gotham City.

'Mr Madigan, this ... this is worse than I expected,' but he said it calmly, as if it were precisely what he had expected.

'Sure is,' Madigan said. 'It's rottener than the septic tank leaking into the kitchen.'

'She's behind it, Mr Madigan. I just know it.'

'She may not be the only one.'

Madigan left Dr Dunne's office almost as puzzled as when he went in, though certain things were beginning to fall into place. He had files but they were the wrong files. It was fair to suppose that Pamela had taken the Professor's cultures and had the info to use them. He still had the bottle he had found in the skip at Pamela O'Neill Crowley's place. But he needed to get a set of prints done on it. He decided to call to Tom Bryan, an old friend of his in the forensic lab down the road from the brewery. He could tell if there was anything interesting in the bottle without alerting the police.

On the way home, he photocopied the papers in an office that smelled of ink and had black powder like radioactive dust on the counters and the floor.

When he got home, he met Lily Bowen on the stairs. She was wearing her best coat and had Keen and Terry in two boxes, one in each hand.

'Wish them well, Michael, my little dears. Wish my little dears well.' She was wearing make-up scraped across her face like an over-iced Christmas cake .

'Why, Lily? Are you taking them away?' Madigan said, secretly hoping for some small feline genocide.

'No, you silly boy, I'm taking them to the cat show. I have high hopes for my Keen here and my little Terry might pick up something in her own class.'

She might pick something up all right, he thought, like a dose of the mange, but he wished them well anyway.

Lily toddled off in her best shoes, a droll little old doll trotting down the street, bumping the boxes against her knees. Whatever chances the cats had of winning the show, they would have none at all by the time she got there.

Madigan went upstairs. The flat was as cold as a presbytery. The usual smells of fried rashers, sleep, stale spunk and sweaty T-shirts were missing due to his long absences. Something reeked in the fridge. It was old cheese. He found a green brick of mouldy bread in the bread bin, sealed it in a plastic bag and flung it along with the cheese into the rubbish bin before pouring half a bottle of curdled milk down the sink.

He switched on his answering machine. There was only one message. It was from Sally. It said that Liam had hurt his arm but was now all right. This could be true or she could be up to something. For once she did not ask for money, but Madigan smelled a rat. He knew she wanted him to phone her to ask if Liam was ok. Then she would drop her expected load of baloney. So he decided not to. Like the cat who ate the cheese and sat outside the mouse hole, he waited with baited breath to see what she would do next.

He phoned all the numbers he had taken down from the mailbox of Pamela's mobile phone. When he got through to the wrong house he just apologised for getting a wrong number. Eventually he hit gold dust. An answering machine said 'this is the Nolan residence'. The machine clicked to take his message.

'Mr Nolan. I have the files you're looking for. Give me a ring at this number.' Madigan left his name and said he could be contacted at the brewery if Nolan wanted his files back.

Then he went back out to the street to look for something to eat. Everyone was at work and the Christmas lights were not yet switched on. The decorations were tassels on the faded beauty of this decaying town. He headed for Abrakebabra. The street was as lonely as a priest's funeral.

TWENTY-FOUR

Calling in the markers. The working life. Middle-age burn out. Farming out the children. The railway station. Bluffing Nolan.
The lights for the crossing of the blind.

Things were bad in the public analyst's lab. Tom Bryan was wearing a lab coat with stains and scorch marks down the side. He had bags under his red eyes from lack of sleep. His wife had cancer and he spent most of his time looking after his two daughters. Like his coat, he was frayed around the edges from too much living, too much caring, too many kicks in the teeth.

The lab smelled of chemicals, ether mostly, and was faded and creaky and old. Samples of drugs well past their best-before date sat gathering dust on dozens of mottled shelves. Tom Bryan owed Madigan a favour. Madigan had once put a little pressure on the consultant who was treating his wife to hurry up with the job and not leave her waiting until she was actually dead before seeing her. Now Madigan enquired about his wife's health and Tom replied resignedly that there was still hope. Madigan gave him the bottle and asked him if he could analyse it and do a set of prints on it. Tom promised to phone with the results as soon as they were available.

Then Madigan phoned the brewery to see if there were any messages for him. A Mr Nolan had called, Ted Plunkett said. He would meet him at 7.00 outside the railway station to pick up the merchandise. If Nolan phoned back, he told Ted to tell him he would be there.

Madigan had the afternoon off and found himself taking a drive to see how things were at his former home. Sally would be at work; he could snoop around as he pleased, just for old time's sake.

He headed south out of Donnybrook, along the dual carriageway, past the new hotels that stood at angles to the older buildings like big cigarette boxes on their sides. He passed RTE. Its mast blinked red in the gloom, like Dublin's answer to the Eiffel Tower. He passed Belfield, his old, though brief, stomping ground. Queues of buses stood in line to pick up those students who did not have their own cars.

He thought about suburban life and the hassle it was. He thought of the assistant bank managers and civil servants, getting up at all hours to be ahead of the traffic to go to stress-filled jobs and then facing the same traffic every evening. He saw them calling into pubs on the way home for a whiskey to settle their nerves before facing into their housefuls of squawking kids. He saw them walk around their houses in the middle of the night wondering why they were so unhappy and creeping to fridge and drinks cabinet in search of something to fill the hollow inside. He saw them waking, stressed out, hours before dawn, wondering where all their dreams had gone and why life was not the appliance-filled paradise that had been promised.

He saw them stumbling into their forties and looking at their wives beside them in bed, and realising they slept every night with a total stranger. And he saw them survey their offices during the day for even the vaguest possibility of a way out, for beautiful secretaries, and some not so beautiful, who, desperate for love, were prepared to time-share a man. He realised that the only people doing well out of this state of affairs were psychologists, lawyers and people like himself, who made a killing out of people's mistrust of each other.

Then he thought about the wives, who, when they realised they too were married to strangers, wondered whether to make a run for it while they were still young enough, or decide, as the vast majority of them did, to stay where they were and do their best to play the hand that fate had dealt them. He saw them take to gin or bridge or religion or golf. He saw them turn into nags and arrive at his own doorstep in droves to find out what their husbands were up to when their backs were turned. And he saw their children, farmed out to crèches, grow up as near-delinquents because of the vagaries of their parents' lives. Yet life could be worse. Madigan, for one, had stumbled on a trade for which there would always be business, at least for the foreseeable future.

The railway station was crowded with young people coming, but mostly going, for the start of the Christmas holidays. Madigan considered how the youth, fearing the lonely bedsits and the hollow bells of Sunday morning, flee the city like lemmings to head for Mammy on weekends and holidays. They go back to all the places that spawned them, jetsam on the tides of the world.

Madigan pulled into the awning by the railway station and parked illegally. High beams of cobwebbed iron supported the roof above the stinking trains. The station was filthy with age, brown with rust and spattered with pigeon shit, the limestone black as graphite from a hundred years of smog. The smell of piss pervaded the platform from loos where you had to pay 20p to pee. A porter with a large belly and a red face ran around to various queues announcing the departure times of trains to various country stations.

He was buying an evening paper when he noticed the wine-coloured Mercedes pull up among the taxis on the road outside. Nolan got out and pressed the central locking on his key ring. The car went blip, the lights winked and then it slept like an expensive hearse. The interior of the Merc at least was now as safe as Fort Knox from the dope heads who hung around the station.

Madigan watched Nolan from behind a stand in the magazine shop. Curvaceous blondes with big tits burst out of the covers of magazines at him. Nolan wore a shiny blue suit like a showband manager or a pet-food magnate. As he got closer, Madigan noticed a black crown topper curled on his head like a camou-flaged rat. Although he wore glasses and the light was bad, his skin looked waxy and sagged a little, as if it were about to come away from his face. He had the small, quick eyes of a stoat and looked to Madigan like he had not sweated for a long time.

Madigan decided to let him wait for a few minutes and watched him while he waited. Nolan was not used to waiting. He moved uneasily around the station. Madigan figured he was doing Nolan's soul a favour by forcing him to practise the virtue of patience. After ten minutes, during which he cooled his heels by walking up and down the platform, he came into the newspaper shop and began looking through the girlie mags.

'*Irish Housewives*. One of your publications?' Madigan asked, pulling a magazine off the shelf beside him and leafing through it.

Nolan looked across the shelf. Not only had he not sweated for a long time, thought Madigan, but he had not smiled either.

'Magnificent, isn't she?' Madigan pointed to a cover of a naked girl with a big ass spread across the seat of a huge motor-cycle.

'Are you Madigan?'

'And who do I have the honour of addressing; Mr Nolan or

Mr Kelly, which is it? Somehow I prefer the former, though I cannot for the life of me say why – maybe because it was the first name I heard.'

'So, you're a smart-ass?'

'People have called me worse.'

'Did you bring the papers, Mr Smart-ass?'

'Now, Nolan, you don't think I'd be foolish enough to give you all the papers just in one go? She might have come down the river on a Honda,' he said, pointing to the girl in the magazine cover, 'but I didn't.'

'Come on, you bastard, don't mess with me. I could have your brains blown out just like that.' He clicked his finger at the efficacy of his brain blowing capabilities. 'Hand those papers over, all of them, now.'

'You're a man of many talents, though I can't say I've heard about your surgical prowess. I think what you're doing is threatening me with bodily harm. Now, if I did come to bodily harm it would look bad, coming from a respectable businessman like yourself. Who knows who I might tell about such threats. The walls have ears, Mr Nolan.'

He looked around furtively. At least Madigan had him thinking he was not alone and took one of the papers in a brown envelope out of the inside pocket of his jacket.

'Now you listen to me, you bastard,' he said, 'and listen well.' Madigan put on his most hard-bitten voice. If it sounded like a growl, all well and good. If it sounded like Mickey Mouse on laughing gas, it would have to do. 'Just to show my sincerity, this envelope contains some of the papers. The others are in a safe place and I'll send them to you by post as soon as I'm safely out of here. I don't want to run into your goon show on the way home tonight, now do I? As an added insurance, I've taken a copy of all the papers, which in the unlikely event of something nasty happening to me will land within hours on the desk in Store Street station, along with a written account of what I've picked up since your little friend Benny paid me a visit.'

'If you know so much, why have you not gone to the police already?'

'Mr Nolan. I'm a peace-loving man.' Madigan went back to his most reasonable voice. 'I don't want the police coming around my life like a swarm of bees, upsetting my peace of mind. All I want is to be left alone, to do my own things in my own little way. I could have used this to blackmail you. I could have sold it back to you, if I had wanted to. I could have run to the police, as you say. But I chose not to. It must be my generally honest nature. I treated your Benny with all the courtesy due to someone like him. I'm liable to treat any more of your friends in the same way. You touch me, Nolan, and this whole baby gets blown sky high, even if my understanding of what's in those papers is no better than yours.'

'Right, Madigan. If the rest of the papers are not in Friday's post then you're in trouble. Now give me that.'

'If the other paper is not in the post by Friday then I suggest you take it up with An Post. I've heard their mail deliveries are sometimes late. They like to have strikes on the run up to Christmas. Now if you'll excuse me, I have other important things to attend to.' Madigan gave him the envelope. He took it and held it tightly, like a big baby minding his soother.

'Now, I suggest you get on your car phone and call off your boys, Nolan. Tell them you've no shift work for them just at the moment. They're going to have no party with me tonight. By the way,' Madigan handed him the girlie magazine, 'you should buy one of these. They're great for clearing the tubes. You could do with a little colour in your face.'

He walked out of the shop and out the high-domed door of the station. A fat man with filthy skin stood at the corner selling newspapers. He used a rock to keep them from being blown away by the wind. He yelled out with an old turkey-like voice: 'Evening peppers, evening peppers, evening peppers.'

It was then that somebody switched on a great light with the help of something heavy and hard to the back of Madigan's head. He went down like a wet sack under a load of gravel. The last thing he remembered thinking was that he no longer owned a pair of legs. As he swam into the calm pool of blue light, he could just about hear the sound of the pedestrian lights going peep peep, peep peep, peep peep, the sound for the crossing of the blind.

Twenty-Five

A Jamaican street party. The Three Stooges. Method acting. Psychopaths
at work. Nolan returns. A dental appointment. Ninety miles an hour
down a dead end street. Silicone Valley revisited.
Shelter from the storm.

Madigan thought he was in Brixton and there was some kind of
street party going on. He was surrounded by four or five Jamaican
girls who were dancing in see-through tops and wore white high
heels and cut-away jeans. He had never been to Brixton, in fact he
only barely knew where it was, and he had never seen Jamaican
girls outside of Bob Marley videos. Yet, here they were, pouting
and licking their lips and flashing their bellies like the black
dancers of MTV. And here he was, surrounded by these beautiful,
half-naked girls in a place of thumping music and a smell of hash
with one hell of a party going on.

The tallest of them approached him, her ripped jeans held up
by some sort of miracle, and began thrusting her pelvis into his
face. She appeared to be wearing nothing underneath and her
pubes were half-visible; she was all belly, brown and beautiful. She
was about to embrace him when he felt what he thought was rain
running down the back of his neck. Then she began to dissolve
and he found himself rising, slowly, oozily, stickily, as if he were a

human-sized wellington boot being dragged suckingly out of a swamp.

First he thought he had no arms, for he could find them nowhere. Then he realised there was pain coming from something that might be arms and began thinking of amputees who feel pain in joints and toes which have long since been consigned to the grave. It came as a shock to him to find that his arms were tied behind his back. He realised that, far from being seduced by beautiful Jamaican girls, he was trussed up like a dead chicken and was lying in a ditch with the rain running down his face. Now Madigan felt barely alive and so cold he could have been locked outside the igloo at the North Pole with no access to the rescue helicopter.

And he had a splitting headache, as if his head was a building site and somebody had been using a kango hammer to rip up the slabs of his brain. He moved his head; the back of his hair was cracking, matted with what he presumed was blood.

Madigan could hear voices and the wind blowing and the sound of a diesel engine running. Slowly he opened his eyes. There were birches over his head shaking eerily as if they were a crowd going wild at a football match in the sky. He realised he was in some kind of parkland or a field or a piece of waste ground; it was suburban, it was orange, it was night and it was raining. And it was near a main road, for he could hear the swish, swish of cars passing in the rain. There was a high bank and an even higher fence between the road and the ditch where he lay, smelling the earth and the trampled grass.

He could just about see three men, about ten feet away, murmuring over the sound of the engine of a new white Ford van. They were playing cards in the light of the back of the van. Madigan could not see their faces in the dark but there was something familiar about them. He pretended to be still unconscious and could hear snatches of their conversation.

'I think we should just do him in, Gary,' one of them said. 'Have it over and done with.'

'OK, you dig the grave, if you're so eager to get saturated on a night like this,' the fellow called Gary said.

'Make him dig the fucking grave himself. Why dig a grave? The cops will find him anyway.'

'Look, there's no need to dig any grave. Besides, how many times do I have to tell you, we can't do anything until Nolan comes back.'

'I could fix him nicely with this, Gary, no bullets, no ballistics, no tracing, nothing but a dead nosey parker.' Madigan did not want to look, so he did not know what 'this' was, but he could just imagine. Suddenly he felt very old. So this is it, Madigan thought. This is the endgame. You skid along through life and suddenly there it is, the wall looming over you and you're doing 90 and there's not a hope in hell of stopping. Surprisingly, he never thought it would happen like this. He had always thought he would die in bed, a crummy old bed perhaps, but a bed for all that, and be taken down the stairs in a nice shiny box. That was how it was supposed to end, not in a wet drain somewhere on the verges of Dublin. He knew he would need luck to get out of this one.

Suddenly, like a blubbering schoolboy, he started to shake, choking back real tears. He had never heard of a private eye doing this. They were not supposed to cry. He knew that the good guys would grit their teeth, try to tough it out and look for a way to escape. He was letting his profession down; this weeping was new territory in the detective business. In a way he was glad he was in a ditch where nobody could see him.

Then he heard the one called Gary say: 'Sheesh, I think he's after coming around.'

'I'll go over and have a look,' the one who sounded like a psycho said.

'Don't clobber him, Derek. Nolan will need to talk to him when he gets back.'

'If he ever gets back,' the third one, who had not spoken before, said.

'He'll come back.'

'I bet he's stuck in the fuckin' traffic.'

Madigan could hear the squelching of feet in the mud as the one called Derek approached. Then he could see a pair of city shoes, fine Italian shoes, covered in muck, and a man in a leather jacket standing over him.

'He's awake,' Derek said.

Madigan tried to speak but there was something around his mouth that he had not noticed before. He was gagged, and just as well.

'This is what you get for messing with the Man,' Derek said, shoving Madigan in the ribs with his foot. Madigan sloshed more deeply into the drain. 'Little boy trying to do big man's business. You're some fuckin' wanker, boy.' He pulled him upright. Madigan swallowed his tears and tried to communicate to him to take off the gag.

'I think he wants me to take off the tape. Do I do it or let him stew?' Derek called out to the others.

'Ask him is he willing to talk – talk the truth, that is,' Gary said.

'Gary says "do you want to talk the truth?" Well, do ya?' He gave Madigan a kick in the belly. It was not hard. The quality of the shoes was too good for heavy kicking. Madigan nodded furiously like a chicken in a bird cage. Derek ripped the gag off. It hurt as much as a Brazilian wax. Madigan realised he had at least two day's beard growth.

'We can make this simple,' Derek said, 'or we can make it hard.'

'Those are nice shoes you got,' Madigan croaked. 'Pity to get them all caked with mud. I'd wait till they're dry before trying to clean them. It'll come off easier then ...' Derek gave him another kick, this time harder.

'What's he talking about?' Gary called.

'He's talking about my fucking shoes.'

'Your shoes? What's he talking about your shoes for? Ask him about the files.'

Madigan decided that his best chance was to play dumb, to act as if the hammering he had got had in some way deranged him. If they thought a screw was missing they might get careless. He swivelled his eyes and lolled his tongue. He decided to play the role of Salvatore in *The Name of the Rose*. He began to make nonsense noises.

'I think this guy is some kind of fuckin' nut, Gary. He's looking damn weird, like somethin' out of "The Exorcist".'

'Don't mind that. Ask him about the files.'

'This is going to get us fucking nowhere.' Derek turned back to Madigan. 'Tell us what you know about the files, man, and no fuckin' nonsense, do you hear?'

'The files, the files, the files.' Suddenly Madigan decided to be Charles Laughton in *The Hunchback of Notre Dame*. 'The files, I remember the files, oh, I do indeed. There were files, files, many, many files.' Then he went back to swivelling his eyes and contorting his face like some creature out of a late night 1940s horror flick.

'What's he saying?'

'He says he remembers the files.'

'Well, tell him to remember a bit more. Tell him what's going to happen to him if the boss doesn't get his hands on them.'

'OK, I'll try.'

Madigan started to get sick, and an empty retching of raw acid filled his mouth. His mouth tried to find saliva but there was none. An egg cup full of green stuff landed on his lapel. He realised his stomach was empty as he suddenly noticed the funny smell. He looked down. He had already been sick. It had dried onto his jacket – a long time, many hours, possibly days, earlier.

'What's he saying?'

'He's parking the tiger.'

'I'd have thought he'd have all that done.'

'Well, he's still trying.'

'Sit him up straight. We don't want him smothering on his own vomit. And untie his hands when you're at it. Let him wipe himself.'

'You sure?'

'I'm sure. He can't run on his hands. Besides, there's nowhere to run to.'

Derek untied Madigan's hands. Madigan left them where they were to give the impression he was too stupid to know they were now free. Besides they were so numb he was afraid to try to move them in case they might break off. He got a good look at Derek. Derek was rough, one of life's failures. Madigan had seen guys like him on the streets and at the graveside orations of the Hoolihans. They were terrible, dangerous men, without the capacity to smile. They did the dirty jobs in times when they were needed. Madigan knew from one look at him that he had what it takes to do the necessary and never have a pang of conscience about it. The Dereks of this world sleep easily in their beds, he thought.

Gary and the third man came over. Suddenly Madigan knew where he remembered them from: they were the two men he had seen at the university delivering the liquid nitrogen to the Professor's lab. Gary was clean cut. He could be your kid brother, the kind of guy you felt you could trust. The other man was older and was shaking, as if he was ill or something.

'Keep away from me, Duffy,' Derek said. 'Duffy's got the fuckin' 'flu and he's dying to pass it on to the rest of us – fuckin' dying, aren't you, Duffy?' Duffy looked too sick to say anything.

Gary leaned over Madigan. Madigan could smell his after-shave; it was not cheap. Gary was the sort of guy who would have a nice sexy girlfriend in an expensive leather coat and tell her that he was in real estate or computer parts or something with genuine prospects.

'OK, now. You got a few things to tell us, Mr Madigan. The Boss says you gave him files. The problem is the Boss isn't sure if the files are real or not. He's had to go away to check them out. Now personally, I wouldn't have any trouble in topping you – in fact, I think it might be the best thing all round. The Boss says you know too much. We have a very simple solution here for people who know too much. Isn't that right, Derek?'

'Yes,' said Derek, 'it's called barging. We drill you, put you on the sewage barge out of Ringsend and drop you with the rest of the dirt into the middle of the Irish Sea. We'll put you where nobody will ever find you – except maybe the dog fish.'

Madigan started to cough.

'Duffy's given this galoot the 'flu too.' Derek said.

Madigan moved his hands and, staring into Gary's eyes as if he was just released from Bedlam, began to cover his own face and let out high animal howls. He was now 'The Scream' by Munch and was surprised at how much his beard had grown and his nails; he must have been unconscious for a couple of days at least, with nothing to eat but his own phlegm.

Suddenly he felt so thirsty he was sure he would die soon if he did not get a drink of water.

'Water,' he gasped. 'Water, food, I need.' He was now an Iraqi in the desert during the Gulf war, hanging out of a bombed tank and speaking broken English.

'I think the guy needs something to drink. He can't speak. Duffy, go over to the van. I think there's a can of coke and a few bags of crisps in the glove compartment. Bring 'em.'

Just as Duffy was opening the front door of the Ford, Madigan saw the headlights of a car flash at the other side of the field and begin to lurch up and down in their general direction.

'Here comes the Boss,' Duffy called out. 'He'll tell us what to do with this chancer.'

It was the wine-coloured Mercedes. When it pulled up beside the van, Nolan got out. He was wearing a different suit to the one he wore in the station. He was under pressure, Madigan thought, the way pale men are under pressure, with the slow, ghost-like anxiety of the bottom feeder.

'You got anything out of that piece of shit?' he asked Gary.

'No. He's playing dumb, pretending to be an idiot.'

'Is he now? Duffy.' He called Duffy who was still standing near Madigan and seemed to be reluctant to be part of the action. 'Duffy. You always said you'd love to have been a dentist, if you'd only had the brains and your parents had the money?'

'Hah, hah,' Derek said.

'Shut up, Derek. Well, now's your chance.' Nolan reached into the front of the van and got out a pair of pliers. 'Mr Private Eye looks in pain. Maybe he's got a toothache. You want to check him out, Duffy? See if he's got a few bad ones?'

'Let me do it, Boss,' Derek said.

'Shut up, Derek. You'll get your chance.'

'I don't have the stomach for it, Boss,' Duffy said. 'I'm not feeling too well.'

'He's not feeling too well, Boss. He's got the fuckin' 'flu.'

'OK, you do it, Derek. But I must talk to him first. Maybe he can tell us something that might allow us to just give him a filling.'

'Hah, hah, very funny, Boss.'

Nolan pulled on a long overcoat, stepped out into the rain and walked over to him, trying to avoid the puddles. There was something about the way he walked that made Madigan feel cocky. Madigan was sure Nolan thought he knew something. His best chance of staying alive was to make sure he kept on believing that. If Nolan found out that he knew very little then Derek would have him on the first sewage barge out of Ringsend the following morning.

'You heard what I said. Derek's a good hand with the pliers. He does nails too, as well as pulling teeth. I'd do it myself but I'd rather not get my clothes ruined. Now the problem is that you gave me files. I don't know if they're right or wrong – not yet. But what I do know is that my boys here borrowed some stuff from the Professor the night before he died – which, by the way, we had nothing to do with.'

'Like the three bears,' Madigan said. 'Only they all died hairy in the wood.'

'Ah, he finds his tongue,' Gary said.

'Let me at him, Boss,' Derek said.

'It doesn't matter whether you believe me or not, Madigan. The point is we know now that the stuff we got was the wrong stuff. And you were there that night, Madigan. All fingers point to you.'

'So I'm singled out for á la carte intimidation?'

'If the files turn out to be false as well, then you're in deep trouble.'

I'm already in deep trouble, he thought, trouble that was deep, wet and cold, like the bottom of a well in the middle of winter. He decided to bluff.

'I suppose your expert is on holidays?' he asked. 'Perhaps in the Canaries? It's hard to sing there this weather, I'd say.'

'What the hell are you talking about? What's this talk about the Canaries?'

'Simon Callaghan goes belly up.'

'What?'

'As I said, Simon Callaghan was killed in Gran Canaria. I kind of assumed you'd done it.' At least now Madigan knew Nolan probably had not killed Simon Callaghan. 'You don't understand the gobbledygook, do you Nolan? You need an expert to tell you whether what you have is valuable or not. That's not very professional.'

'You can save me the trouble with one sentence, Madigan, or you can lose a few teeth to begin with – and a lot more. You have the answers.'

'I have the answer,' Madigan said. 'Here.' He whispered.

Nolan leaned down. Madigan whispered into his ear. 'I'll tell you what the answer is, Nolan. The answer is wet Jamaican pussy, the answer to all our problems. It's up to you to find the question.' Nolan suddenly sprang upright and struck Madigan across the face. It stung, like big hail in the middle of November. He had a few rings on.

'Right, you bastard, you've asked for it. Derek, come here.'

Derek came over with the pliers and caught Madigan around the neck. He tried to shove the pliers into his mouth but Madigan would not open it. The pliers were hard and cold and sharp and were cutting his face; he started to struggle.

'What's keeping you, Derek, can't you get a simple job done?'

'It's too dark here and he keeps squirming. I can't get the

fuckin' pliers into his mouth.'

'Then bring him over to the light of the van, you fool.'

Derek began to drag Madigan by the underarms towards the van. 'You're a heavy bastard, aren't you?' he grunted.

'Size is everything,' Madigan said, repeating himself to an entirely different audience. He would probably never have the opportunity of saying it again though, he thought.

It was then that Derek made his first mistake of the night. He held on to the pliers as he dragged Madigan across the field. The others were too lazy to help. Madigan waited till they were near the van. Then he snatched the pliers from Derek and with all the strength he had left in him he hit Derek as hard as he could with the pliers across the temple. There was the kind of dull clunk you get when you kick a large turnip. Derek went down. Madigan was lucky. His legs were tied together with wire, Derek's second mistake. The pliers went through the wire in a second. In another second Madigan was in the van where the gang had made their third mistake by leaving the engine running.

By the time Nolan and the others had realised what was happening, Madigan was already in second gear, moving into third and following the tracks of the Merc across the field. The diesel was sluggish but he was well out on the road before they started to go after him.

He knew he would not get away from them with the commercial wheels he was driving. A Ford Transit is a useful van but it will not outrun a Merc, not on the open road. And there was an open road, for once, a dual carriageway.

Madigan turned left. He had no idea what direction he was headed in. He past a concrete factory and swung around a familiar roundabout. Suddenly he knew where he was. He was outside Tymon Park. By this time the Merc was right up behind him. All it needed was a traffic jam and they were straight in through the rear door. Madigan's only hope was to find a housing estate that had a lot of dead ends. He could lose them in a maze, if he could find one.

Then he remembered the estate where Vikki Morgan lived and drove there like a madman, hitting traffic ramps and crossing at least two schoolyards at 70mph. For once he prayed for traffic cops but they were never there when you needed them.

He passed Vikki's house. Vikki would be in slumber land, her big body warm in the nest. But Madigan flew past like a mad dog just freed from an electric fence. Then he remembered a cul de sac between two others where he had once got lost. He could turn the van there and wait for the gang to catch up. Then, while they were trying to turn, he would drive like hell out the one exit he knew was there. There were two chances in three they would end up facing a six-foot wall.

Madigan pulled into the drive, turned the van and waited for them to come around the corner. The Merc screeched as it took the bend. Madigan saw their faces as they past. Gary was driving. The Merc squealed again as it past. Madigan put the boot to the floor of the Ford and shot out of the drive and around the corner. He was out on the road before Gary even got into reverse.

Madigan went back the way he came. As he passed the dead end where he had turned he looked over the wall and sure enough, there they were, turning the Merc in one of the cul de sacs. By the time they got out, he would be half way to town.

Then he realised they would probably follow the van to his flat, or if they had been tracking him all along, either to the Combat Zone or to Marika's place. He did not want to draw trouble on either Marika or Lily Bowen, so he pulled in and parked the van in somebody's drive. There was a mobile phone on the dash. He pocketed it, hid behind a wall and a minute later watched the Merc hit the dual carriageway and head into town. Then he limped and crept, crept and limped, slowly and painfully, his joints cold and numb as if he had been wedged in the icebox for a week, to Vikki's house. He hoped she was alone. Not that it mattered too much. Either way, she would be surprised to see him at such short notice.

Madigan rang the doorbell. It took Vikki five minutes to come down and she was still half asleep. The top of her nightgown was undone – her breasts were more than visible. Despite his exhaustion, Madigan knew he was back in the land of the living, looking down Shrangri La into the heart of Silicone Valley.

'My God!' she exclaimed. She did not seem to recognise Madigan at first. 'Mike? What happened to you? Look at your face.'

'I had a run in with a few old friends.'

'You look like you almost died.'

'You could say that.'

'And you're frozen with the cold.'

'Maybe I'm dead and this is the afterlife,' Madigan said, trying to avert his eyes from her bosom. She shook her head.

'Come in, for God's sake. I'll put on the kettle and run a bath.'

Madigan went inside. It felt strange to be in a warm house. Suddenly he had a premonition of what heaven would be like, or should be like: Vikki running a hot bath for him and giving him comfort in his hour of need; angel of mercy, pneumatic paradise, gliding hands, pure warm flesh.

Madigan took out the mobile phone and rang an old friend of his in Cleveland, Ohio. He asked him not to put the phone back on the hook for as long as he could so as to run up a big bill on Nolan's mobile. It would not be much revenge but it would be better than nothing.

TWENTY-SIX

Marlowe paints a different picture. Madigan over-reacts. Denouement.
Global possibilities. 'Everybody was watching everybody all the time.'
QED. The road to recovery.

Madigan figured he had a few days, a week at most, to get to the
bottom of the case before Nolan found out that the papers he had
given him were bogus. He was shaken by the events of Tymon
Park - his knees were still wobbly, his wrists were sore and he had
bruises on his cheeks where Derek had struck him with the pliers.

What mattered now, as Madigan saw it, was that the case be
made public. He wanted the press and the television and radio
companies to have the story as soon as possible. Publicity would
be his only immunity from whatever surprises Nolan might have
in store for him. If going to the press caused problems for
Marlowe, then he was going to have to live with it.

Madigan decided to call on Marlowe during his lunch break
and drop a few clangers and see what the echo might bring in.
Marlowe was smoking his pipe and wading through a pile of documents when Madigan got there.

'A grand job,' Madigan said.

'What?' Marlowe looked up from his sheaf of papers.

'The building. You guys made a fine job of the building

outside. I'm surprised you could afford it.' The police station had been repainted. It no longer looked like Poland.

'Oh, you mean the painting? Yes, it's not a bad job. The Minister made an election promise. The Department came up with the money. You know how it is. Keep the heritage lobby happy, pick up a few votes in the process, fire a few grand at a police station. It would have been more useful to use the money to build a few more cells but we had no choice in the matter. Still, I suppose it does brighten the place up a bit.'

'Yes, I did think the place looked a little more like heaven.'

'I've good news, Mike. We picked up Nolan and a few of his boys.'

So, Madigan thought, that was why they did not keep after me.

'Like Gary and Derek and Duffy; Curly, Larry and Mo?'

'You know them?'

'Let's just say I've made their acquaintance. Nice boys.'

Madigan went on to tell him of his experience in Tymon Park.

'You were lucky,' he said.

'I can still feel the luck running down my trouser leg.'

'We think we've got Nolan for Benny's death, though. The papers you gave him were bogus but he didn't know enough about the topic to tell whether they were bogus or not. If he had the real papers maybe we'd have got him for the Prof's death as well.'

'Maybe you mightn't.'

'What do you mean?'

'I'm just saying I'm not sure if Nolan killed the Prof and I don't think Nolan killed Simon Callaghan either. I doubt if he ever even heard of him. I dropped it into the middle of our little conversation in Tymon Park. I knew by his reaction that he didn't know who I was talking about. Also he got the wrong stuff in the Prof's house that night. Somebody sold Nolan a dummy and he thinks it's me. Somehow I think we'll find it's our beautiful friend, Miss Ireland.'

'But we've nothing to pin it on her, nothing substantial. She'd have that stuff, those cultures you talk about, anyway, and the papers too.'

'What about Simon Callaghan?'

'The Spanish authorities say he just drowned.'

'What's all this got to do with the Hoolihan family, Marlowe? Don't bullshit me now.'

Marlowe looked like he had just been kicked in the balls.

'What do you mean?'

'The fucking Hoolihan family. Miss Ireland. You know exactly what I mean. She's one of them, and you let me poke around in her life as if she was just a goddamn professor's wife. You know as well as I do what the Hoolihan family are like. They'd wipe me out of the way as easily as they'd wipe a snot on the underside of a car seat.'

'Calm yourself. You're overreacting.'

'Overreacting? Me overreacting? You know how ruthless those fuckers are. If I had even the slightest notion that there was a Hoolihan connection I'd have run from this faster than you could say "the long goodbye".'

'Nothing has happened yet.'

'You call what I went through in Tymon Park nothing? Three people are now dead! Go right in there and ask for the files, you said. It's worth trying, you said. It's a foolproof case, you said. If it's foolproof, then I'm the fool. And all this horseshit that you told me was going on, all this crap about confidential police business. It's codswollop, man, codswollop. Now, you'd better come clean with me, Marlowe, or this whole story is going to the press before the day is out.'

'OK. Take it easy. I can explain everything.' Marlowe looked to Madigan like a husband who has been unfaithful and now wants to get it all off his chest and make everything right again.

'It'd better be good, Marlowe.'

'It's a long story, Mike.'

'That's all right. I've plenty of time for long stories. The brewery can look after itself for an hour or two.'

Marlowe leaned back on his chair and put his feet up on the desk in front of him. He offered Madigan a cigar and began to light his pipe again. Madigan declined the offer, though he wanted a smoke more than anything else in the world. However, he had no objection to Marlowe filling the room with the smell of the aromatic weed. Passive smoking is a small pleasure, he thought, not as good as, say, masturbation, but a pleasure for all that.

'OK, Mike, I'll level with you, starting from the top, right?'

'Right.'

'We've known for a long time that the Professor's work was very valuable. That whoever got control of the patent on MDC would make a lot of money out of it. We also knew that it would make all other drugs for treating depression obsolete, so that the makers of the existing drugs would lose a fortune. We knew Nolan was looking for the means of making it. It's simple industrial espionage. According to our contacts, he's working on the QT for an American multinational whose main product line is, you've guessed it, cyclocon. He was also trying to sell it to the Hoolihans, double-crossing the Americans.

'You see, the problem they all had with the Professor was that he was going to hand this new knowledge over to medical science, in other words, put it in the public domain. A fair gesture from him, you may say, generous. And I would have to say I agree. But the problem with people like the Professor is that they're out of contact with the real world. If the Professor's findings went public by the traditional means of publication, then the whole basis for many of the treatments used up until now would be as useless as yesterday's news. And cyclocon would be wiped out as well.'

'But why couldn't the existing companies use this new MDC treatment instead of their own? Why not simply trade in the old method for the new, if and when the new became common currency?'

'In theory, yes, they could. But it would take a complete reworking of their product lines and that would take years and hundreds of millions of pounds, dollars, you name it. We're talking instant cure here, complete irreversible cure without further need for drug treatment. Traditional drug companies produce chemicals. What we're dealing with here is molecular biology. The companies that could produce such technology in the short term are small campus companies. Whichever one of them got in ahead of the posse in the development of MDC would clean up on a grand scale. We're talking mega bucks here; the global possibilities are huge. And the technique would lead them to the treatment of other genetic diseases as well. So you can see what's going on.'

He puffed rolls of smoke like small sheep so that the air around Madigan was as steep with longing as hillsides.

'Of course, the technology could be bought, or one of the big multis could simply take over a campus company which had developed such techniques. But all that would take time, and time is money. Shareholders are not patient people, Mike. If the knowledge became public in a few years time then maybe the problem for the drug companies would not be so great. By then they would be gearing themselves up in any case. It's a case of bad timing, you see, too much knowledge coming too early.'

'You knew all this all along?'

'Well, our main contact was Simon Callaghan. He came to us

because he was worried at what might happen if the Professor's work got into the wrong hands. He was also concerned that the Professor had been so secretive about the work. The fewer who knew about it, the more they were at risk. Simon Callaghan wanted step-by-step publication of the work as it went along. In that way it would all leak out as it was being done. But the Professor was concerned that by partially publishing he would give away enough that would allow somebody else to get in ahead of him with the main findings. Perhaps he saw a Nobel Prize in it for himself, who knows, but he sure as hell wanted to get the credit for it, and I suppose, who can blame him. After all, he did do the work.'

'Where does that leave Nolan?'

'As I said earlier, Nolan was trying to get the papers for an American company. Nolan will get up to any scams so long as there's money in them. The assumption is that the drug company paid him well for his services. Nolan is just a gopher, to all intents and purposes.' And then he tried to sell back to Pamela what was effectively already hers.

'So Nolan never found out that the papers I gave him were the wrong ones?'

'Probably not. And if the papers you gave him were well substituted they might persuade his sponsors that what the Professor had discovered was not really that important; at least they might think that for a year or two. My guess is that you unwittingly got rid of that half of the problem by giving him the files.'

'Was that why you sent me to Pamela to get the files in the first place?'

'Partly. You see, you came along just at the right time from our point of view. We had been watching the goings-on in the university for a long time. Our contacts told us that both Nolan and the Hoolihans were getting interested in work that was going on there.

226

Taking that and the worries that Simon Callaghan had about the Professor into consideration, it was easy to put two and two together and come to the conclusion that they were both interested in the same thing. We were keeping round-the-clock surveillance on both the Professor and Simon Callaghan. We figured they were both in danger from Nolan, and possibly from the Hoolihans.'

Marlowe got up and walked around the room, holding his pipe in his hand and using it as a pointer.

'Your arrival on the scene was useful to us, because it meant there was another layer of watching going on. The chances were that you might pick up some information that might be of value, either about the Professor or about his wife. You see, everything would be all right once those papers were published. The Professor and Simon Callaghan would be able to live away normally from then on. The horse would already have bolted. Our hope was to keep the stable door open. But it didn't work out like that.'

'So all this time, Nolan is the only African American racial minority member in the woodpile, if you'll pardon my PC non-compliance.'

'He was the only one we knew about then. We were keeping a very close watch on his comings and goings at the time and also everybody we knew who worked for him. None of them were doing anything suspicious on the night the Professor died. We also suggested to Simon Callaghan that he take a holiday until the papers were safely in the hands of the publishers. Unfortunately, the ploy was not entirely successful.'

'Simon Callaghan becomes shark-feed in the Canaries?'

'Precisely. Death by a convenient accident. But at least he survived longer than the Professor.'

'Some consolation. You say I was useful in terms of picking up pieces of loose information, even though I think I picked up very little. What was Nolan doing chasing me for the files?'

'Nolan found out that Pamela had been seeing you, so he presumed that you were in on whatever was going on. So he sent his man to search your flat and the rest you know. And, of course, you were there the night he robbed the liquid-nitrogen cylinder with the wrong cultures in it from the university. So you had to be a prime target.'

'Yet despite all your care, the Professor dies and you've nothing to link Nolan to the case, and Pamela is out of the country on the same night so she would appear to be in the clear as well. Looks like you were not doing your job very well.'

'It looks like that. However, we could find no evidence that his death was murder. The blood tests on the body showed that there was no elevated level of insulin at the time of death. The coroner's report showed that the man's heart just stopped. He just suffered a heart attack. End of story. There was no case from then on. We were strongly advised to stop the investigation.'

'Yet it was highly suspicious?'

'It was highly suspicious and if I had my way, I would have followed through with the case. But as you know, we were called off.'

'But surely the fact that Pamela was originally a Hoolihan should have meant that you could at least have kept the case open. You seemed to be pointing the finger pretty strongly at her at one stage.'

'You see Mike, dealing with the Hoolihans in this country is difficult. They have contacts all over the place, influence in every stratum of society. There are even certain government ministers who are secret Hoolihan supporters. There is a certain nostalgia for Hoolihanism in many quarters. It's the soft underbelly of our society. There's not a town or village in the country that does not have one or two Hoolihan sympathisers. Everyone knows who their supporters are but nobody says anything, for they know their lives would not be worth living if they did. Hoolihanism is the wild card around here, the invisible living among the blind, so to speak.'

'Yet at one stage you gave me the impression you were fairly sure of her complicity in the Professor's death?'

'I was and to be quite honest, I still am. But with Nolan beating around the edges I could never be quite sure who was chasing whom. Nolan had a higher profile as a gangster, so it was logical that we focus on him. Besides, as far as we knew, Pamela had ceased to be a real Hoolihan long ago. She would have been trying to distance herself from them. Hoolihanism would never be part of her image nowadays. Our perception of her was that she had long since been on the straight and narrow and that, if anything, they would be an embarrassment to her. But I suppose a leopard never changes its spots.'

'Even though you told me at the time that she was to all intents and purposes sleeping her way to the top?'

'Sleeping with people is not a crime Mike, though there are some in this country who still think it is.'

'You said at one stage that you thought there might be a cover-up going on, especially when you were called off the case so suddenly.'

'Well, we were called off the case rather quickly, but then we had nothing to pin on anybody. We thought we could nail Nolan but as I said before, Nolan was on the wrong track too. Mind you, he's not going to get away lightly from the death of Benny Mulligan. We think we may have enough to convict him, and your seeing Nolan coming out of Mulligan's house is part of that evidence. So I'm afraid you may be seeing Mr Nolan again, Mike, if only across the witness stand.'

'So you've completely abandoned the idea of a cover-up?'

'Not abandoned it. It's just that there were several perfectly good reasons for closing the case.'

'Just one more thing. Could I have a look at the voting register?'

Marlowe picked up the phone and called Jim, the same piggy policeman that Madigan had seen the first day he called in connection with the case. Jim looked at Madigan with his small, porcine eyes, making him feel as if he was storing up resentment for the next time he might have a parking fine.

'Jim, could you bring in the voting registers. Mr Madigan would like to look something up.' Jim went out again.

'What do you make of the fact that I was called in originally because the wife believed the Professor was having an affair?'

'All she wanted in reality was to have him watched. You would report on what you saw, or rather what you didn't see and you would be in a position to let her know where the Professor was at any one time and what he was doing.'

'Looks like everybody was watching everybody all the time.'

'Sounds like that, but I suppose somebody is always watching no matter what we do.'

Jim turned up with leather-bound folders the size of four King James Bibles. He placed them on the desk in front of Madigan who opened one and turned the heavy pages until he found the address he had followed Pamela to in Rathfarnam. And there it was, right in front of his eyes: the needle in the haystack and the snake plonked right in the middle of the grass.

'Who's PHP, Marlowe?' he asked.

'Chief of Staff of the Hoolihans. Why do you ask?'

'Looks like we're in the shit so,' Madigan said, matter-of-factly, 'right up to our oxters.'

Marlowe looked surprised for the second time that day, as if some high bird had dropped something black and white and spattery on him.

'You remember what I said about my visit to Pamela where I was given the fake files? What I neglected to mention was that I put a little pressure on her, made her think I knew something when in fact I didn't.'

'You didn't threaten her, did you?'

'Not at all, just dropped a few gentle hints like I usually do. Wondering if I could find the pressure points, you know, like acupuncture. In another life I'd have been a Chinese medic.'

'We'd all like to be in other lives from time to time. I hope you were more subtle than you were with Benny Mulligan.'

'I'm the essence of subtlety, Marlowe, especially with women. That night I panicked her a bit, cut her phone lines and disabled her mobile phone. I imagined that if she were in collusion with anybody she'd have to hit the road to warn whoever it might be that I'd be on to something. And by God, did she hit it: broke the speed limit in that Beamer on every 200-yard stretch. It took me to the pin of my collar to keep up with her. And where do you think she ended up? At this fellow's place.'

'PHP?'

'Precisely. QED.' Madigan smiled for the first time in a week. 'I was going to keep it up my sleeve until I had checked it out myself and until I had a few more facts. But you've been straight with me today, so I figured I could be straight with you. She stayed there all night, as far as I could tell. I went home when I got tired of waiting.'

Madigan went out, leaving Marlowe to ponder his new predicament. The sky had cleared. It was blue and cold. The streets of Dublin were shiny and black as deep ice. The wind hit him like an interrogator's slap. A small slice of new moon sat over the cathedral like a piece of half-chewed orange peel. It was a nice small moon on a nice small day, marching listlessly into mid-December. He still had the pain in the back of his head and the ache in his joints but he was well on the road to recovery.

TWENTY-SEVEN

Midnight visitors. The Lord of the Flies. We're not gangsters.
Significant progress. A hint of dark deeds. For ourselves and
those who are dear to us. Madigan gets a look into
the black soul of his native land.

Madigan had worked out what he would have to do. He would blow the MDC story all over the papers so that neither Nolan nor Pamela would have a place to hide. As he went to sleep that night, in what would be his last night in the Combat Zone, he knew exactly who he would contact the following morning. However, by the time the following morning actually arrived, he contacted nobody. By then he had learned the virtues of whole new levels of circumspection, whole storeys, whole floors, whole warehouses in the big skyscraper of silence.

It began when a bullet came from across the road over the late night traffic and went through his window which collapsed in a curtain of shattered glass, though the blind hung exactly as it was, leaving just a tiny hole full of light. The bullet ricocheted off the ceiling and three walls and landed on Madigan's bedside locker like a blunt lump of melted coin. That little journey of a small piece of lead was enough to change his mind about a lot of things – because before he had time to pick up the phone, they were through the door. It was terror time. Old yellow fingers must have let them in.

Madigan had been asleep. He was pyjamas vulnerable, sleep vulnerable, nightmare vulnerable. He thought it was a dream and was wondering how long it would take before he would wake up in Brixton with more naked Jamaican girls dancing around him. Then the lights came on and a cold draught came in the broken window and he knew that if it was a dream, it was a bad one. At first there were only two of them and they burst through the door as if it were made from eggshells. They were big hefty fellows and they both had handguns that pointed at Madigan like a pair of piggy eyes. He heard the low purr of the BMW outside. Soon Pamela and another man in a well-cut suit and thin-rimmed glasses joined them. Mr Good-suit and Pamela appeared to Madigan to be unarmed.

'I think you know who we are, Mr Madigan,' Mr Good-suit said. He was a tall man in his mid-thirties with a neat haircut and an upright bearing and expensive gloves. He had a smooth face and looked the type who was used to telling people what to do and who did not have much trouble in getting them to do it.

'Pádraig Pearse, I presume,' Madigan said, echoing Stanley in deepest darkest, 'or is it PHP?' He pulled down his T-shirt under the bedclothes to cover his balls, realising as he did so that that would make no difference to whatever they had in store for him.

'My name need not concern you, Mr Madigan. I am, as it were, the man with no name.'

'Suit yourself.'

'Pamela, you know, I believe?'

'We've met.'

Pamela nodded. She was dressed the same way she had been the first time Madigan met her, as if she were coming from a party and organising a killing at the same time. He did not want to think about it.

'Mr Madigan. Unfortunately, we need to talk. I say unfortunately because some of the people we talk to don't often get the chance to talk again. Mind you, that's usually their own fault. In any case, it's important that we understand each other from the outset and that there be no misconceptions. Do you know what I mean?'

'I'll probably get the hang of it after a while.'

'It's like this, Mr Madigan. We see ourselves as supplying a social service in these communities, to what you would no doubt call the lower classes. We provide services that the State either won't or cannot provide. We allow people to sleep in their beds, ordinary people, Mr Madigan, good, working-class, God-fearing citizens. There are others in our community, and I say the word community in the decent, old-fashioned sense of the word, who will not allow good people to live their lives in peace. We believe in peace, Mr Madigan, peace with a big P. We're talking here about drug pushers, we're talking child molesters, rapists, petty thieves, drug addicts with AIDS, we're talking about people who get their sexual thrills in public toilets. Can you imagine that, Mr Madigan, men going to public toilets to get their kicks? What we're talking about here, not to make too fine a point of it, is scum. One of our aims, and it's only one of our many aims, as you know, is to take the scum off our streets. The law fails to do it, as we see it. So the job, and it's not a pleasant job, comes down to us. It's a cleaning up job: refuse collection, so to speak, a cleansing of certain toxins, an environmental issue.

'And the people want us to do it, Mr Madigan. They ask us to come in and sort this filth out. They want their children to go to school without having to avoid pushers in the school yard, they want to walk outside their doors at night, they want to park their cars in safety. And the State, this so-called Free State, has failed them in this, Mr Madigan, failed them miserably.'

Madigan hoped he was going to get to the point a little more quickly; he felt if he was going to die, he did not want to spend his last minutes listening to a political diatribe against the iniquities of society. As he saw it, society was about as equal as a fixed greyhound race. There was little point in worrying about it or trying to do anything to change it, for the big guys always got you in the end.

'Now, you've been in contact with Nolan, I believe. Nolan is one of the people we're trying to rid this city of. He has avoided us so far but sooner or later we'll get him, just like we've got a fair few of his equals. Nolan is a parasite of the worst possible description, a pariah. He's a gangster, Mr Madigan, and a thoroughly evil man. And he has been very lucky of late to be taken into police custody. He's safe, though not entirely safe, in jail. But if we want to get him, we can get him in jail too.

'Now the reason we've had to make this call on you, is that you've been fishing around in very dirty waters of late.'

'I was paid to do so by herself over there.' Madigan nodded at Pamela, who was smoking a cigarette. She said nothing.

'You were actually paid by us, Mr Madigan, though you did not know it at the time. To help us in our struggle we need cash, and Pamela here has developed a lucrative and indeed perfectly legal way of making an awful lot of it. You're not perhaps the world's best private detective but you are, how shall I put it, resilient. You have the capacity of the slow, dumb animal to plug away at something, blindly, blindly, Mr Madigan, as a young puppy dog. But it would appear in this case, against all the odds, that you have been relatively effective. Now we'd like to make you an offer. We'd like you to work for us, Mr Madigan. We pay well. We believe you have some good contacts in the police force. You pass on what you learn from your good friend, Mr Marlowe, to us and your standard of living will, how shall I put it, go through the roof.'

'What if I don't?'

'It's very dangerous not to do business with us, Mr Madigan. People don't turn us down. It's as simple as that.'

Madigan decided to bluff.

'You can put a bullet in me now, in that case. I'm not going to work for you. Even if I did, sooner or later, you'd end up putting a bullet in me anyway. I'd be living around too many shadows. Life isn't worth that.'

'But you might get a year or two, maybe ten years, maybe even a lifetime, if you help us.'

Madigan said nothing.

Padraig H. Pearse thought for a moment and looked at him.

'You're no fool, Madigan. Having people on our payroll is an excellent way of keeping control of things. But you're free, of course, to turn us down. It is, after all, a free world, though not of course a free country. Now seeing as my little sales pitch did nothing for you, I want to get down to the nitty-gritty, the nuts and bolts, the brass tacks, as it were, of why we're here. And before I say anything else, I want to put your position in context. If you don't answer the questions I'm going to ask you now we'll shoot you straight between the eyes as you lie there and we'll walk out that door and nobody will ever be any the wiser.'

As he said this, one of the goons quietly put a silencer on his gun. He raised his arm. The long shadow of the arm crossed the bed. Madigan remembered 'The Saint' on television when he was a child.

'You see, we have all the necessary prerequisites for a quiet execution. This is not a threat, Mr Madigan. This is a simple fact. We deal in facts, not slogans, though we can deal with slogans too when we have to. You would be found dead tomorrow morning or perhaps, who knows, in a week's time. By then, no doubt, the rats would have eaten your fingers off. The guns my men have are brand new and untraceable. And the man downstairs, the owner of this place, is on our payroll so he'll say nothing. We're not gangsters like Nolan, threatening people with this or that. We're not fools with nail guns or mere drug smugglers. We just do what we have to do for the greater good. The rules of the game are very clear.

'Also remember, if you tell us lies and we find out they are lies, then we will get you sooner or later. I needn't tell you that we always get our enemies. You will never have a good night's sleep again.

'Now for the truth, Mr Madigan. It's time to get down to actualities. We'll start with what you know about our MDC operation.'

Madigan told him what he knew, which was not an awful lot. There was no point in trying to hide anything. The best he could hope for was that if he spilled everything, they might let him go.

'What do the police think is going on?'

He told him what Marlowe believed was happening.

'Mr Marlowe is a shrewd operator. We didn't, of course, kill the Professor. The poor Professor, well he just died. His lifestyle, it wasn't exactly healthy now, was it? All those sweets! As for poor Simon Callaghan, he just swam too far out to sea. Now it seems to me that you have overstepped the mark by staying on the case after Pamela, on our behalf, paid you your money. What did you hope to gain by this?'

'I wanted to get to the bottom of what was going on.'

'Well it looks like you have.'

'I didn't quite anticipate that it was leading here though.'

'We never do, Mr Madigan, do we? Life is like that, isn't it? We take on something and we don't know what's around the corner and then we're up against a wall or somebody is chasing us down a narrow alley with a gun in his hand. Life's a bitch sometimes. Isn't that what they say in Anglo-Saxon cliché land, or is that a phrase coined by our American friends?'

'That's it.'

'Life as we know it, you might say. We know a few things about you too, Mr Madigan, and one of them is that, whatever else you do, you would never work for nothing. Is that true?'

'It's true. I can't afford to work for nothing.'

'You confirm something I have long believed: that every man, I'm talking here about empty cans of men, mere containers, men with no substance, weak-washy, everyday types, that every man can be bought. The watery man, Mr Madigan, is just a drone. He feeds the machine of commerce, he consumes, he is a mere cog. He needs to be led, much like a domestic animal on a leash for the good of society.' He raised his little finger and moved it slowly in an arc to illustrate what he meant. 'And if circumstances dictate that he be put down, he will be put down, if that's what is deemed necessary for the greater good. There is an old curse in the Irish language, Mr Madigan – our beloved Gaeilge, the authentic voice of the Irish people – not the foreign tepid speech of the invader. The curse says *bás na bpisíní ort*, which literally means may you die as unwanted kittens die. Now I'm not wishing the curse on you or on any one belonging to you but we all know how unwanted kittens die. The ordinary man is like the unwanted kitten, Mr Madigan. He may be allowed to live or he may be helped to die, for the common good. Any farmer will tell you that to maximise yields he has to cull the weaker members of his herd. We sometimes have to cull the herd for purity's sake. This is everyday common sense but common sense is often, as we know only too well, uncommon wisdom.

'Anyway, I digress. Would I be right in assuming you were not working for nothing when, in spite of being paid, you kept on poking your nose around in what did not concern you?'

'Marlowe promised me a few bob out of a slush fund he had to try to get to the bottom of the case.'

'Ah, we're making progress. And what was your plan when you had, as you people put it, solved the case?'

'I was going to go to the papers with it.'

'On the assumption that the courts might not have enough evidence to convict anybody for the poor Professor's death?'

'More or less.'

'And yet the law of the land states that everyone is innocent until proven guilty. You're saying you would act as judge and jury and publish a whole raft of allegations against what are, in effect innocent people?'

Madigan wanted to say that that was his stock-in-trade and far worse but he managed to keep his mouth shut.

'Put like that, yes.'

'Do you still plan to do this? That is, if you get out of here alive.'

Madigan thought for a few seconds.

'Probably not.'

'This is indeed significant progress, Mr Madigan. You are not as foolish as we thought you were. This is extremely good news, both for us and for you and indeed for other people too.'

'Other people?'

'We believe you may have a new girlfriend, a very attractive young woman, by all accounts. You've been seen with her on a number of occasions of late. It would be a shame if anything were to happen to her, wouldn't it? But of course, we now know nothing will happen to her, don't we, that you would do nothing to endanger her life?' He leaned over Madigan, who could smell his breath. It was cool and dry, a combination of disinfectant and Polo mints. 'You are no doubt familiar with Sandford Park school in

Ranelagh, one of the more progressive schools in Dublin, where all the up-and-coming young couples send their children?'

'That's where Liam goes to school.' Madigan felt a sudden sinking feeling. This was the sucker punch, right in the middle of the belly.

'Precisely. A school for future leaders. Your little boy, a fine, good-looking boy too, so I'm told. He gets dropped off there by his *máthair* every morning at 9.15 and is picked up again at 3.00. Now I don't know what your relationship with your former wife is, but I'm sure you would not wish any harm to come to either of them, especially that little boy. And it's a terrible thing to say but accidents can happen. *An dtigeann tú?*'

'I think I get the picture.'

'Good. Good. Excellent. I think we understand each other.'

'You can do what you like with me but leave Liam and Marika out of it. Don't hurt them.'

'It's not a question of hurt, Mr Madigan,' he said silkily. 'It's a question of necessity. We have no wish to hurt anybody. They are and indeed should remain, entirely innocent. In fact, one of our aims is to make the world a better place for young people like your son or your young lady. But if you should be, well, foolish enough to try anything stupid, like getting what you know published, well let's just say we'll do whatever it takes to get back at you. And nobody connected with you will be safe. That confers a big responsibility on you, Mr Madigan, one you should exercise with no small amount of caution. *An dtigeann tú?*'

'*Tigim.*'

Madigan did understand. There was no way he couldn't.

'Good, good. I believe we have an understanding. You are very lucky, Mr Madigan, and very wise. We could very easily leave you here with a hole in your head and we would have no more trouble from you. But we like people to see reason. There is no need for bloodshed in this world when it can be avoided. I'm a peaceful man, Mr Madigan – as I say, peace with a capital P – and I prefer to debate and discuss things rather than act rashly. It's all about dialogue at the end of the day, procedure and debate, talking to people and getting them to come around to see one's point of view.

'We will leave now. You will be breathing. And let us hope that in two months time or in six months time you will still be breathing. This is entirely up to you. Silence is a greatly underestimated virtue, Mr Madigan, believe me. Silence, in this case, is indeed golden.'

'You bitch,' Madigan blurted out to Pamela. 'You got me into this. I should have known.' He was fresh out of further clichés.

'She is under instructions not to reply to you, Mr Madigan. So save your breath for cooling your porridge, now that it looks like you may live long enough to have breakfast. We will leave now. Thank you for your time. You are now living but that will not always be the case. This is true of all life, isn't it? Just remember.'

With that, he turned on his heels and, with Pamela by his side, went out the door. The goons cased the guns under their jackets and followed, shutting the door quietly behind them, as if afraid of disturbing somebody's sleep.

Madigan lay there, quiet as the countryside on a Saturday night. After about ten minutes, the owner knocked and came quietly in. He said he was sorry about the intruders and about the window getting broken but he would see to it that it was fixed straightaway. He nailed a sheet of plywood to the frame to keep the wind out and left without saying another word. Madigan lay in bed for a long time after the yellow-fingered man left. He would not have been able to get out even if he had wanted to.

Twenty-eight

Omertà. The triumph of evil. Bringing it all back home. Tom Bryan
phones. Potassium chloride. Madigan adapts to the new reality and
begins to believe in his luck. Learning not to care. *Ave atque vale.*

Madigan moved out of the Combat Zone the following day and
went back to his own place. He was frightened, but glad to be
alive. He was a coward, he decided, but then cowards' brood are a
brood who survive. He quoted Bob Hope to himself: heroes run
in my family. Would anyone else do any different?

The air in his flat was dead and dusty as an old tomb but he
felt lucky, like a cancer patient with a tumour in remission. He
knew he was fortunate to be breathing and felt he was now living
in a sort of afterlife of good fortune.

Though it was before Christmas, he was full of new year res-
olutions and they all revolved around keeping his mouth shut. He
was, of course, about to give in to terrorism, but life is sweet. As
long as he said nothing, the Hoolihans would leave him alone.
Nolan was on remand, facing trial.

He knew he would never see a conviction in the case, of
course, not when the Hoolihans put pressure on people, as they
usually did. He suspected that Pamela and her friends would get
clean away with whatever she had done, that nothing would ever

be proven, that the Professor and Simon Callaghan's deaths would never be solved. Madigan had seen such things happen many times. Any connection with the Hoolihans meant immunity from prosecution – silence descends and truth is choked before it can be uttered. The Hoolihans were too powerful. They needed the State, but the State needed them too, if only because they kept order in places where the police could no longer go.

And in the shady world of racketeering, there were always going to be wars between the likes of Nolan and the Hoolihans, with the latter getting brownie points from the locals by polishing off an odd drug peddler while at the same time extracting protection money from every illegal caper in town.

Madigan had wandered by accident onto the fringes of such a war, where the company was anything but edifying. It made his stomach queasy, his kneecaps itch and the flesh between his ribs seemed suddenly easy to puncture. As he rooted in the bag of white bread he had bought for his supper and smeared on the Marmite, he was glad just to be alive.

Then the phone rang.

It was Tom Bryan.

'That bottle you gave me,' he said, 'It's very odd. It's completely clean. There are no prints whatsoever on it. Either it was left out in the rain for ages or it must have been well wiped before being dumped.'

'That's a pity,' Madigan said, 'I was hoping it might yield something. Thanks for trying anyway.' He wanted to cut him off. He did not need to know anything else about the case.

'By the way,' the phone line was crackling. Tom's voice came in and out of focus as if he was in an echo chamber and somebody was regularly cutting off the echoes. 'Do you mind my asking, why were you interested in a bottle of potassium chloride? If it were a bottle of cyanide or strychnine or even weedkiller I'd understand. But KCl is about as innocuous as you can get. It makes a good salt substitute.'

'Anything else on it?'

'Well, the septum was punctured once, but the solution was still sterile. About half the volume was used, maybe 25ml.'

'Could it be used to kill somebody?'

'Well, if it were injected intravenously, then anybody's a dead duck.'

'What?' Madigan sat up. Suddenly his mind stopped drifting.

'Well, if you give somebody intravenous potassium chloride you'll stop his heart in seconds, death by lethal injection, used for executions in many countries.'

'And would that not be detectable?'

'Well the potassium wouldn't, because it's in the bloodstream anyway and it would be absorbed into the tissues after death. Besides, nobody would be looking for it. If he was sedated first, say by a sleeping tablet, he could be injected without ever knowing it. The sedative would be detected, if somebody looked hard enough. But even if it was, the levels would be so low they would not lead to suspicion. You can sedate a guy with innocuous levels of a hundred and one drugs. But if you raise his potassium levels at the same time, then bingo, the heart goes bang and he heads off for the long holidays.'

'Well Tom, looks like you've just made my day.'

'If you say so, Mike.'

Madigan hung up.

So it seemed that, in spite of everything, he had solved the case of the Prof's death, more or less. Not that anyone would ever know how he had died, except for himself and Pamela and her boys. That put Madigan in pretty good company. The only other person who might have known was Simon Callaghan and he would not be talking either. It was, all in all, a nice little white-wash. Nolan would go to jail for Benny's death but 'the boys' and their lucky lady would be free to go on doing what they had always done. It was justice, Irish style – the falling cloud of silence. There was only one thing for it. He needed some nihilism, so he put Warren Zevon in the stereo and turned the volume up so as to pretend he lived in a rock and roll world.

Madigan decided to turn down Spratt's offer of promotion in the brewery. There was more money to be made from snooping into other people's lives and getting paid for it under the counter than there would ever be in the new job. There was no point in break-ing his ass working just to pay for somebody else's unemployment benefit, while the snooping was tax-free.

After he got over his fright, he realised he was beginning to enjoy his little sideline. It allowed him to meet people he would not otherwise meet. It opened new horizons on what was going on in the world and took him out of the class-ridden confines of the brewery. The snoop pokes his way into all levels of society. If he is devious and lucky, he survives. Madigan was devious enough and, he felt, after Tymon Park and his close shave with the Hoolihans, he began to believe in his luck. He did not care if he never solved anything, as long as he got paid. He did not care if his work ever led to any convictions, for no sooner have you taken one corrupt politician or racketeer out of the system than another takes his place.

The baddies always win, as well as having the best lines. This was simple pragmatism. You do the best you can and you hope to stay alive. Compromise is part of the ageing process.

At least in the snooping, he was himself. Looked at objectively, the world was full of people who never learned to become themselves. They remained the agents of stronger forces. He himself had been that way for years, stretched like a piece of perished canvas between Sally and the brewery. The world was all upside down and the notion of rest was something other people did. Now he was inclined to let the brewery go whistle and do the bare minimum when it came to work. As for Sally, well, as far as he was concerned, Sally was now somebody else's problem. His son was growing up and he would defy Sally and try and see more of him than he had done heretofore.

In the days before Christmas he got a phone call from Marlowe letting him know that the big trial bike would be available for collection in the first week of the new year. But it would be more than the new year, it would also be the new century and the new millennium. The world would move on, getting more and more choked with traffic, the broadbands choked with porn, the ants in their motorised anthills looking for virtual lives. But now Madigan did not care. He would have his new bike. He could chase the cops and robbers up the pavements and along the grass margins if he had to. He could do stairwells and pedestrian exits to get out of trouble. To become the solver of the world's problems all he needed was a helmet and a good pair of warm gloves.

The world is strange, he thought. If everybody in Dublin rode motorbikes and bicycles, rather than cars, like the Chinese, then there would be no traffic problems: a simple solution under everybody's nose, yet nobody took that option. Perhaps Pearse was right and people are docile sheep, each following the other, even into the gap of madness.

Not that Madigan cared. He was in love for once in his life. From being a walking horn head full of bitterness towards Sally, he had developed an attitude of distance to the world. He was learning not to care and got a lot more done as a result. He would suit himself within his limitations and play to his strengths when he got the chance. He could not escape the brewery completely, for the need to make a living imposed its own constraints. But this did not matter much, for he had come to the conclusion that freedom was nothing more than an illusion anyway.

Things were now slack in the brewery on account of the Christmas trade having gone out three weeks earlier. Alan Spratt called Madigan into his office for a Christmas drink. Madigan told him he would not be accepting his offer of a promotion.

'You can't expect such an offer again, you do know that?' he asked, with a serious, regretful expression on his pudgy face.

'I understand that.' Madigan smiled.

The Christmas lights came on at 3.00. Madigan bought some wrapping paper for Liam's present and then searched the shops for something special for Marika. He was to spend Christmas with her, emigrant Moldovans having no homes to go to. On Christmas Day, he planned to have Lily Bowen, Marika and Tom Bryan around for Christmas dinner. He would have liked to have Ted Plunkett too and perhaps Vikki Morgan, but Ted had his own family and Vikki was too sexy to risk having her in the same room as Marika. You could not predict the chemistry of such an encounter. This was one of the small compromises he knew he would have to make in the name of love. Still, they would have the streamers and the party hats and slice the turkey and eat the pud and drink the wine. His was a small but vibrant community, he knew, and you are dead unless you belong to some community.

When he got home there was a message from another woman looking for him to do a little investigation for her. So the world went on, full of little infidelities and people ripping off whatever they could. It was boom time, house-price inflation time; a carpenter could charge a fortune to hang a door. It was that kind of time, an epoch that when it ended, people would scarcely believe it had ever happened. People were working harder and living harder than they had done since the nineteenth century, when the life expectancy was sixteen. It was millennium madness. Christmas was coming and some of the geese were getting fat, while the rest were being screwed for everything they had. There would be no shortage of business for Madigan. Who knows, he thought, with marriages caving in all over the place from all the pressure, maybe some day he too might become rich as a result of this unhappy state of affairs. There is always a silver lining, even in the heart of misery.

Though he tried hard enough, Marlowe was never able to pin the murder of Professor Crowley on Pamela or anyone else. Without Madigan's evidence from the bottle, he had no case. According to official statistics, the Professor had died of natural causes.

However, it looked like Marlowe did his career no good by trying to move against her. He was told he would never again get a promotion. This was not the end of the world for Marlowe, for he was always a man for the shadows and he preferred the quiet life in any case. And he could not be moved out of his position for he had too high a profile. To do so would only arouse further suspicions. He took the whole thing in his stride. His attitude was simple: you do your job as best you can but you cannot solve everything and you cannot solve everybody's problems. You build a small sand castle and the tide comes in and washes it away, but you keep on trying, like old Sisyphus with his shoulder to the stone.

As regards Pamela O'Neill Crowley, she changed her name back to O'Neill, still pretending in public that Hoolihanism was in her past while it was patently obvious it was not, despite her middle-class pretensions. For Madigan, this showed up most pointedly in her relentless pursuit of the fast buck and the fact that she could send her children away when it suited her without giving it a second thought. She had mutated into the breed of entrepreneurial spirit who stop at nothing to get their way. She sold the house she inherited from the Professor and set up a campus company to exploit the findings made by her husband. The story in financial circles was that she was well on her way to becoming a billionaire from the potential sales of MDC. What she did with the money was her own business; it certainly wasn't Madigan's.

Madigan saw her one more time. He was at Dublin airport, flying to London for an operations meeting with Spratt. He spotted her coming down an escalator. She was all poise, wore a navy business suit and had a briefcase in her hand. She had a couple of senior politicians with her. She looked like she had finally hit the jackpot. She glanced in Madigan's direction but did not seem to recognise him, or if she did, she pretended otherwise. She was moving on to the next killing. She had forgotten her past. The future was on her side. She could pass for any one of the thousands of newly rich. She walked out of the airport building, hailed a taxi, and was gone.